JACK FLEET HOUSE

By

John Dean

Contents

Jamie

A loud crash woke Jamie. His first thought was "Not again!" Aaron was a bully and, as hard as Jamie tried, he could not tell anyone about it. The last time Aaron came into his room, he set fire to a piece of cardboard. Because of his blindness, Jamie didn't know that the cardboard was not going to cause a major problem, because Aaron had placed it inside a used cocoa jar. However, Jamie was quite calm, went to the sink in the bathroom, wet a towel and was able to find the flames due to his exceptional hearing.

"No! Is that you Aaron?" No answer. He got back into bed and the next thing he knew, Mrs. Herbert was waking him.

"Come on, Jamie. You'll be late for breakfast. And what's this on the floor?" She found his mirror had fallen from its position on the wall and smashed.

"Something woke me last night, Ada. What is it?" Jamie asked her curiously.

"It's only that old barometer," Ada replied "I'll get Percy to hang it back up later. Come on now, all the bacon will have burnt to pieces."

Jamie was nine years old. He came to Jack Fleet House when he was just five. Nobody had lived in Jack Fleet as long as Jamie. He refused to accept that he was still in residence because of his blindness. He was, for his age, very intelligent, and could find his way around all twenty-five rooms and memorise who was staying where. Frustration doesn't really explain how Jamie was feeling. He was very popular with everyone he met, but all too often friendships that were made were soon broken because children were "ambered".

This is a term used by Jamie. Ian, who was Jamie's best friend for the three months that he stayed in Jack Fleet, came up with the name as a parody linked to Foster's Lager (the Amber Nectar).

Ian had been gone four days now.

"I wonder what he's doing," Jamie thought to himself.

"Is your bacon alright, Jamie? Ada asked.

"It's fine thank you. Could I have some more orange juice, please?"

"Certainly," said Ada.

"Is anybody leaving today, Ada?" Jamie asked, hoping she would say "Yes, Aaron".

"I don't think so. Sharon is expecting a third visit from that Welsh couple. You know, the ones that told you about the bleeding tree."

"Ah yes, the tree where some man was hanged hundreds of years ago. And they later found out he was innocent."

"Yes, that's right, since the hanging..." Ada replied, but Jamie butted in.

"The tree has oozed a red sap, so they've called it The Bleeding Tree."

"Quite right, Jamie," Ada laughed.

Sharon, Jamie thought, had quickly taken over from Ian. She soon realised, however, that Jamie was very independent.

"I'll do that for you, Jamie," Sharon said.

"It's okay, Sharon, I can manage."

Jamie was replacing one of his many books back onto the bookcase. Braille was fantastic, almost as good as the radio. Many times, when Ada came into his room in the morning, she would find him sound asleep with his headphones on.

Ada spent her own money on batteries for Jamie's radio. She realised how much of a comfort it was for him.

"We should get him some more of them story CDs, Percy," she said, while Percy was reading his daily paper.

"Who?" replied Percy, looking up from the sports pages.

"Jamie, of course," Ada shouted.

"Yes, my love. He would love that. I'll see what I can find Saturday morning."

Percy and Ada had been married twenty-seven years. They met at Fenchurch Street Station during the Second World War. Ada was working at Euston Station in the buffet bar with her best friend, Topsy, and every Friday night they had to run for the last train. One night they were there with a couple of minutes to spare. They noticed a sailor asleep on the bench. Knowing full well that their train was the last one, Ada boldly woke the sailor up. It was Percy.

Jamie loved hearing the story of how Percy and Ada first met. It was only recently that Ada had told Jamie what happened that first night. When they got off the train at Tilbury, Ada pointed to the docks, showing Percy the direction he had to go, saying, "We go this way, in the other direction."

Jamie asked, "Did Percy kiss you goodnight?"

Ada laughed. "We were kissing on the train!"

Jamie found his way to Sharon's room and knocked. Hearing that someone was moving around in the room, Jamie opened the door. "Sharon?" No reply. The next thing Jamie knew, he was pushed to the ground.

"Don't you say a word to anyone, do you hear me?" Aaron was twelve years old and much bigger than Jamie.

"What are you doing in Sharon's room? If you've hurt her, I'll...."

Aaron blurted out "You'll what, you little wimp. You'll say nothing, that's what you'll do."

A few seconds later, he heard Sharon's voice, but couldn't get to his feet quick enough.

"Jamie, are you alright? What happened?"

"I'm okay. I tripped on something, I don't know what".

Sharon looked at him. There was something not quite right. In the short time she had known Jamie, she knew he was very steady on his feet and hardly ever tripped as he had said. Still, as long as he was alright, she wouldn't press the point any further.

"I've just had my third meeting with Bill and Tricia. You know, the Welsh couple, Jamie."

Jamie tried to be positive for Sharon. "Oh good. How did it go? They seem really nice."

Sharon thought for a minute. "Jamie, I don't want to be ambered. I want to stay here with you."

Jamie saw red. "What! What do you mean? Are you stupid or what?"

"Jamie!" Sharon cowered.

"Sharon, you have got to realise what's in front of you. You have a lovely couple of people who want to give you everything. They live on a farm in Brentwood, and they have no other children. You are very special to them. Wake up and smell the coffee, Sharon." Jamie walked to the door and turned around. "I'm sorry for shouting, but you cannot let this opportunity pass Sharon. I'll see you later."

Sharon knew Jamie was right. She was missing the point. Bill and Tricia were very special. She switched on her TV and found her favourite programme. "Poor Jamie," she thought. "He can't even watch TV."

The Bad News

Sharon was leaving. Sharon was leaving and, as hard as Jamie tried, he couldn't stop thinking about her.

Bill and Tricia had been to see Percy and finalised all the details. It would be just three more days and she would be gone.

"Yet again," Jamie thought to himself. "Yet again." How many more times would he be heartbroken? "You idiot!" Jamie said to himself. "It's what Sharon wants deep down. Alright. She said she wanted to stay, but you know the truth."

There was a knock on Jamie's door. "Come in. Who is it?"

"It's only me, Jamie." It was Harry, the new lad. Harry was eleven and just a little bit overweight. He too, unknown to Jamie, was being bullied by Aaron.

"Jamie, did you hear about Sharon?"

Jamie smiled. "Of course I did. She leaves in three days."

"No," Harry said, "Somebody stole her diary and records. She's really upset."

"Aaron!" Jamie shouted.

Harry had his own ideas and it was exactly what he was thinking. "Why do you say Aaron, Jamie?"

Jamie cursed his outburst. "I didn't mean Aaron did it, I mean…"

Harry cut in. "You know as well as I do Aaron is the one who did it. There's nobody else here that would be so naughty. We've got to tell Percy."

"No!" Jamie said, "We have to find another way."

Percy was in his study, going through his mail. All the usual stuff was there. Bills for this, demands for that. Ada walked in. "Sharon has had some stuff stolen from her room, a diary and some records."

Percy carried on going through his mail.

"Percy!" snapped Ada. "I said Sharon has had some stuff stolen from her room."

"I don't believe it," said Percy.

"What do you mean you don't believe it? She has lost things out of her room."

Percy sat upright at his desk. "Sorry Ada. I didn't mean…. I mean I heard what you said. It's this letter from the Governors I…." Percy took a deep breath.

"What is it?" Ada said, noticing that Percy was really upset.

"The council have informed the Governors that we have been short listed for a new development of apartments to be built on this plot. The likelihood is that we may have to close within the next three months, and that there is nothing anybody can do. The Governors have known about this for over a week and cannot see a way round it."

Ada was stunned. This was a real shock. They had given their life to Jack Fleet, had really changed people's lives. So many children had benefited from the efforts of everybody concerned in the running of the home.

"There must be something…. somebody who can help us," Ada cried. This was about as much as she could take.

"There," Percy put an arm around Ada. For the first time in a long time, he really didn't know what else to say.

Percy thought for a minute. There must be a way, but who on the council could help him? Most of the councillors were, unfortunately, in the pocket of the newly elected Mayor, Jock McBride. There had been some real battles with him when he was just a councillor. Now he was Mayor. It seemed to Percy that the situation was beyond repair.

"What about Barry?" Ada said, in desperation more than anything. "He has been a good ally in the past, and you know what he thinks of the kids, especially Jamie."

"I know, Ada, but he has a lot on his plate with his business. I don't know if he has the time."

"He'll find time when you tell him what's happened, Percy, I know he will." Ada was sure she was right.

Barry Wilson was indeed a very busy man. Apart from running the area's biggest plumbing supply shop and trade counter, he and his wife Angela also bred African grey parrots. They started breeding three years ago on a small scale, and it very soon took off. He now had twenty-nine pairs, which meant at any time he would have more than fifteen to twenty chicks. All were hand reared and fed up to five times a day. It was taking its toll on Angela and things were stressed between them.

Percy was sceptical. "I don't want to get Barry involved. He has far too much on his plate and, anyway, he's just one councillor. What can he do?"

Farewell Sharon

Jaime was on his bed, listening to his favourite radio show.

"Jamie." It was Harry. "Turn it off, quick. Listen." Jamie took his earphones off.

"What's up Harry?" Jamie said, annoyed that he had been disturbed.

"Sorry Jamie. I thought you would want to know. Sharon is being picked up in about fifteen minutes. She's really confused." Harry could see Jamie was upset.

"I can't help her. She hasn't got a choice," Jamie said. At that moment, Ada came into the room.

"Alright boys. Listen. We all have to go to the main hall. Percy has something to tell us all."

"Tell us what, Ada?" Jamie asked. This was most unusual. Probably some new addition, or a new rule from the council.

Nearly everyone was in the hall when they got there, except for Sharon. When Harry told Jamie she wasn't there, he just switched off and didn't listen to what Percy was saying.

Jamie didn't hear the moans from everybody. He was just thinking about Sharon. He had to see her. He left the hall and was about to go upstairs when Sharon called him from the front door.

"Jamie!" Sharon was crying. "Jamie, I have to go now, but Bill and Tricia have said they will bring me up to see you until you leave."

"That's okay, then," Jamie thought sarcastically. "It's best if you just go and live your life, Sharon. There's no point in the odd visit. And anyway, I'll be gone soon and who knows how far away we'll be from each other."

Sharon was hurt. Why was he being like this? "Jamie, I've given Bill and Tricia's number to Ada. Please tell me you'll keep in touch."

"Sharon love, we have to go," Tricia called, "Say goodbye to Jamie." It was hard for both of them.

"You look after yourself, Sharon. Don't worry, I'll be fine." Jamie just wanted her to go now. "I'll call. I promise."

"Thank you, Jamie. I'll call before you do, I bet." At that, she was in the car and gone.

Jamie went back inside. Harry came running up to him "What's gonna happen to us now?" he cried.

Jamie said, "What's up, Harry?"

"They are gonna close us down. The home is closing down in three months they reckon." Harry was crying.

"They can't Harry. The council... Percy wouldn't let that happen. He'll sort it out." Jamie wasn't unduly concerned. There had been scares like this before. It would all work out in the end.

****

Barry Wilson sat in his office, not knowing what he was going to say to Percy and Ada. He'd had the memo from the estates office a couple of days now. He just didn't like the idea of speaking to his good friends at Jack Fleet. He phoned Angela.

"Have you spoken to Percy?" she asked.

Barry replied, "What do you think?"

"You can't put it off indefinitely, Barry. They're our friends." She was exactly right.

"That's why it's so hard, Ange. I don't know if there's anything I can do."

Angela replied "You've never ducked an issue in your life, Barry. For god's sake, phone him at least."

Barry had made his mind up. He wouldn't phone. He would call round and see them. Besides, it would be an excuse to see the kids, especially Jamie.

Barry and Angela had a lot of time for Jamie. They admired him so much, never complaining, just being as helpful to everybody at Jack Fleet as he could.

He quickly phoned Angie again. "What are you doing later, about 6:30?" he asked.

"Nothing. Only your tea." It was Tuesday. He always had kippers on Tuesdays.

"Can you meet me outside the gates of Jack Fleet at 6:30?" he asked.

"You want me to come as well? Okay, see you at 6:30," she replied.

He sighed with relief. At least she'd be with him.

****

Barry arrived at almost the same time as Angela. She put an arm round him as he got out of his car. "I've baked some scones for the kids." She smiled.

"They'll love that. Make sure the kids get them before Percy does." He laughed.

Percy was in his study when Barry and Angela walked in.

"Barry and Angela! Well, what a lovely surprise." He shook Barry's hand and gave Angela a big cuddle. "How are you both? Well I hope. It's lovely to see you." Percy was being genuine. He thought so much of them.

Barry said, "Thanks Percy. Have you heard..."

Percy cut in, "How can they do this Barry? It's so unfair... I mean, haven't they given any consideration to the kids?"

"Look Percy, it's got through the initial stage, but they have much more standing in their way than they realise. Why, public opinion could make an enormous difference. And even if it only slows the process down, it would be something. Yes, that's what we need to do. Get the locals behind us. Most of them know how much you've done for the kids and the local community. I'm sure we could lobby the county council and even get the local MP involved."

Barry took a deep breath. "I know what this means to you and Ada, Percy. I know we will not let this matter be breezed through the local council without a fight. You have my word."

****

Jock McBride was impatiently waiting for the call. He'd promised to call, after all. Wasn't it his idea to get together? Jock was his own man. He did not care too much for anybody, unless they were going to be useful to him in some way. He'd been this way for most of his life. It had led to him being one of those people who wouldn't think twice about walking all over someone if there was gain or profit at the end of it. Jock was now approaching his 60th year, but he had lost none of his ways. He was brought up in Glasgow and had a tough upbringing. His family, two brothers and one sister, had all disowned him. He just didn't care who he hurt.

The phone rang. "Hello, Jock here." It was him.

"I'll meet you at the King's Arms in half an hour, okay?"

Jock said "Okay," and put the phone down.

The situation was moving very fast. It had only been one month ago when he found the offer in amongst the tenders for the land. "Who wouldn't?" he thought to himself. "Who wouldn't? It's too good an offer to turn down." He was near retiring age and a hundred grand was too good an offer. Nobody would have turned it down. He was about to leave his office when Shirley, his secretary, buzzed.

"Jock, it's Percy Herbert on the phone."

"Tell him I'm busy and to call me tomorrow." Jock did not want to hear Percy Herbert whinging. He and his fat wife should have retired long ago.

"He said he'll come and see you tomorrow."

"Whatever." Jock did not give Jack Fleet a second thought when he set the wheels in motion. He knew he would have to face Percy eventually and was not overly concerned about it. He could handle Percy Herbert.

He parked his car in the King's Arms car park. It was a quiet time of the day, and the pub being out in the country was an ideal place to meet him. He had ordered a pint of best when he turned up.

"What you having? The bitter is nice."

Terry Watson was forty-two years old, a self-made millionaire. He owned property all over the world and, like Jock, had no scruples at all when it came to doing business. There were his kind of people, or there were wasters.

"I'll have the same as you, Jock. Cheers." They took a seat in the corner.

"How's things your end?" Terry asked.

"Well, I've got it through the biggest hurdle, so I think we can say we are well on the way."

"Any problems with the fella at the school?" Terry asked.

"He tried to contact me today. Apparently he's coming in tomorrow. He's not a problem. We could have more problems with a couple of councillors. You know the two I'm talking about," Jock replied.

"That parrot breeding plumber. What's his name, Barry something isn't it?" Terry laughed.

"Yeah, that's right. And the other spanner in the works is Terry Brown. He's too straight for his own good."

The two of them discussed pros and cons for a while longer before they went their separate ways. They had secretly offered different bonuses to four or five councillors. The odd one or two had some skeletons in the cupboard that they could work on to help their plan get through. Everything was in place.

****

Aaron Clark was not a nice person. He had a chip on his shoulder. Losing his father at the age of six was a real body blow, as it would be to anyone his age. His mum, Marie, tried her best, but got in with the wrong company and ended up on drugs and lost her two boys. Aaron's brother, Stephen, was older by six years and had done well at school. By the time he left college, he had seven GCSEs and was doing really well at the local power station, where he was nearing the end of his apprenticeship as an electrical engineer.

Stephen's phone rang. It was six o'clock in the morning. He'd only been in bed about three hours due to a breakdown, which meant he'd had to stay on after his two till ten shift.

"Hello, who's that?" said Stephen, trying not to be annoyed.

Silence. This was happening too often, normally during the day though. He thought for a second. "Aaron, is that you?" The line went dead. He promised himself he would call the home and make sure Aaron was okay.

He was glad the call hadn't woken Aunt Beryl. She would have gone potty. He went to the bathroom, then returned to bed.

Aaron crept back to his room without anyone noticing. He really needed to speak to his brother. It was just breaking the ice and, hopefully, not having Stephen lecturing him as he usually did. The last words Stephen had said to him were "That's your lot, Aaron. You won't get another chance." With the likelihood of being moved out of the area, Aaron was clinging to the hope that Stephen would change his mind and give him another chance, one which he promised himself he wouldn't waste.

Aaron was envious of his brother, but had blown his chances of living with him and his Auntie Beryl by his behaviour on several occasions. He had been given chance after chance.

He was also envious of Jamie. Everyone loved Jamie, poor little blind boy. He was determined to hurt Jamie as much as he could. He had sorted Harry out. He was no problem.

He sold Sharon's records to get some more money for ciggies as well. He also knew that Jamie was scared of him, and laughed when he heard the news about the home closing down. What would poor little Jamie do? He would love to go somewhere else and start all over again. Chances were that they would all be relocated to the same home, and he would carry on just as he did at Jack Fleet. He went to see Percy. "What's going to happen to us?" he asked Percy.

Percy was caught off guard. Aaron never showed any emotion about anything and Percy was sure he just didn't care about anything or anyone. "I really don't know what's going to happen, Aaron. But we will not give up without a fight, you can be sure of that."

"That's okay then," Aaron said.

Percy was indeed confused. Aaron was acting out of character.

Percy was tense. He didn't like what was happening and he didn't like who was causing it. Jock McBride. He was a sneaky, nasty piece of work and, although Percy knew it was futile, even seeing him, he had little or no choice.

Barry and Percy had both agreed not to lay all their cards on the table. They had, in their wisdom, decided that Percy alone would be the one to confront the Mayor. "The Mayor, he's a mare alright," Percy thought to himself. No, they wouldn't give him the satisfaction of pleading to his better nature, as there wasn't one. Instead, they would use a different tactic, hopefully to get some more time and then use that time to gain more public awareness. And hopefully support. He was due at the Mayor's office at 11:30. It was only 9:15, so he had plenty of time. He decided to phone Barry.

"I was about to phone you," Barry answered. "How are you?"

"I'm tighter than a drum, but I am not going to be beaten, Barry. I've been awake half the night and am convinced of one thing."

"What's that, Percy?" Barry asked.

"We can and we will win through at the end of the day."

Barry thought for a moment. "Percy, are you sure you don't want me to come? It's not a problem really. I can get Ange to cover me here?"

Percy quickly replied. "No Barry, I don't want to let him know who, if anybody, is supporting us. I'd just as soon keep him in the dark."

Barry agreed but said "He's probably worked out for himself that I would be in your camp on this one Percy, and it would surely come as no surprise to him if you did tell him. But I think you're right. Let's keep him guessing, okay? Anyway, I've got a customer waiting. Please call me as soon as you get back."

"I will. Don't worry."

Barry served his customers, then sat in his office. He just didn't see how they could resolve this and keep everyone happy. There had to be a way. His main concern after the actual closing, if indeed it did come to that, was Jamie.

Percy arrived at the council offices with fifteen minutes to spare and was offered coffee in the Mayor's lounge.

Jock McBride was sitting in his office reading the local paper. Nothing, he thought, nothing about Jack Fleet. He really was convinced this would be a breeze. Percy Herbert would be a walkover.

"Good morning to you, Percy. How are you doing? And how is that lovely wife of yours?" Jock said trying to sound sincere.

"We are both fine. Thank you for asking." Percy was trying to stay calm and that was not easy.

"Let me guess why you are here Percy," Jock said.

"You are joking, Mr. Mayor, aren't you? You don't have to be a rocket scientist to work that one out. Just explain to me how…. how you could let this happen, knowing how much Jack Fleet has done for the local community, and how damaging this will be to the kids? I just can't believe you aren't doing anything to stop this from happening."

"Hold it right there, Percy. That's exactly the point. I am doing something, okay? So calm down."

"Like what? What have you done? Or are you just paying lip service?" Percy shouted.

"If you are not going to calm down, Percy, I'm afraid I'll have to ask you to leave." Jock paused. "Thank you. Now listen. I've set up a special committee to see what we can do about Jack Fleet." He carried on, naming four councillors who were on the inquiry team.

Percy bit his tongue. Two councillors who would have made a difference were not on the committee. Percy just walked out and sat in his car.

Percy was all over the place. He needed a drink. He thought for a minute. Somewhere quiet. The bar was half empty when he got there and, very shortly, it was just Percy and the barman. "How long you worked here then?" Percy asked.

"I've had the King's Arms about three years now. It's been up and down, which is normal for the pub game. By the way, my name's Ronnie. What's yours?"

Percy smiled. "Thanks very much. I'll have another pint of bitter. That's very kind of you."

The pair of them laughed and Ronnie did buy Percy another pint.

"What's it all about, Ronnie? I mean, why can't life be more er...... I mean why do terrible things happen? Life's too short, isn't it?"

Percy went on to explain his predicament about Jack Fleet and the problem and, before he knew it, he'd had another couple of pints. Ronnie seemed like a nice fella with a more than sympathetic ear. Percy finally said his goodbyes and promised to call back. He felt better having talked to Ronnie and wondered to himself why there weren't more people like him.

He was about five minutes from home when he was stopped by the police. Oh no. He was distraught. The officers were nice enough but Percy, to his horror, was over the limit. By the time he had been taken to the police station and given his statement and urine sample, he was extremely late. Consequently, by the time he got home, Ada was in a real mess. When Percy explained his day, she was ready to throttle him.

"What were you thinking, Percy? You never drink and drive. I don't believe you." Ada really was fuming.

"Ada, I just had a bellyful of the Mayor, listening to his drivel. It just pissed me off and I needed a drink. I'm sorry. I'm really sorry."

"Sorry doesn't cut it Percy, does it? People are relying on you to be strong. Well this is a really good start."

Percy was in the office when the phone rang.

"How you doing Percy? Ronnie here."

When Percy explained what had happened, Ronnie was really upset. "I'm sorry Percy. I feel responsible, I..."

"Don't be silly, Ronnie. You run a pub, people drink. You can't be responsible. Besides, it was the middle of the day. It was just one of those things."

"Even so Percy, I feel partly to blame. But I may have some good news for you."

Percy smiled to himself. "Good news? Wouldn't that be something?" Okay, my friend, go ahead, cheer me up." Percy was naturally sceptical.

Ronnie explained. "My wife, Barbara, when I explained your predicament to her, said something that you may want to hear. Apparently, I don't know if you know, but Jack Fleet was a local businessman about 40 or 50 years ago, and he was always doing good for people, helping them in whatever way he could. Anyway, to cut a long story short, he had a daughter, Emily, who lived in the area until a few years ago until she emigrated.

"Apparently, there was a story going around that the site where Jack Fleet was built was actually built on Fleet land and that, even when the home was originally built, there were complaints from within the local community that the council built on land that wasn't theirs in the first place."

Percy thought for a moment. "What's his point? They objected to the home. Why, how can this help the current problem?" Percy said, "I don't see."

Ronnie cut him off. "Percy, don't you see? If the council have upset the Fleet family in the past and we can locate Emily Fleet, maybe, just maybe, she can have sweet revenge on the same council who upset them years ago. It's got to be worth a try, surely." Ronnie was very convincing.

"Let me think about this for a while, Ronnie. Thanks very much, I do appreciate it."

"It's the least I can do, Percy. Speak to you soon."

Unknown to Percy, Ada had been listening for some time and was keen to hear what the conversation was about.

Percy's Problems

Ada woke with a start. What time was it? She slowly turned over, trying not to disturb Percy, till she noticed he wasn't in bed. It was half past three. She was just putting on her dressing gown when Percy came into the bedroom.

"Sorry, love. Didn't wake you, did I?" he asked.

"No, I…. I don't think so pet. I just turned over and noticed you weren't in bed, so I thought I'd check you were okay. What's up? Did you fall asleep in your armchair?"

He smiled and nodded his head unconvincingly, so she asked again.

This time he hesitated. "Ada, I don't know what's going to happen with Jack Fleet. I don't know what's going to happen to the kids, to Jamie… and I'm probably going to lose my licence. It's just everything getting on top of me and you just keep everything together. You're always there for the kids and me, and all I do is keep messing things up. I…"

Ada stopped him. "Percy, what's brought this on? Nothing else has happened, has it? We'll be okay. Has someone told you something and you've kept it to yourself? Because if you have, you will hear me. You know how I feel about being honest with me. A problem shared is a problem halved and all that."

There was an uneasy pause. She was right, but there wasn't any one thing that was getting him down. It was just everything, and nothing to give them any hope.

"Oh Ada. He just half fell into her arms and started crying.

"Come on now, pet. This isn't like you. Are you sure you're telling me everything?"

He wasn't hiding anything, he told her, and assured her he'd be okay and would try to be more positive and proactive in the future. They cuddled up closely and, eventually, Percy fell asleep.

Ada was now the troubled one, and this was not good. Percy was always the worrier, and it would be hard to lift him out of this mood. She too eventually went to sleep.

****

They were both awakened by the ringing of the front door bell. Aaron had beaten them to it, and was halfway up the stairs when Percy arrived on the landing.

"Percy, it's Bill and Tricia. They've come to see us, but Sharon's not with them. Don't think Jamie will be pleased," he ranted.

"Hold it right there, Aaron." He was right, but was over-excited and needed to calm down.

He calmly walked down the stairs to the study. "Good morning, Bill. How are you? Tricia, it's lovely to see you. You're both looking well. How's life treating you?" He was genuinely pleased to see them.

Bill said, "We're both fine, Percy. You look tired. How are things?"

Percy was about to relate the doom and gloom when Ada walked in the room with a smile as wide as a child's on Christmas morn.

"Tricia and Bill! What a lovely surprise. You should have told us you were coming. We'd have got up earlier and laid on a bit of breakfast for you."

"It's alright, Ada," Tricia replied. "We had a bite on the way down. How are you? You both look like you had a rough night, if you don't mind me saying."

Tricia had no qualms about speaking her mind. Ada knew that much about her, but she liked that in a person and was herself a very forthright person. She didn't hesitate to put them both in the picture and bring them up to speed, as it were, on their current plight.

They all agreed that nothing was to be gained from being down and depressed. Bill wondered if they could all meet up later and put their heads together. Ada thought it a promising idea, and said she'd try to get all of Jack Fleet's supporters around a table for a 'way forward' meeting, for want of a better name for it. Percy said he'd get straight on the phone to Barry and the two Ronnies to see if they could make it.

****

Stephen Clark was on the late shift. Aaron had not returned his calls and he was concerned. Even though Aaron, it seemed, would never change, he did feel obligated to help him as much as he could.

When he spoke to Percy, he was surprised that Aaron had shown some concern over what was going to happen at Jack Fleet. Usually, he just went from home to home, not seemingly concerned about anything. Maybe he was starting to grow up and find something more important than ciggies and computer games.

Maybe Auntie Beryl would reconsider. You never know. Aaron was a real pain and it was, in fact, Stephen who banned him from coming to their home. But to be fair, Beryl had no problem agreeing with Stephen.

The biggest problem Stephen had was his work. As he was on a five-shift rota, it would mean Beryl would have to handle Aaron at night, at least seven nights a month. She, understandably, had refused to do it and Stephen reluctantly agreed. He was tempted to ask for a transfer to the day shift, but the loss of money added to the benefits of being on shift, such as golf and the like, stopped him from considering it after a minute or two. No, there had to be a better solution. He set off for work early, but had to call in at the local plumbing supply centre for some shower cable.

"I'd like six metres of shower cable, please," Stephen said.

Barry was out on council business, so Angela was minding the shop. "Do you have a trade card?" she asked.

"No, I didn't realise, I mean how do you qualify for one? I mean, I'm not in the business. I'm just doing a job for my friend."

Angie and Barry were pretty lenient as regards who was eligible for a discount. After all, someone who knew what he was about was always likely to be a repeat customer.

"Well," Angie answered, "if you spend this sort of money in the next two months, I'll give you some discount."

"Thank you very much. That's very kind of you. I do the odd job now and then, and I'll certainly give you some more business if that's okay."

Angie smiled, "You're more than welcome. Do you live nearby?"

"I'm about half a mile away from the Orsett Cock pub. It's a bit remote, but my Auntie has been there for years. Stephen felt a bit embarrassed saying he lived with his Aunt.

"Well, we live in Horndon. Do you know Horndon?" Angie asked.

"I know of it, but we are the other side of the motorway. It's okay there, though sometimes it's a bit too quiet." Stephen said his goodbyes and set off to finish his private job.

Angie was going through the day's invoices. There was something familiar about that young man and it was beginning to bug her.

The Campaign Starts

"Barry just called me on my mobile, said he couldn't get through. Have you been on the phone, sweetheart?" Ada asked.

"Sorry, love. Yes, I was talking to Ronnie, you know, the governor of the King's Arms."

"What did he want? He's..."

Percy stopped Ada in her tracks. "Ada, Ronnie is a really nice fella. He's found out some info about Jack Fleet and has just relayed the news to me and, while it may be something or nothing, it could make a significant difference to us."

"I'm sorry, Percy. It's just this drink driving thing. He should have been more sensible."

"Hold it right there, Ada. I was the guilty party, not Ronnie. He's in the business of selling drinks and, having said that, he feels really bad about what happened. It may even be that how he feels has been the catalyst for what he's just told me. So, don't condemn the man. He is a really nice, good hearted gentleman."

****

Ronnie Dexter's office was a mess. He had worked on the Thurrock Gazette for over twenty years. He had his own very distinctive style of reporting and he'd had several offers from national papers but had declined them all.

"Sensationalists" he called them. Quite what they would have made of his filing system one wonders, and his eating and drinking habits left much to be desired.

His secretary, Lucy, had long ago given up on trying to organise Ronnie, realising that he was far too set in his ways. Lucy entered the office with some trepidation. Ronnie was tucking into a Big Mac and fries. It was eleven-thirty.

"What is it now, Lucy?" he said, swallowing the last of the burger.

"Sorry to trouble you, Ronnie. Did you read the memo I left about Barry Wilson re the Jack Fleet children's home?"

"Jack Fleet? I don't remember seeing that."

Lucy wasn't surprised. "I left it on your phone when I left last night. Did you not see it when you came in this morning? Mr. Wilson seemed quite concerned and feels that we could help him with this predicament." Lucy was used to this, but it really didn't upset her because, when Ronnie did get his teeth into something, he was an excellent journalist.

Ronnie looked bemused, lifting up the empty McDonald's bags until he finally noticed the memo on the floor. "Got it," he said. "Leave it with me. I'll give him a call."

Lucy turned to leave the office. "Oh, by the way," she said, "the number's on the back of the memo."

Ronnie picked up his coffee. He'd call Barry Wilson later. He needed to finish off his green belt article.

****

Barry and Angela were, before the brown stuff hit the fan, looking for property in the south west of England, Devon or Cornwall. Although not quite ready to retire, semi-retirement seemed like a sensible option. Barry thought they could continue to breed African greys, which would generally bring in enough with what they already had put by, to have a nice comfortable life in a much nicer part of the world.

"Barry," Angela called. "Ronnie Dexter's on the phone. Will you take it down there?"

"I've got it Ange, thanks." "Ronnie," Barry almost sighed. It had been three days since he left a message with Ronnie's secretary.

"Barry, I'm really sorry it's taken a while to get back to you. You know how it is, don't you?"

Barry laughed. "Of course I do. I'm as guilty as the next man for not calling people back. It must be an age thing Ronnie. What do you reckon?"

"You have it in a nutshell, Barry. Anyway, what can I do for you?"

Barry paused for a moment. He didn't want to come across as emotional. Logical, yes. Emotional, no. He felt emotional about it, but Ronnie Dexter was a reporter, a very good reporter, and logical, Barry felt, was the way to go.

"Ronnie, I presume you know about the Jack Fleet thing, the shutting down and everything?"

Ronnie said "Of course. I think it's wrong Barry, but..."

Barry cut in. "Hold on, Ronnie. I'm sorry. There are no buts here. This council, under Jock McBride and his cronies, is bent. You know that. You've said it enough times in your paper, so don't give me buts."

It was Ronnie's turn to butt in. "Barry!" Despite all he had said to Angela, he did end up getting emotional. Ronnie took a breath. "Right. Now listen to me. I agree 100 percent with you about Mr. McBride. What I'm saying is, you are between a rock and a hard place. He has half the councillors in his pocket. You're really going to be up against it."

Barry couldn't argue. He knew he was right. "Ronnie, I have some information coming to me that may give us an advantage. I'm meeting someone tomorrow night who reckons he can add weight to our cause. What I need from you, Ronnie, is just to know that you will give us some publicity when the time is right. That's all I'm asking. Are you okay with that?"

Ronnie didn't hesitate. "Barry, I don't know if you know. We have a young lad, our office boy at the Gazette. Liam is his name. Four years ago, he was in Jack Fleet. He's a wonderful, well balanced young man who will tell you how much he has to thank Percy and Ada for. The lad was going nowhere, always in trouble, heading for a life of crime. When I look at him, I know he has the potential to go a long way in this business. Of course, he has an advantage. He's learning from the master!"

"Ronnie, you're a star, and very modest too. But seriously, I thank you for your support and will speak to you soon. Keep your fingers crossed that the news I get tomorrow night will be a definite plus for us all."

"I'll do that, Barry. Call me when you know more." Ronnie was genuinely pleased for Barry.

"I'll do that, Ronnie, no problem." Barry smiled for the first time in a long while.

Kids Concerned

Jamie was pleased to hear from Sharon. He heard all about her horse riding experiences and how she loved her chestnut mare and loved even more the work involved in looking after a horse. He was genuinely pleased for her. She was very special to him and he would be seeing her soon as Bill and Tricia were coming to Jack Fleet to lend their support for the cause.

Aaron was still a problem and Jamie would rather sort it with Aaron instead of telling Percy and Ada what was going on. He was endlessly telling Harry to calm down and not be paranoid about Aaron, but his words seemed to land on deaf ears. Harry was slowly becoming a nervous wreck. He was even scared to go to the washroom by himself and often asked Jamie to go with him. Quite what Jamie could do if Aaron started something was beyond him, but Jamie was Harry's right-hand man and would not see him come to any harm.

"Jamie," Harry said. "Do you think they will close Jack Fleet down?"

Jamie thought for a moment. "I don't know. I don't think so, but at the moment it's not looking good. And Ada, well, she's just not on the same planet these days."

They both, as if by instinct, sighed together. The door burst open. It was Aaron.

"Which one of you told Percy? Come on! Who's man enough to say? I know it was one of you."

Jamie and Harry just stared with vacant expressions.

"I don't know what you're on about Aaron. Calm down." Jamie pleaded.

"You! You teacher's pet. Goody two shoes. I know it was you. , Well, I'll tell you now. You are in for it. I'm gonna sort you right out and take your queer friend with you. Enjoy your sleep. If you get any, that is." He left the room laughing.

"What do we do now, Jamie?" Harry cried.

Jamie just nodded. "Don't worry, Harry. We'll sort it."

Reflections

The tide was on its way out. It was just breaking into dawn. The rain had stopped; the wind had died down. Roker Beach was deserted, except for a few coal prospectors picking up the black stuff that was continually being washed up on the shore.

Sam was packing his tackle away in a mood of quiet contentment. Half a dozen coalies would do, but it was more about the feeling of being with nature than the number of fish he was able to catch.

Peace.

The alarm clock went off. It was so real. He missed the northeast. He missed Sunderland, the banter with the magpies. To a lesser extent, he missed the southerners.

He moved to the south when the shipyards started to dry up for work. Some of his friends chastised him for going to join the "dumb southerners", as Frank Johnson called them.

"You'll not like it down there," he used to say.

Sam said, "Aye, you're probably right, Frankie boy."

It all seemed a far cry from South America where he had moved to in the sixties. His brother, George, wished him bon voyage from Tilbury, where he joined the P & O ship Orcades, with an agreement from the company that he could work his passage. So, emigrating was very inexpensive. In fact, it was very enjoyable. He worked just four hours a day, and enjoyed the work also as a deck hand.

So here he was. He still didn't know why he settled in Peru. Was it the people or Lima itself? He wasn't quite sure. But, over the years, he had become reasonably well known by not only Peruvians, but also many Europeans. They included Emily Fleet, who was his closest friend.

He had stayed in Tilbury for too long, especially since his dear Annie had died. Something inside him was nagging at him to travel and he couldn't ignore the feeling. So when Annie departed, he could not stop himself. Annie had been against the move to Tilbury at first, but soon came around. Even so, she had made it very clear to Sam that she would move no more.

Sam's thoughts often went to Sunderland and, while he conceded the friendliness of the southerners was okay, it just wasn't the same as the northeast. Still, never mind. He kept himself busy now early mornings and late evenings tending his roof garden, his pride and joy. He found himself, more and more, adopting the locals' siesta habits, especially through the peak summer months. Consequently, late nights were occurring more often, too.

He lived on the outskirts of Lima in a three-story villa. The three floors were starting to tire him out. He knew deep down that he would soon have to find alternative accommodation. The problem was, though, he would struggle to find something with a garden.

All the neighbours looked out for Sam. He had won them over completely with his soft-spoken, laid back , northeast accent. Even the local children loved him. They did struggle with his name, though. One youngster, Paco, would call out "Hunkle Sangy, play football" and usually Sam would kick the ball a few times, though it was never enough. The kids, like all kids, couldn't understand the complications of old age. But Sam, to his credit, didn't look his age. He found it hard to believe he was nearly eighty.

Emily used to say that if she was twenty years older, she'd fancy him. It always made Sam laugh. "Try fifty, pet. You'd be about right then."

"What do you miss about England?" Sam asked Emily one day.

"I suppose it's the little things, Sam. You know, believe it or not, sometimes I miss the weather. Crazy, isn't it?" she laughed.

Sam could see her point. We always seem to want what we can't have, and he agreed with Emily too. The climate was generally much hotter here, but he missed walking in the rain.

"What about your family, Emily? Don't you miss them?" Emily went quiet.

Sam said, "You do have family Emily, don't you, young girl like you?"

Emily paused before speaking. "Sam, I have no real family, haven't for a few years now. My father died shortly after marrying my step-mum. My real mum left home when I was very young and, to this day, I haven't a clue where she is. Neither do I know the whereabouts of my brother, Peter. Last I heard, he was in Australia somewhere. So I have no real reason to go home. I mean, home to me now is here. I've travelled, as you know, and like you, I've fallen in love with Peru, especially Lima. So, it looks like I'll grow old here, too."

"Old like me, you mean?" Sam laughed. She laughed with him. Sam often recalled his conversations with Emily. She was really easy to talk to. He hadn't seen her for a while, but she seemed really settled in Lima too.

Sam's brother, George, kept in touch regularly and also sent the local Gazette, so Sam could keep up with the news and what was going on generally.

"Bowls!" he thought to himself. He missed his bowling. Given that he wasn't very good, his old friends probably missed him too, seeing as he liked to play for money and invariably lost. He had only played the game when he moved to Tilbury and became a bit of an addict.

"Still," he thought, "the fishing is better here." There was a jetty and also the rocks held some real fun. Strangely though, it didn't seem very popular with the locals until Sam started offering his catch to his neighbours. Then he found he couldn't go on his own. The neighbours' efforts to palm their kids off on him usually worked.

Life In Lima

Emily Fleet left the U.K. over twenty-five years ago. She had been used to a very good lifestyle, but felt she wanted to see the world.

In the last ten years, she had been to South America, calling in at Peru, where she camped out on the mountains. She taught aerobics in Chile during the Falklands War. She was designated her own llama in Brazil, where she revelled in the festivals in Rio de Janeiro. Yes, she had left behind her roots, but they were roots and she would be able to pick the trail up anytime, so she was not too concerned.

She was currently staying in Lima where she met, believe it or not, Sam Allison, a Geordie, who had left England over forty years ago.

Sam was a lovely man. He had the chance to go to London with his brother, George. They were both ship builders, but he decided to emigrate. He worked his passage to South America, which literally cost peanuts, and settled down in Peru. The two of them hit it off straight away.

It was only in passing that Sam mentioned that his brother George sent out the local paper, which just happened to be the Thurrock Gazette. Although Emily had been away for such a long time, she asked Sam if he would let her browse through his most recent papers.

Sam was only too pleased to oblige. George religiously sent the gazette every week and Sam admitted to Emily that he didn't read every edition and that he felt guilty.

Emily comforted Sam. "The news in these papers is old. It's old now and it will be old tomorrow. It doesn't matter when you read them. It only matters that you do, at some point, have a look through them. You never know what might appear in front of you." Sam just nodded his head.

Emily often thought of her time in Thurrock. It was often turbulent, often amusing, never dull. The thought of reading about what was going on in her old domain excited her.

Where Is She?....What's The Mayor Up To?

Barry was apprehensive. Would this be good news or not? He was and had been for most of his life a positive thinking kind of person. But something was nagging at his positivity and he couldn't shake it. He had arranged to meet Ronnie at his pub in Orsett. Provided it didn't get too busy, Ronnie said he'd be able to give Barry some time.

Barry arrived about fifteen minutes early, but the pub was really busy. There had been a sort of festival about the gardens in the town and all the locals retreated to Ronnie's pub after the judging. It was nearly 8:30 when Ronnie finally sat down with Barry.

"Would you like another?" Ronnie asked. Barry held his flat hand over his drink and moved it from side to side. "I'm fine Ronnie, thanks."

Ronnie sat across the table from Barry and began to tell the story of Emily Fleet and the "legacy" of the ground that Jack Fleet House was built on. Barry listened with interest, but gradually realised there could be a down side to this news.

So, when was the last time Emily was heard of? I mean, she could be anywhere, Ronnie."

"Ronnie nodded his head in agreement. "I really don't know. I've been asking my regulars, especially the older ones who come in here, and as yet I have nothing concrete to go on. There is one thing, though, that may be of use to you, coming at it from a different angle." Barry leaned forward, still sceptical though.

"About three or four weeks ago, Terry Watson, you know the fellow I mean."

Barry cut in. "Oh, too right I know who you mean. The man's an animal. He has no scruples at all."

It was Ronnie's turn to cut in. "Well, he came in one lunch time and sat down with Jock McBride, our wonderful Mayor. They chatted for around forty-five minutes and then left."

"Well, well," Barry thought, "the plot thickens."

"Did you manage to hear what they were talking about, Ronnie?"

Ronnie sighed. "Unfortunately, I wasn't here. Carol, our lunchtime barmaid, mentioned it to Barb in passing and she only mentioned it to me a couple of days ago."

They both looked at each other and were thinking the same thing.

"It's possible," Barry said.

"You bet your life it's possible," Ronnie replied.

They both sat there weighing up what they had: a crooked Mayor and a nasty piece of work in Terry Watson, who was well known for his ruthlessness when it came to the building game.

"Barry, I'll have to get back behind the bar. The girls are running their legs off. Keep in touch, yeah, and I'll keep asking about Emily, okay?"

Barry hadn't touched his drink since Ronnie sat down. He thanked Ronnie, finished his drink and went outside to the car park. "Jock McBride and Terry Watson," he thought to himself and just shook his head. By the time he got home, Angie was just finishing the night feed of the chicks that stayed in the house. Angela was as shocked as Barry when she heard what Ronnie had told him.

"Speak to the Gazette. Ronnie Dexter will love this," she said.

"Ange, we can't do anything. We need proof. We'd have a libel writ slapped on us as quick as lightning. No way. We need proof." He made them both a drink and sat mulling over the events of the day for a while, then went to bed. He struggled for hours to get to sleep, tossing and turning. Surely there was some way to get in touch with Emily Fleet. He decided he would contact the Gazette and put an ad in there. It was a risk, as somebody could put two and two together, but he decided to do it anyway.

Young And Old

Emily jumped at the sound of a knock on her door. She didn't get many callers and was pleasantly surprised to see Sam standing there.

"Sam! What a lovely surprise. Come in."

Sam was out of breath. Emily's home was at the top of a small hill and it was quite warm out.

"Would you like a drink?" she asked.

Sam gasped, then laughed. "A cup of tea would be lovely, Emily. Thanks."

"No problem. Take a seat." she replied.

Sam really admired Emily. She was a very intelligent woman who had crammed so much into her life.

"You take one sugar Sam, don't you?" she called from her kitchen.

"One and a bit please, Emily."

Moments later, Emily returned with two mugs of tea and sat down. She had a lot of time for Sam. He was a very interesting old man. Sometimes he would tell her stories about when he was a youngster.

He and his brother, George, would get up to some things that surprised her, but it was generally acceptable in the northeast in those days.

She laughed when Sam talked about picking up coal on Roker Beach. Their bags had holes in them, and usually George and he would race back to their house in Grindon and end up with next to nothing in the sacks. Then they would have to go back and get some more.

"I've brought you a couple of months' supply of Gazettes that George sent me, Emily. You said you would enjoy reading about your, or should I say our, old town."

"Oh lovely, Sam. I'll read them from cover to cover. Thank you." She picked up one of them and flicked through a few pages and seemed, Sam thought, genuinely interested.

"It's a hot one today, Emily," Sam said, still perspiring. It was quite a walk for him.

Emily replied, "Well you won't have to walk back, Sam. I'll drop you in town. I have to go out anyway."

"Thanks." Sam was grateful. He was in his seventies now and Lima was the right climate for his arthritis. He could manage much better here than in dear old England.

Emily was currently between jobs, but was never out of work for very long. She had, over the years, worked hard and gained a lot of respect for her unique style of physical education and aerobics. She almost methodically called back on old work places and almost always was taken back for a few months at a time.

After dropping Sam off home, she herself had a couple of chores to do, then returned home herself. Whilst out, she thought about the papers that Sam had brought and was looking forward to having a trip down memory lane.

Courage Of Jamie

Jamie wasn't well. Ada was looking after him, but he was sweating one minute and shivering the next. "Do you want me to get some Lucozade, Jamie?" she asked.

"If you don't mind, Ada. Thanks." The thought of Lucozade sounded good.

"Sharon's been on the phone again, Jamie. Why don't you call her back?"

Jamie thought for a moment. "I don't want anyone fussing over me, Ada, except you that is. She means well, but I'd rather just lay here and get rid of this bug. Give her my apologies would you please, Ada? Is Percy over his problem yet?"

Ada just shook her head. "No, not at all. He's a worse patient than you, Jamie. I'd better get back to the poor so and so. I'll get your Lucozade when I'm out, okay?" She hurried off.

"Thanks, Ada," Jamie called, but he didn't think she heard him.

Jamie's thoughts turned to Aaron. The main benefit of being poorly was that he saw less of Aaron, although, from what Harry told him, Aaron had seemed quieter of late and nothing like as nasty. He even seemed genuinely concerned about the closure of the home.

He wondered what was going to happen. He knew there were efforts being made to fight the closure and get the support of the town behind them. You never know. Maybe, just maybe, something could be done.

Harry entered the room. "You have a visitor, Jamie." Harry stood back, and Barry walked in the room.

"How are you, Jamie?" Barry asked.

"I'm not too bad thanks, Mr. Wilson. How's it looking about the closure plans? Any news?"

Barry just shook his head. "Nothing as yet, son. But we'll keep trying till something gives. We certainly won't give up without a fight, that's for sure."

Jamie felt that, if anyone could prevent the closure, it would be Barry and Angela.

"Jamie, I have to ask for your help. We need to involve the local paper at some stage and I was wondering if you would let the Gazette interview you about your time at Jack Fleet House." Jamie sat quietly. Barry took his time. "You don't have to do it if you don't want to, Jamie, but being the most senior boy/man here, it would seem logical that the locals should know how you feel about what the council are trying to do."

Jamie sat up straight. "Of course I will Barry. Just give me a couple of days to get over this illness. I'll do what you want."

"You're a good lad, Jamie, but don't panic. It won't be for a while yet. We have some other avenues to explore first. I just needed to know that you were up for it. Well done. I'll see you soon, okay?" Barry turned to leave the room.

"Barry," Jamie called loudly.

"Yes, son."

"Will Angela come next time, if she's not too busy?"

"That's a promise, son, that's a promise." Barry laughed quietly to himself as he walked down the stairs. Jamie liked them both, but he adored Angela.

"How did you get on?" Ada enquired.

"He's gonna do it. He seemed apprehensive at first, but he'll do it, no problem." Barry was pleased with Jamie's response and it showed. "How's Percy doing?" he asked, knowing full well what the reply was going to be.

"Predictably," Ada sighed. "Oh, you know, he's dying. He's only got a temperature but he's dying. You men make me laugh. Barry, are you as bad as him?"

Barry nodded. "Speak to Angie. She'd agree with you, Ada." He laughed, said his goodbyes, clicked the button on his car keys and opened the door of his XJR.

He loved his car. He always said to Angie "I'll know I've made it when I've got myself a Jag." Sure enough, he was very successful and liked the nice things in life. They had decided to move to the southwest, but house hunting was put on hold due to the trouble at Jack Fleet. They both felt that this problem needed their fullest possible attention. He pulled into his drive and was surprised at what he saw: the Mayor's chauffeur–driven vehicle. How long had he been here, and what did he want?

Angela met him at the front door. "Jock's here, Barry. He's only just arrived. I was about to phone you."

"What's he said, anything?" Barry asked.

"Just small talk, love. He gives me the creeps. Be careful what you say to him. He's slippery."

Barry thought, "You're too right there, me darling." Jock smiled when Barry entered the lounge.

"Mr. McBride. What a surprise. What brings you here? Nothing wrong, I hope."

"On the contrary, Barry. I have no problems with you at all. In fact, I'm here to help you."

"Really," Barry thought. "Pull the other one."

"Okay, what can you do for me then, Mr. Mayor?"

"Well, it's like this. You know this new building project? Well I .... I mean we thought we would like to give local businesses first refusal on tendering for supplies to the builders. And you, being the only local plumbing business, we thought you would like to offer your services. I'm sure you would appreciate that this would mean a considerable increase in your turnover for around two-and –a-half to three years, not forgetting perks and incentives that may be included..."

Barry cut in. "Hold it right there, Mr. Mayor. If you think I'm gonna jump into your pocket, you've got another think coming and, as for your project, I wouldn't count my chickens if I were you. Now I would like you to leave.... Angie, show him out."

Jock wasn't used to people turning him down. "If you change your..."

Barry was getting annoyed. "Don't hold your breath, Mr. Mayor. You'll keel over before I jump into bed with you. Now, goodbye."

Barry gave a big sigh. Angie never said a word. She just put her arms around him and held him tight.

Downtime For Percy

Percy wasn't well. Ada sensed it was more to do with all the hassle, and she found it very difficult to motivate Percy into doing anything positive. He would just shrug his shoulders and say, "What's the point?" Ada was beginning to lose her patience with him. Of course he was hurting, she understood that, but it was like having somebody laying on the floor holding on to your leg everywhere you went.

"Percy!" Ada yelled. "When are you going to snap out of it. I know we only have a couple of weeks, but you can't sit around moping. For Christ's sake, start fighting back instead of letting everyone walk all over you." Percy just sat motionless. "You're just giving up, aren't you? You say you care." Percy's face went red. "I'm sorry. I know you care." Ada realised straight away she'd overstepped the mark. "It's just not like you, Percy. You've never been a quitter but, right at this moment, you seem to be just that."

Percy thought for a moment. She was right, as usual. He'd all but given up the fight. "Ada, I'm so sorry. It's just everything's building up and I don't know how to handle it."

There was a knock on their door. Ada went and opened it. It was Jamie.

"Hello love. Come in. What's up?"

Jamie wasn't backwards in coming forward. He came straight to the point. "I want to know what's happening. What do you think is gonna happen to Jack Fleet and all of us?" Jamie sighed. "All of us," he thought. There was hardly anyone left to worry about, just Harry, Aaron and himself. Since the notice to shut down, no new children were coming in and the last few were being ambered very quickly.

"Jamie," Ada said. "I'm not going to lie to you. It's not looking good. Although there is some... sorry, not some... a lot of effort being made to prevent this horrible thing from happening. It seems that we are between a rock and a hard place. I mean, we don't seem to have any way around it." Ada paused. She felt so bad for Jamie. He was hurting and was going to be hurt even more as far as she could see.

"Jamie," Percy stood up "Jamie, I give you my word. We will not let the council run all over us. In the past, when we've had problems, we've fought and fought hard to get through them. And I'll tell you something else. No jumped-up, crooked, Scottish dwarf of a mayor is gonna get the better of me!"

Ada and Jamie were stunned. Percy left the room.

"Jamie, how about that!" Ada cried.

"I think he believes he can do something Ada, don't you?" Jamie asked

"Yes Jamie. I think you're right."

Percy was on the phone. "Okay Barry, see you there."

Ada walked in. "See you where, Percy?"

"I'm gonna see the two Ronnies and Barry at the pub. We are gonna beat this."

"Angie," Barry called.

"Yes, love." Angie was feeding the chicks.

"Percy's just been on the phone. He wants us all to meet at the pub. You gonna come?"

Angie shook her head. "You go, love. I'll clean up here and sort us out some food for when you come back."

"That's just it sweetheart. I don't know how long I'm gonna be. He sounded very angry. I wouldn't like to put a time on it."

"That's alright. I'll sort something to eat that won't be too sad to go in the microwave." Barry smiled. "Are you sure?"

"Not a problem, babe. Just give Percy my love and do your best for him."

She was a wonderful woman, Barry thought to himself. She never ever complained about anything or anyone.... Well except Jock McBride. So, with Angie's blessing, Barry set off for the pub by taxi. He knew what a long night this could turn out to be.

"How are you guv'nor?" asked the taxi driver.

Barry gave the taxi driver the whole story during the ride to the pub. It was quite easy, said the driver, to see why Barry was so wound up.

"Good luck," said the driver, "I hope it all works out, mate. That's £7.50 please."

Barry gave him a ten-pound note. "Keep the change, fella. Mind how you go." Barry had a soft spot for cab drivers. After all, it was a tough job. Not because of having to pick up people who, more often than not, were worse for wear, but because of the long hours they had to do.

Barry entered the lounge bar. Ronnie J was behind the bar. He gave a knowing smile. There was no sign of Percy yet.

"Hi, Barry." It was Ronnie Dexter. "What's this all about?" he asked.

Barry shrugged his shoulders. "I know as much as you. Percy phoned me about half an hour ago. That's all I know. Anyway, what you having Ronnie?"

Ronnie shook his head. "I'll just have an orange juice, Barry, please. I'm driving to Brentwood tonight when this is over, so I'll pass if that's okay."

Ronnie Dexter was a very nice man. Barry thought to himself that he should be on one of the national newspapers with his talent, rather than a local rag. Still, if it meant more power to their cause, then he would settle for that.

"Where's Percy?" Ronnie Jackson asked as he sat down with Ronnie and Barry. "He phoned me giving it the big 'un and he ain't even here. What's going on boys?"

Barry replied, "Let's just wait and see."

Percy was on edge. He was so annoyed with himself. He had been so negative, so despondent, he could kick himself. When he entered the pub, he was pleased to see they were all there.

"Hi guys," he yelled "Sorry I'm late. Can I get you a drink?"

Barry said, "I'll have a pint, cheers Perce."

Ronnie said, "Go on then, just one more. I've been here since eleven this morning. Bloody dreymen were useless today."

"Stop whinging, Ronnie," said Ronnie Dexter. "You've cracked it with this pub. The food's good I've heard. Judging by the punters in here tonight, I'd say the beer's good too!"

Ronnie grudgingly smiled and nodded his head. He was right. Ron and Barb had really turned the pub around. You couldn't get a meal unless you booked six weeks in advance, so they were definitely doing something right.

They all sat in the bay window area of the pub.

"Right," Percy said. "We, us, are going to pull out all the stops. Call in favours. Do whatever it takes to stop this corrupt council from shutting down Jack Fleet. I know that I can count on you three to do your level best, and I want to apologise for my lack of effort over the last couple of weeks. I.... I suppose I was just brow beaten into thinking that we wouldn't be able to stop this closure from happening. Well, I want you three to know, we are gonna beat this.... Jock McBride won't know what's hit him."

"It's about time we had some sign of fight from you, Percy," Ronnie Jackson said.

Percy agreed. "I don't know what's been going on in my head, fellas, but all I can say is that I'm through the worst of it now and all my energy is going to go into saving Jack Fleet House and, with your support, I just can't see us being beaten."

"Like your style," Barry said. "Angie's ready to help, as I'm sure Barb is a well."

"The one thing that's bugging me," Ronnie J said, "is this Emily Fleet thing. How are we gonna find her? She could be the answer to all our prayers."

They all agreed and discussed different methods or angles they could use to find Emily Fleet.

Looking For Emily

The alarm clock went off. He hit the snooze button. It was a late night. Angie was asleep on the sofa when he got home. It was good that Percy was more like his old self. He was a bit of a tiger in the old days. Barry thought to himself, "If we're gonna do this, we need everyone to be 'in the zone' so to speak."

"Do you want a cuppa Doll?" Angie nodded. Doll was his name for Angie, and Angie didn't mind him calling her that, but got annoyed if anybody else did. He had almost left the bedroom when she called out, "Don't burn the bacon, love."

Barry stopped and gave her a look, turned and smiled. He made his way to the kitchen and got the frying pan out. After breakfast, he cleaned while Angie fed the babies. She asked what had happened at the meeting the night before.

"Well, Percy seems to have snapped out of it. It seems that Jamie lit the fuse and I don't know what he said, but he certainly seems to be like the old Percy."

Barry went and sat in the garden. He thought about the meeting and which way they could go to at least slow down the council. Ronnie Dexter had an idea about doing a search through the archives on a couple of issues, such as who holds the deeds on Jack Fleet and looking up the Fleet family tree. The first was probably a non-starter as access would be almost impossible. If there was a possibility of the ownership causing a problem for the council, the deeds and proof of ownership would probably disappear, conveniently. The search on the Fleet family tree was more promising. Sure, they all knew about Emily, but it was more than possible that there was still family living locally. This, indeed, needed looking into, but discreetly. He didn't want the crooked Scotsman finding out.

"That's a good idea," Angie said. Barry agreed but wasn't too sure how to go about it.

Angie had an idea.

A short while later, Angie called Barry while he was down with the parrots. "Baz, I've just spoken to Barb and she has told me of a company where you can look up your family tree and everything." She was so excited. Barry calmed her down with a hug.

"Well done, babe. Well done."

It was something. He didn't know what would come of it, but it was something. He had better tell the two Ronnies and Percy. In fact, Ronnie Dexter was the ideal person to talk to, with his knowledge. Yes, that's what he'd do. It took a while to speak to Ronnie Dexter. He left messages on his mobile, office and home and eventually he got the call back.

"Barry, how are you?" Ronnie asked. Barry started to tell him about the company and was just about to ask Ronnie what he thought when Ronnie stopped him in his tracks.

"Barry, hold on. I've already tried that company. Lucy in our office spent some time looking into it for me. She has traced her family and so, when I was talking to my colleagues about everything, she got me excited as you are. Sadly, we had no joy. The only living family members are Emily and Peter, but nobody knows where the hell they are. Sorry, mate."

Barry was stunned. "Okay, Ronnie. We'll keep on somehow. I don't know where we'll turn next, but we will keep trying. Thanks again, Ronnie."

Angie entered the room. She could tell Barry was down. "What's up, love?" she asked caringly.

"The family tree is no good; no clues. Ronnie Dexter has already tried it. Another dead end. I don't know which way to go next, love. It's getting to the point where you just......"

"Barry Wilson, don't you dare talk like that. I will not let you give in." She was determined, she was right, and he knew it.

"I won't give in, Ange. It's just that right now I can't see a way to stop this terrible thing from happening."

Lucy's A Nice Girl

Lucy McGregor had only worked for Ronnie Dexter for a few months. Starting off as a temp, she had impressed Ronnie so much that he took her on full time.

She was twenty-six years old, blonde and quite pretty. Ronnie's usual comment was 'If I was twenty years younger, I'd...' She would usually stop him there and tease him. She had really made an impression, so when Ronnie asked her to accompany him on a trip to Jack Fleet House, she was only too pleased to say yes.

Ronnie, as everyone requested, was to do an article on the home and go to print at a time they all felt would benefit their cause the most.

It was while they were in the grounds of Jack Fleet that the penny dropped, so to speak.

Ronnie said out loud, not really talking to anybody, "Emily Fleet, where are you?"

Lucy felt sick. She looked terrible, all of a sudden. So much so that Ronnie asked, "Are you alright, love? You look as if you've seen a ghost?"

Lucy shook her head. "I've got a bit of a headache, Ronnie, that's all. I'll be okay."

Ronnie said, "We can do this another time, Lucy. It doesn't have to be done right now."

Lucy looked down at the ground and then at the building. She noticed a boy with dark glasses gazing out of the window. He looked so sad.

"Who's that, Ronnie?" she asked

Ronnie looked up. "It must be Jamie. He's the blind boy who has been here longer than anybody and, to be honest, he is the focal point of our campaign."

That wasn't what Lucy wanted to hear. This was getting worse. She would go and see her uncle at the first possible opportunity. She managed to finish the tour of Jack Fleet nevertheless.

Jock McBride's private phone rang. He picked it up. It was his niece, Lucy. "Hello Lucy. How are you?" Jock said with a smile.

"Uncle Jock, you have been lying to me. You.... "

Jock cut in. "I beg your pardon. Now listen to me."

"Uncle Jock, you never said you were trying to get the kids home shut down when you asked your little favour. You said it was..." She was stopped abruptly.

"Hold on, young lady. I get you sorted with a job and a flat and this is how you go on? I asked you to do one little thing for me and this is how you repay me?"

"Okay, but you lied about why you wanted me to do it. Why didn't you tell me?" she asked.

Jock thought for a minute. "Lucy, you must understand that Ronnie and that paper crucify me for every little misdemeanour. Surely you understand I want a little revenge."

"Uncle Jock, listen to yourself. Revenge? We are talking about young kids here. All they have is Jack Fleet House and you're going on about..."

Jock interrupted. "Lucy, I'm sorry ... I never thought. I just got so wound up with the local paper and I know Dexter is behind most of the bad press I get. It just makes me angry, that's all."

He had a problem and he knew it. He really needed Lucy to be on his side and it was not looking good. "Lucy, I'm going to help the kids find somewhere real soon. I know you would like the place to stay open, but I really can't see how it can be done. I'm only one person on the council, contrary to what Mr. Dexter and his cronies may say. I don't run the bloody council. I'm just a member. I don't even get a vote unless there is a stalemate. Then I use my casting vote."

Lucy was not convinced. She did try to understand what her uncle said, but she was still very angry that he had lied to her.

"Uncle, I'm not happy. I need to think about this. I have to give myself some time to sort this mess out. I'm going home. I'll speak to you tomorrow." She ended the call.

"What to do now?" she asked herself. "What to do?" First of all, she needed to do what her boss had asked her to do. Get in touch with the company and try to find any family still living locally who were related to the Fleet family. That's it. As soon as she got home, she would start researching. She was determined to help the cause, as much as possible. She did owe her uncle, but you have to draw the line somewhere, she thought.

About half an hour later her phone rang. It was Barry Wilson.

"Hello, Barry. This is a pleasant surprise. How are you?" She had liked Barry from the first moment she met him at a fund-raising dance which he had organised for the local hospice.

"Lucy, my love. I'm fine. How are you?" he replied

She paused. She had been better. "Oh, I'm just the same as usual. What can I do for you?" She hoped it would be something that meant spending some time with him.

"Well, I was talking to your boss Ronnie, and he told me that you didn't have any luck searching for links to the Fleet family and I..."

Lucy interrupted. "Barry, I did have a little look, but not a comprehensive one. In fact, I'm about to spend some time this evening to see if I can't have some success."

"That's great, Lucy. Do you need a hand? I could pop round if you like, give you some support?"

Lucy found herself blushing, "Well, there's not much you can do, Barry, but if you're wanting to, I don't mind. As long as your wife doesn't mind." She was trembling.

"What's your address? I'll try to pop round after dinner, say about eightish. Is that okay?"

"Yes, of course. I'll see you then." She put the phone down and ran to the bathroom.

Barry, to be fair, didn't have a clue how Lucy felt about him.

What's Cooking?

Ada was busy preparing the evening meals and, even though there were fewer children, it was her busiest time of the day.

Percy walked into the kitchen. "How're you doing pet? What delights have we got tonight?"

Ada smiled. "Percy, you know full well what's cooking. You requested it yesterday, remember?"

"Well, my love, I only asked. I take it that means 'tattie hash'."

"Correct, as if you didn't know, you old scoundrel." She couldn't be hard on him. She loved him so much and was only too aware of what he was going through with the threatened closure and everything.

Jamie and Harry poked their heads around the door. "What's for tea?" they said together.

Ada laughed. "Frogs legs and toenails if you don't leave me alone. Now be off with you."

Jamie and Harry giggled and went into the dining area. Dinner was not due for an hour or so, but Percy had told them it was 'tattie hash' and it was their favourite meal also, so they were anxious to get stuck in. As they sat at a table, Harry turned and noticed Aaron sitting in the corner. After a minute or so, he plucked up the courage to speak to him.

"Hey, Aaron. Why don't you join us?" Harry asked.

Aaron just sat and ignored the question.

Jamie and Harry had noticed that Aaron had gone from a bully to almost a recluse in just a few weeks.

To his surprise, Jamie found himself asking the same question. "Come on, Aaron. Come over and join us."

Aaron stood up and stared at the two of them. "It's alright for you, ain't it? You won't be homeless. It's me who's gonna suffer. Just leave me alone." With that, he stormed out of the dining room.

Almost immediately, Percy was standing in front of them. "Are we okay, then? Ready for some tattie hash?"

They both nodded and said they were. Then Jamie said, "Percy, what's the matter with Aaron?"

Percy seemed surprised at the question. "I'm sorry. Am I hearing right? You're concerned about Aaron?" Percy was indeed surprised. He didn't have anything concrete, but he was sure Aaron wasn't being the best of friends to Jamie and Harry.

"Percy," Jamie interrupted. "Aaron is not my favourite person, I'm sure you are aware, but he is definitely not behaving the same way he usually does. I don't know why, but he's not himself." Harry nodded in agreement.

Percy thought for a moment. He also had noticed a change in Aaron, so much so that he'd been in touch with Aaron's brother Stephen who, to be honest, didn't seem too interested when told of his current unusual behaviour. Still, what more could he do? He found it very difficult to talk to Aaron. Funnily enough, it was Ada who seemed to be the only one to get close to him and even she found it difficult. He needed to sort this one out. Fantastic, he thought. With everything else, he had another problem that seemed almost impossible to solve.

"Grub up!" Ada yelled.

Percy smiled as, one by one, the remaining children entered as if they were waiting around the corner. For the next ten minutes or so, all you could hear was the sound of cutlery on plates as they all tucked in.

Surely Not

The doorbell rang in Lucy's flat. "Oh, god." She was so nervous. She opened the door.

"Hello, Lucy. How are you? I've brought a bottle for you. You don't have to open it now. It's just a gesture to say thank you."

"You're too kind, Barry. It's my favourite as well. I'll put it in the freezer for ten minutes or so. Won't you come on in? Take a seat." She was so nervous. She hoped it didn't show.

"How's your job going at the Gazette, Lucy? I've not seen Ronnie for a little while."

"Oh, I think I'm doing okay. It's a very busy little job. There's always something to do, and no two days are the same, which helps the day go quicker." Small talk, she thought to herself. We're making small talk. "How's Angie, Barry?" She really didn't want to know but the words came out anyway.

"She's fine, sweetheart. She's just fine. She'll have her whinge about the babies, but she's a good 'un. They broke the mould when they made her."

Barry was being genuine. Angie really was special. "I don't know how she puts up with an old codger like me. Hardly ever home, always something to do when I do get home. That's why coming round here tonight for me was a nice idea. It's a break from routine. Nice young lady and a good cause to chase up on the old computer. Makes a nice change."

Lucy thought for a moment. "You can come here anytime, Barry. I think Angela's a very lucky lady. You're a lovely man." What was she saying? Where did that come from, she thought?

"Thank you, sweetheart. I'll tell you what. If I was twenty years younger, you might change your tune." He laughed.

"Age has nothing to do with it, Barry. It makes no difference to me." There, she had crossed the line. That wasn't too painful. She had only said what anyone would have said in the same situation.

Barry seemed to go quiet.

"Right, Barry, shall we start?" Lucy smiled.

"Okay, what do we have to do? I mean, how do we begin?" Barry laughed. He still didn't understand computers. Sure, he could play solitaire and pinball but, as for anything else, he was hopeless.

"Well, we have a few options. There's a website for almost anything. As you probably know, it's just finding the right niche. But I think if we start with Registrar of Births and Deaths, we can build a picture from there."

"I wouldn't have thought of that, Lucy. So, we get a list of members of the Fleet family and see if they are still alive. Great." Barry seemed pleased with himself.

"Well, not exactly Barry. We'll be able to find if there are any more family members that we are not aware of but, as to whether they're still alive or not, unless they died in this area, we won't know. Do you see?"

Barry stroked his chin. He did see. "I'm not much use am I, pet?" he said disappointedly.

"That's okay." Lucy said with a smile. "Two heads are still better than one. You'll be alright." Lucy clicked on the mouse and they sat next to each other.

The registrar idea did not bear any fruit at all. They also tried the 'Census' website, but there were no Fleet names in the last twenty years.

"Ah well, we tried," said Barry. He was optimistic an hour ago. Now he was just feeling down.

Lucy smiled. "Well, well! Is that all it takes to get you all disappointed, Barry Wilson. We have lots of avenues to try yet but, if you want to give up, that's up to you." She laughed at him.

He too saw the funny side. "Alright, alright. I get your point. What do we do next?"

"Well, we have a break and a nice glass of wine."

A loud bang came from the kitchen.

"Oh, no." Lucy shouted.

"What was that?" Barry replied.

"I forgot to take the wine out of the freezer."

They both ran to the kitchen. Sure enough, on opening the door, the wine was everywhere and, being a chest freezer, it had covered everything. Lucy didn't panic. She started taking everything out and putting it on the draining board.

"It'll take some getting rid of…. the smell, I mean. Hopefully it shouldn't affect the taste of anything," she said.

"You'll be okay, pet. The smell will soon go. Do you want me to go and get another bottle?"

"No, it's alright Barry. I'm not fussed. Don't go on my behalf."

After another half hour or so of searching, they decided to call it a day.

"Lucy, thanks for trying pet. Seems there's not much we're gonna be able to do with this one." Barry was now feeling very low. Lucy sensed it too.

She gave him a hug. "We won't give up. Well, I won't give up. Look at you. There's still a chance we'll find something."

Barry squeezed her tight. His mind went elsewhere. She was right. She was also beautiful. "Cor, look at me," he said.

Lucy smiled. "What?"

"I'm nearly twice your age and I'm cuddling you. You're a beautiful young lady. I…. I better be off."

Before he could let go of her, she kissed him briefly on the lips. He almost returned the kiss as she pulled away. They looked at each other and nervously smiled.

"Barry, you're a lovely man. Don't put yourself down about your age. I could say I was born too late, couldn't I?"

Barry looked a little puzzled.

"Now, off you go. I'll keep in touch. I've a few more ideas. I'll let you know if I have any joy," Lucy said reassuringly.

At that, they said their goodbyes.

After he'd gone, she just stood with her back to the front door. He was very special, but he was also married.

Barry sat in his car for about five minutes contemplating the evening, then went home. It was only a short drive home. It was just after 10:30. He hadn't realised the time. He was just pulling onto his drive when his mobile rung. It was Lucy.

"Hello love, what's up?" Barry asked.

"Nothing's up. I just had an idea. I don't know why I didn't think of it before. What about an ad in the Gazette to see if anyone knows the whereabouts of Emily Fleet, or indeed any of the Fleet family?" She sounded really excited.

"Lucy, my love. We've already done it. Your guv'nor suggested it a couple of months ago."

"Oh, I'm sorry Barry. I thought…"

Barry interrupted her. "Don't apologise for trying to help the situation, sweetheart. And thanks for this evening. Although it was fruitless, it was nice spending time with you. I'll speak to you soon. Bye love."

She returned his wishes and hung up. Two hours later she was still awake.

Break For Emily And....

Emily Fleet was so relieved. Another term was over at last. She had found the last couple of months quite a strain. Well at least now she could make some plans about how to spend the next six or seven weeks.

Sam had been up a couple of times in the last few weeks, and she had a pile of Gazettes to read through. First of all, though, it was chill out time, off to the coast. Her favourite haunt was a place called Piura, about two hundred and fifty miles up the coast. It was paradise. She would make sure Sam was okay and see if he needed running anywhere before she went. That should clear the way for a trouble-free week or so, giving her a chance to recharge her batteries. She arranged to pick Sam up at 9:30 in the morning. He needed a few bits and was most grateful she had phoned.

Sam was sitting on the wall outside his house. Locals called it a villa, but to Sam it was his house, his home, and he loved it. And his garden at the rear was beautiful, although he always told Emily that his roof garden was his pride and joy.

"Morning, my little darling. How are you today?" Sam seemed very chirpy.

"I'm fine. Finished term yesterday. Looking forward to a nice rest." That was an understatement, to say the least.

"You enjoy it darling. You deserve it." Sam liked her a lot. She had been a really good friend over the last year or so.

The drive into town was always a little bumpy. Some of the areas they had to drive through were really run down. A vast number of Lima's ten million inhabitants didn't have electricity, or even fresh running water.

As they parked in the centre of town, Sam asked, "Have you read the Gazettes I brought up to you, darling?"

Emily shook her head. "I'm going to take them up to Guayaquil with me and read them while I'm getting my tan sorted, Sam."

He laughed. "Ah, you sun worshippers are all the same. Now you listen. That's very hot up there this time of the year. Make sure you don't get too much midday sun."

Emily nodded her head. "Don't worry. I'll be careful." Sam was right though. It was very hot. For ten months of the year, most of Peru was covered in low cloud, but in January and February, it cleared and became red hot.

Sam asked, "Why don't you go on the Gazette's website? Not that I know anything about computers, but it's all you read and hear about these days. Wibbly wobbly dot something or other, I don't know."

Emily laughed out loud. "Sam, www.com, not wibbly wobbly. I don't know where you get that from."

They both laughed together. Sam didn't take too long to get his bits and pieces together and it was around lunchtime when they got back to his place.

"Thanks, Emily. Do you want a drink of something before you go darling?"

It was a good idea. She wasn't going to see Sam for a week or so, so she agreed. "A nice cup of tea would hit the spot, Sam, if you don't mind."

"No problem. I'll show you my roof garden, darling. You'll love it." Sam was very house proud. There wasn't a thing out of place. Ornaments he'd brought from England mingled with local pottery and pictures. It gave the house a really warm feel.

They walked the three flights of stairs to the roof garden. Sam was a little out of breath.

"See, Emily, this time of year the extra few degrees make all the difference. It's so hot."

"Sam, this is beautiful. You must really have worked hard."

"I can't spend as much time up here as usual, darling. Early mornings and late evenings have to do. I can't bear the heat any other time."

They returned to the ground floor. Emily noticed a Gazette on the dining room table.

"Came yesterday, that one. You can take it if you want. I haven't read it yet, though," Sam exclaimed.

Emily shook her head. "No Sam, you read it. I've got plenty to be going on with. I'll read this one when I get back."

He gave her a hug as she left his front door. She was about to get into her car when she turned and went back to Sam.

"Sam, have you got a piece of paper and a pen?" she asked.

"Why yes, love. What for?"

"Well, I know you've got my mobile, but the reception is not great." Sam handed her a pen and his notebook.

"So, this is the number of the place I am staying if you have any problems. I should only be a week or so, but you never know. I might stay longer." She really did care for him.

"Thanks, pet. I'll not bother you though, but I understand why."

"It's just for me really, to know that you can get hold of me. Selfish really."

"Don't be daft. Now you get off. You have a long journey ahead of you. Have a great time."

She gave him a big hug and set off back to her apartment.

It was two p.m. A bit late really, but she decided to leave today anyway. If she was lucky with her connections, she could be there by eightish. She just caught the train in time. The first couple of hours were stop free. The ocean was to the left, the Andes to the right. It was beautiful, save for the odd areas where run down shanties popped up out of nowhere. The train had just stopped in Chiclayo when her mobile rang. It was Sam.

"Sam, what's up?" she asked, concerned as she hadn't been gone long.

"Can you hear me, darling? It's Sam. You're breaking up…. Hello…" Silence.

She couldn't get a signal. She would call him from a land line when she arrived, although he sounded okay. It was nearly ten o'clock by the time she arrived at her hotel. She decided not to ring Sam. She would leave it till the morning.

She had stayed here on her first visit last year and was pleased that Helmut, the manager/receptionist/porter remembered her.

"Madame Fleet, how are you? It's lovely to see you again." Helmut was Swedish, though many thought that, because of his name, he was German.

"Lovely to see you too, Helmut. Are you well?"

"It is …. how you say, must not grumble. Is that correct?"

Emily laughed, "Yes, that's it, Helmut."

They exchanged a few more pleasantries, then Helmut showed her to her room.

"I've booked you into a room with a view of the ocean. I hope it is to your liking, my dear."

Emily walked out onto the balcony. Beautiful, she thought.

"It's lovely, Helmut. Thank you."

Helmut was smiling. "I've a small meal of salad saved for you downstairs. Oh and I nearly forgot. There is a message for you. I'll go and get it." He was gone before she could say she would come down and get it. Never mind.

When she arrived downstairs, Helmut was just about to come up to her.

"There, there is your message. It is from Stan or Sam."

"Sam it will be, Helmut, thank you." She walked into the restaurant and read the note.

Pressing Times

Tuesdays were always a busy day at the Gazette, and today was no different. The sports section was always busy but, with Ronnie Dexter at the helm, it always seemed to fall into place. He never seemed that busy to Lucy, but he knew everything that was going on and where to find whatever was needed without any problem. During one of the quieter moments, Lucy approached his desk and asked, "Ronnie, do you have a minute?"

Ronnie looked up from his Times crossword. "Well, here I am, as you can see, very busy," and started laughing. "Go ahead, what's up?"

"I don't know if you know, but I spent some time with Barry Wilson the other evening, trying to find anything we could on Emily Fleet's whereabouts and I was wondering when the ad was placed in our paper and if there was any feedback at all?"

Ronnie shook his head. "I for one don't know of any feedback, Lucy, and, as for when, just look it up on your computer. But it has to be a couple of months at least, I would have thought."

Lucy shrugged her shoulders. "I just wondered if it was worth doing again. I mean two months is quite a while. Can we run it again?"

"I don't see why not. Do you want to deal with it?"

She nodded excitely.

"Good. That's settled then. I'll clear the path for you. You can get it in this week's, can't you?"

"Thanks, Ronnie. I'll sort it straight away." Lucy dealt with the matter promptly. "I know," she thought , "I'll phone Barry. He'll be pleased."

"Hello, Barry Wilson's mobile. Can I help you?" It was Angie.

"Oh hello, Mrs. Wilson. It's Lucy at the Gazette. Is Barry busy?"

"Well, not really busy, Lucy. He's in the aviary with the birds. I can get him on the intercom if you can hold?"

"No, it's okay, Mrs. Wilson, I'll…. Well could you ask him to call me when he has a minute please?"

"No problem Lucy, and Lucy.."

"Yes," Lucy replied.

"Lucy, my name is Angie. Please call me Angie."

"Okay…. Angie. Thank you.

About forty-five minutes later, while she was tidying her desk and getting ready to leave work, her mobile rang.

"Hello, Lucy. How're you doing? Any news?"

"I'm fine, Barry. I just thought I'd let you know. We're running the Emily Fleet ad again this week. It's been nearly three months since the last one. I spoke to Ronnie and he has agreed to run it again. That's good news, isn't it"?

"That's great, Lucy. On behalf of everyone at the home, I'd like to thank you for your efforts."

"No need to thank me. It's for a really worthy cause and I don't subscribe to the 'progress at any price' attitude that some people seem to have in this area. I'll be glad to help anyway I can." Oops, she thought, went a bit over the top there. Normally just say enough.

"Well, Lucy, all I can say is that, if you feel like that, we'd better get you right on our side. Are you free Thursday evening?" Lucy didn't hesitate, "Yes, what's going on?"

Barry informed her that there was a council meeting, and that all interested parties would be there. The public gallery was sure to be full also. So, if she could come along and listen, he sure would appreciate it.

Lucy thought for a moment before finally agreeing to attend. There was the small matter of Uncle Jock, the Mayor. Difficult, but she was only going to listen. Her uncle probably wouldn't even know she was there, so she said she would be there.

"Good girl. It's usually over around 9:30. We go for a couple of drinks afterwards, if you fancy it. I'll run you home afterwards."

"Okay," Lucy said. What was she doing? She only had to be in Barry's company and she felt all funny. And when he spoke, or even put his arm on her shoulder, she felt like she was melting. She really had not experienced that feeling before. Yes, he was married. She kept telling herself this, but…. Didn't he go out of his way to be nice to her and was constantly praising her? He must think something of her or why all the fuss? We'll see what happens, she thought to herself. That's it. We'll wait and see.

Contact...At Last

Emily rose at around 9:30 and walked out to the balcony. "Ah, beautiful," she whispered to herself. And beautiful it was. It was maybe two or three miles to the sea, and she had a clear view from her lofty position. After a light breakfast, she decided to phone Sam. Although the message did not convey any urgency, she thought she should get it out of the way so the rest of the day could be hers.

"Hello," Sam shouted.

"Hi Sam, it's me Emily. Is everything alright?"

"Oh, Emily. How are you? I'm really sorry to trouble you. It's just the Gazette..."

"The Gazette? What do you mean?" she interrupted.

"Well," Sam said. "Well, it seems that somebody wants to get in touch with you. There's an ad in the Gazette asking if anyone knows the whereabouts of Emily Fleet or any other Fleet family member, but it doesn't say what the reason is for this."

"I haven't got a clue," Emily replied. As far as she knew, there were no remaining family members in the area.

Sam was about to speak again. "Do you...."

Emily butted in. "Sam, when I come back, I'll come up and see you and we'll sort it out. Is that okay?"

Sam agreed, and they said their goodbyes.

Emily was curious and, being inquisitive, opened her case and pulled out the bag that Sam had given her with the Gazettes in. There were maybe a dozen or more. She decided to browse through them while she was tanning herself.

About an hour or so later, she found the same ad in one of those Gazettes. Somebody was quite keen to find her. They had placed the ad two or three months apart, as the only Gazette Sam had was the one that had just arrived. There was no quick way of dealing with the matter. No e-mail address or fax number. So she felt it would be prudent to wait till she returned to Lima when maybe she could even phone the Gazette to find out what this was all about.

Emily had been in the sun too long. She remembered Sam's words and thought to herself that he would have really laid into her about too much midday sun. It was around four in the afternoon and, already, she could feel the heat, especially on her shoulders. So much so that she decided to have a shower and cover her burnt areas with after-sun lotion. There was a knock on her door. She put on her dressing gown and went to answer it.

It was Helmut. "I am so sorry to disturb you. There is a Mr. Mason in reception now. I hope you don't mind. He came to the restaurant last night and asked me if I knew anyone who could help with his shoulder injury. I did mention that you were staying here, and you were a physio, and he would like you to look and see if you could help him. I'm sorry, I hope you don't mind."

Emily smiled. "It's alright, Helmut. Tell him I'll be down in five minutes."

She had done physio work as part of her training and had, from time to time, been able to assist people with muscular injuries. Helmut himself had benefited from her experience.

When Emily arrived at reception, there was nobody there. Helmut suddenly appeared from his office.

"Emily, my dear. I'm afraid Mr. Mason has had to leave. He may be back later, but I know he is due to fly to Japan tomorrow, so he may not."

Emily was quite disappointed. Although she wasn't a fully-fledged physio, she did have a knack for quick, short, sharp treatments that seemed to do the trick. "Oh well, Helmut, can you do me a favour and put on your barman hat? I fancy a..."

Helmut stopped her. "Southern Comfort with lime and lemonade?"

"Perfect," Emily said. It had been her tipple for quite a while now, and Helmut had obviously remembered it from last year.

They both laughed and entered the small bar area.

"Do you know what, Emily? I think I'm going to join you."

Emily laughed. "What, you and Southern comfort? I don't believe you."

It was Helmut's turn to laugh. "No, no, it's too sweet for me. I have a bottle of Napoleon Brandy, which I have had for about eight or nine months. It was given to me as a thank you for services rendered from a customer last year. So, I think it's time I opened it."

Emily smiled. "Good for you, Helmut. We'll get drunk together."

At that, the portable CD player went on and, in a very short space of time, the pair of them were dancing and singing to their hearts' content. They were both quite merry when he walked in. At first, they didn't notice him.

"May I join you?"

Both Emily and Helmut jumped. The bar was hardly the brightest room. Helmut believed in soft lighting.

"Ah, Mr. Mason. Emily, this is Mr. Mason."

Emily smiled at the stranger. He was quite a handsome man, she thought, maybe early forties. "Pleased to meet you, Mr. Mason." Emily offered her hand, which he grasped firmly.

"Lionel, call me Lionel. You guys celebrating something?" he laughed.

Emily laughed with him. "No, no, we are just enjoying a quiet evening. I couldn't be bothered to go out for a meal, so I... Well, we just thought a few drinks in the bar would do tonight. How's your shoulder?"

Lionel thought to himself that first impressions could sometimes be way off the mark, but she seemed really nice. "Oh, it's not so bad. Don't worry about it. It will clear up in a day or so."

Helmut asked, "Are you off to Japan tomorrow, Lionel?"

"No, there's been a change of plan. Seems I need to extend my stay, if that's okay. Perhaps another week or so. Would that be alright?"

Helmut said, "I'll just nip and check. Give me five minutes," and was gone in a flash.

"What do you do?" Emily asked.

"Nothing exciting I'm afraid. Computers. Pretty boring really. What do you do, Emily?"

Emily smiled. "Well, I'm a gym/aerobics teacher and, as Helmut told you, a sort of physio, though I don't have all of my qualifications yet." There was a slight pause. "I could look at your shoulder tomorrow, if you like? Can't promise anything, though."

"I'll see how it is in the morning. Thank you. That's very kind of you."

Helmut came back into the bar. "Next couple of days will be okay. Not sure about the rest. I need to receive confirmation. We'll sort something out though. If I can't help, I'll speak to my brother-in-law. Between us we'll find somewhere."

They spent the rest of the evening getting to know each other. Pretty soon it was just Emily and Lionel, as Helmut was busy serving the rest of the hotel guests.

Eventually Helmut came over. "You two okay? It's 2am. I really must go to bed. You can help yourself to another drink if you like. I don't mind."

"Thank you, Helmut," Emily said. "Would you like another drink, Lionel?"

"Providing I'm not drinking on my own."

Helmut laughed. "Good. I'll see you in the morning. Goodnight."

They both said goodnight and moved to the bar. Emily sat on a stool, while Lionel went behind the bar to pour some drinks.

"Southern Comfort isn't it, Emily?"

"Yes please," she said, "with a dash of lime and lemonade."

He seemed fascinated by Emily's stories of her world travel exploits and genuinely interested, but when Emily asked personal questions about him, he was not very forthcoming. "Ah well," she thought, "I won't push it."

It was just gone three when they retired. Lionel was on the top floor. As they walked up the stairs, trying to be quiet, Emily took to a fit of giggling.

"What is it?" Lionel whispered.

"Nothing," Emily laughed. Then she got the hiccups and that made it even worse. "This is my room, number 13. Unlucky for some …hic." Another fit of giggling.

"I'll see you in the morning," Lionel laughed. "Hold your breath for half an hour."

Emily was still laughing. "Goodnight, Lionel."

"Goodnight, Emily," he replied, pecking her on the cheek.

Ailing…. But Why?

Jamie woke up earlier than usual. Most mornings he arose at around eight o'clock, but today he was wide awake at six-thirty. Ada had told him yesterday he should go to bed earlier instead of listening to his radio and he would feel much better. Ada had mentioned to Percy how Jamie had been looking run down lately.

Jamie went downstairs and walked into the kitchen, which made Ada jump out of her skin.

"Jamie, you really frightened me. What are you doing up so early?"

"I'm not feeling too good. Been awake for ages. My throat is sore, and I've been to the toilet twice in the last couple of hours."

Ada sighed, "Oh, it's probably a bug or something. What… "

Jamie cut in. "Ada, my stomach's really sore."

Ada sensed it was more than a bug. "Jamie, let me take you to your room. I'll get the doctor out."

Percy said, "You'll be lucky. He won't come out. I'll take Jamie to the surgery. It'll be quicker in the end."

The doctors were very busy, but Percy was right. This was the best way to do it. Eventually they entered the doctor's surgery. Percy was quite put out. The surgery, for years, had been very good but, just recently, there had been complaints aired in the local paper. So when he walked in to see a total stranger in the chair, he just sighed.

On their return to Jack Fleet, Ada was on edge. She was genuinely concerned. Jamie had not looked well for some time.

Ada opened the front door. "Well?" she said.

Percy sighed. "He has to go to the hospital for some blood tests, love. Bloody locum at the surgery. I felt like he really didn't give a…"

"Percy, he's only doing his job," Ada interrupted.

Percy replied "Why hasn't he got his own surgery? What's happened to Dr. Pat? He knows everything about Jamie, and Jamie is used to him."

Ada sighed with Percy, trying not to make Jamie feel too down. "Oh well, Jamie, you don't mind a few needles when Dracula takes some blood from you do you?" Ada was trying to make light of the situation.

Jamie was not convinced. "Ada, I think I'll go to my room. I feel tired."

Ada replied, "Okay, my boy. How about a nice cup of tea?" Ada waited for Jamie to reply as she went to the cupboard to get some teabags when she heard a thump behind her. Jamie was lying on the floor.

"Percy, Percy. Quick!" Ada screamed.

Percy came running into the kitchen. "Oh my god, I'll call an ambulance."

Ada knelt down. Jamie was white as a sheet. She put him into the recovery position, and monitored his breathing and pulse. They didn't seem too bad.

"Ambulance is on its way, love," Percy said.

"Make sure the gates are open, and leave the front door open, too. What's going on Percy? What's this now? As if he hasn't got enough problems."

The ambulance arrived around fifteen minutes later. As usual, the paramedics were excellent. Ada thought to herself that it gives you hope that it's not all doom and gloom with the NHS. Ada travelled in the ambulance, while Percy tried to find someone to look after the home. Although there were only seven children left now, it was still a big responsibility. Percy arrived at the hospital about an hour later and, on arrival, could not find any trace of Ada, so he went to reception. The receptionist gave him directions to where Jamie was being treated.

When he got there, Ada was sitting in a bay with no bed in it, crying her eyes out.

"Ada, what's happened?" he cried.

"Oh Percy, I don't know. Jamie came round in the ambulance and didn't seem too bad, but when we got here, he passed out again. Percy, I'm really scared. He looked as white as a sheet."

"It's alright, my love. He's in the best place. They will sort him out," Percy said reassuringly.

It seemed like an eternity. They both sat there, not knowing anything, fearing the worst. Suddenly there he was. His bed trolley was being wheeled back into position, and Jamie was awake.

"Oh Jamie, are you alright? I've been so worried about you."

"I'm feeling a bit sick, Ada. I don't know what's up with me. How did I get here? I'm…."

Percy interrupted. "Jamie, son, don't worry. You'll be okay now."

At that moment, the doctor arrived. Ada feared the worst. The doctor introduced himself, and asked Percy and Ada to follow him to his office. There was an eerie silence as they sat down.

"I know you are concerned about Jamie and I wish I could give you some good news, but we really are stumped about Jamie's condition." We have done tests and, unfortunately, nothing has come to light as of yet. We are continuing with our tests. Jamie is comfortable at the moment. That's all I can say. I know it's not enough, but that's where we are for now."

Ada and Percy looked at each other with vacant expressions.

"Look," the doctor spoke tenderly. "We are on the case. We are monitoring Jamie constantly and we will continue to do so. I suggest you prepare yourselves for a few days of anxious waiting. We'll keep you informed of what's going on. In fact, I'll call you myself tomorrow morning to give you an update."

"Can we see Jamie?" Ada asked.

"Of course, but just for a few minutes, okay?"

Percy said, "Okay, doctor, okay."

They went to see Jamie, but he was asleep. Ada kissed him on the cheek and whispered, "I love you."

Forbidden Fruit

Lucy found her keys and was about to lock the office when Barry walked in.

"Hello, petal. Am I too late?" He gave Lucy a smile.

"Not at all, Barry, although I was nearly done. I've had a very busy day one way or another." She had indeed. The Gazette was relatively a small concern, but Lucy felt they were under-staffed. She herself had many responsibilities, but the upside of that was that the days went quicker. "What can I do for you, Barry?" She thought to herself "Be there for you? Kiss and cuddle you when you come home from work?" She just smiled.

Barry said, "I was just passing and was wondering if there was any response to the ad, only it's been a little while, so I just thought."

"I'm afraid there's been nothing yet." 'Yet' meant that Lucy hoped, as did Barry that somehow, someone would respond.

Barry had a resigned look on his face. Lucy walked towards him, put her hand on his shoulder, looked into his eyes and said, "Barry, something will come up. I'm sure of it."

Barry shrugged his shoulders. Lucy wanted to hold him, but he was married, wasn't he, and she liked Angela very much. She wasn't ready for what happened next.

Barry pulled her towards him. He could smell her perfume. Her head was on his chest.

"Lucy," Barry whispered.

"Yes, Barry?" Lucy waited on his reply.

"Lucy, I...." At that moment, Barry's mobile rang. He took it out of his pocket. It was Angela. She was very upset.

"Baz, it's Jamie. He's in hospital. Ada has just rung me. Where are you?"

"I'm in town, love. I'll get straight over there. I'll call you when I know what's going on."

Angela was not having that. "No, you'll come and pick me up. I'll see you then. How long you gonna be?"

Barry wasn't thinking straight. Of course Angie would want to be there. "About quarter of an hour, love, okay?"

Lucy asked, "What's up?"

Barry explained, and Lucy understood. Barry left straight away. Lucy locked the office door, leant her back against it and sighed. What was he going to say, she wondered to herself. Was he...?

Angie was ready when Barry got home. They were at the hospital in no time, as Barry hardly ever used the main roads during rush hour. It actually took them longer to find Ada and Percy than it did to get to the hospital.

"What's happening, darling?" Barry enquired.

"Ada's worrying over nothing," Percy butted in.

"What do you mean, nothing? They don't know what's wrong, so it must be serious," Ada shouted.

It was Barry's turn to butt in. "Ada, Ada, calm down. Has the doctor said anything yet?"

Percy explained what the doctor had told them.

"Okay, then," said Barry, "we'll wait. Now who wants a drink? There's a machine over there."

Angie looked at Barry. He was being his usual unflappable self. He was such a good person to have around in a crisis.

They all sat waiting for what seemed ages.

Love In The Sun

Emily slept really late. It was nearly eleven by the time she got to the restaurant. Helmut was nowhere to be seen, so she helped herself to some juice and sat near the French doors. The sea was a few miles away, but Emily swore she could smell it. The view was…. well, words failed her. Everywhere she looked, there was beauty. Inland, the Andes, the town below and the sea beyond. She would love to spend more time here, live here in fact. Well, we can't always have what we want, can we?

"Emily, at last! How are you feeling? You have a hungover this morning?" Helmut was his usual bubbly self.

"Helmut, I'm hungover, but it's called a hangover, and I should really go back to bed." Emily was serious. She hardly ever indulged in anything, least of all drink and, boy, was she paying for it now.

"No, no, no, young lady. You are not disappearing, no way." Emily hadn't seen Lionel enter. He added, "You're going to show me the sights. We agreed last night, don't you remember?"

Emily smiled. "Last night is, well, a bit of a blur. If I said I'd show you the sights, then I will, though you will have to let me get some food in my stomach first, Lionel."

"Okay," he said. "What would you like? A full English breakfast?" Before Emily could reply, Lionel said, "Make it two, please Helmut; make it two." He was very assured.

Emily tried to protest, but Helmut was already on his way.

Emily looked at Lionel. He was a very handsome man and, as far as she could tell, he also had a pleasant way about him.

"How are you feeling, Emily?" Lionel was genuinely concerned.

Emily thought for a moment. "You are a very persuasive man. All I want to do is chill out for the rest of the day, and you have me promising to do a tour of the local hotspots." Emily tried to sound stern, but couldn't carry it off.

"Emily, Emily, you only have yourself to think about. Don't worry about the tour today. I myself have plenty of time. I have a few more days here yet to see the sights. Really, don't push yourself if you're not up to it."

Why was he so understanding? She would have taken him round, but he didn't make it easy for her to say no. But that's exactly what she did.

Lionel was completely in agreement. He admitted to Emily he wasn't feeling too great either, which made Emily laugh when he told her.

Helmut was aware of what was going on here and was ready with a suggestion. "Emily, why don't you and Lionel go up to the roof garden? It's a nice, but not too hot day and, when the sun moves round, you could water my plants for me."

"Helmut, you crafty old sausage. Can you believe that, Lionel?" She laughed and so did Lionel.

"I'm game if you are Emily. Sounds perfect. I might even help you if you're lucky."

"Oh, I see. Men ganging up on the lady. Very nicely done, Helmut. Did you plan this?"

Helmut shook his head. "No, not at all Emily, but it does seem like a good idea. And besides, I think my bar needs replenishing after your little late-night drinks last night. If you two disappear, it will give me a chance to do it."

Building Blocks

"Lucy, Lucy," Angela shouted. Lucy didn't hear her. It was noisier than she realised, so she walked a bit faster. Lucy must be on her lunch hour, she thought to herself. She finally caught up with her. "Lucy, where are you off to in such a hurry? I could hardly catch you."

"Oh, Mrs. Wilson."

Angie looked at her in a semi-stern way.

"Sorry.... Angela, I keep forgetting."

"That's okay, Lucy. Are you on your lunch break?"

"Yes," Lucy replied. "I'm just about to grab a coffee. Will you join me?"

Angie smiled. "You took the words right out of my mouth."

Lucy didn't feel that she was too close to Angela, probably because of how she felt about Barry. She was very nice though, and so easy to talk to.

"Lucy, I've got a little problem and was wondering if you could help me out?"

"I'll try Angela. What's up?"

Angela explained that she and Barry were planning a short break and were hoping that she, Lucy, would look after however many chicks (baby African grey parrots) there were at the time.

"I don't know anything about looking after parrots, Angela."

Angela cut in. "Don't worry about that. You can come up to the house whenever you like and get some practice in, if that's all you're worried about."

Lucy didn't hesitate. "Okay then. You sure Barry is okay with the idea, only.... "

Angela laughed. "It was his idea to ask you. He said something about you being really interested in birds."

Lucy went all tingly inside. Maybe there was a chance for her and Barry.... Don't be silly, she thought.

"Are you okay then?" Angie noticed Lucy was a little quiet.

"Oh yes, Angela, I'm fine. How often do they need feeding?"

"Well that is the 64000 Dollar question. It will depend on how old they are. But don't worry. If they're very young, you can stay at the house. And as we're just going away for the weekend, it won't interfere with your work commitments. Is that okay?"

"That would be great, Angela, just great. Look, I have to go back to work now, so..."

Angela interrupted, "Okay, I'll get Barry to get in touch with you when we know more, okay?"

"Okay." Lucy was really excited. Not just about the job of looking after the parrots. That was going to be enjoyable. No, it was the thought of Barry showing her how and what to do. Also, their house was beautiful. She went back to work with a spring in her step.

Meanwhile, Angie was on the phone to Barry. The pair of them were really pleased that Lucy had agreed to their request. Now they could plan their weekend.

The plan was to take Angela's mum, Connie, away for the weekend. To where, they weren't sure yet, but it would be good for all three of them.

Barry was very, very busy. Added to that was the whole mess that was Jack Fleet House and not forgetting his increasingly randy parrots. He didn't seem to get a minute to himself. Lucy, what a great kid, he thought to himself. If only I was a bit younger....

There was a knock at the door.

It was Ronnie Jackson. "Alright, boy. What you up to? Are you busy?"

"Never too busy to see you, Ronnie. How are you? Come in."

They walked through the house and into the back garden.

"Coffee or a beer?" Barry asked.

"Oh, no beer. Pool match last night, wasn't it? No, coffee will be fine," Ronnie replied.

Barry returned with two cups of coffee, sat down and said, "What's happening then, Ronnie? Is this a social call or what?"

Ronnie said, "Well sort of. I ain't seen ya for a while anyway, but it's our wonderful Mayor. He's been seeing rather a lot of that crooked builder, Terry Watson. I'm sure he's behind this home closure."

"You can bet your life on that, Ronnie," Barry said. If we could just find out what it is that they're up to. I mean, we know what they're up to, but we need proof, don't we?"

They mulled over the idea, or ways they could break their plans, but it would be difficult. Jock McBride was a very clever man. Barry had watched him rise from nothing, get on to the council, eventually becoming Mayor about two years ago.

Barry had tried to resurrect the law that states that each Mayor must stand down after one year in office, but was voted down by the crooked Scotsman's cronies. No, this was a real problem.

Kids!

Aaron coughed, then he coughed again. When he took his hand away, he saw blood…. and then he was violently sick.

Harry was passing Aaron's room as this happened and quickly found Ada, who was in the kitchen. When they walked into his room, Aaron was lying on the floor crying, holding his stomach.

"Aaron, you poor thing. What's happened?" Ada hadn't noticed the sick on the floor next to his bed.

"I feel really ill, Ada. Help me," Aaron cried.

Ada felt his brow. He was hot and sweaty, but he was shivering too. "Stay here, Harry. I'm going to call the doctor."

Harry looked at Aaron. Yes, he was a bully, but he did feel for him.

Five minutes later, Ada and Percy returned.

"Can you stand up?" Percy said. "We'll take you to A and E. Sod waiting for the doctor."

"I think I may be sick again," Aaron replied.

"Just call an ambulance, Percy. That's the best thing. They're used to dealing with situations like this."

Percy hesitated, but then agreed with his wife. He left them to make the call.

Ada sat with Aaron and dabbed his forehead with a cold flannel. Harry was genuinely concerned for his tormentor-in-chief and was struggling with that thought. It took twenty-five minutes for the ambulance to arrive, and Aaron had been sick twice more while they were waiting. Ada had a brief conversation with the paramedics and went with them to the hospital, after telling Percy she would call him to let him know what was happening and when she would need picking up.

Percy made himself a cup of tea and wondered why and what had happened, because it wasn't just Aaron, was it? Jamie was already in hospital with similar symptoms. He checked on everyone over the next hour or so and told them not to drink any tap water until further notice, just in case.

At the hospital, Aaron looked pale. Ada was by his trolley and impatiently waiting for someone to attend to him.

"What's keeping them?" Ada said when she was told that someone would be there soon to tend to Aaron.

"I'm really sorry, but we are extremely busy. If he gets any worse, please let us know at the nurses' station."

Ada grudgingly accepted their excuses and at last sat next to Aarons' trolley.

Just seconds after sitting down, Aaron sat up and threw up very badly, not only lots of it, but it was a dark red colour.

"Nurse, come quick, nurse!"

It was four in the morning when Ada phoned Percy. She was outside A and E when he got there.

"Well…?" Percy asked.

"They don't know Perce… They just don't know what has caused this. I told them about Jamie as well and…" she paused.

"What?" Percy said.

"Well, now they're going to send Environmental Health round." She sighed.

"What for?" Percy shouted.

"Don't shout at me, Percy Herbert." Ada was fuming. This was not going to help their cause one little bit. "Once the council hear about this, there will be hell to pay," Ada said.

They both looked at each other and sighed as they passed the hospital gates.

Harry hadn't slept properly for a few nights, certainly since Jamie had been in hospital. He heard Percy's car pull up and ran downstairs.

"Go to bed, Harry. He's okay. Well, he's in the right place anyway. Go to bed," Ada shouted as he reached the bottom of the stairs.

As Harry was making his way back up the stairs, Ada said, "Harry, are you okay?"

"I'm fine, Ada, just not sleeping enough," he replied.

"Well, you go and have a lie in. In the morning, don't bother with the usual breakfast time. I'll sort you out when you get up."

Neither Ada nor Percy were able to sleep, with the worry about the kids and now the Environmental Health too.

Dual Personality

Lionel Mason was a much travelled, very successful business man, specialising in....well, whatever people needed. He seemed to be able to turn his hand to anything and give the impression that he had been involved with the product all his life.

He loved South America, especially Peru. This was his second summer here and he could see himself settling down here eventually. He had considered moving on after just a couple of days until he met Emily Fleet. He felt he needed to find out more about her and, consequently, tapped Helmut for some info about her. He made up the story about his shoulder and then let the idea of physio go away, as he found it so easy to talk to Emily.

"So, what brought you to Peru, Emily?" he had asked.

Emily paused. She thought for a second. "Fate .... I don't know really. All I do know is it sort of feels like it's right. It's home for me now and for the foreseeable future." She found it easy to talk to Lionel too. She was attracted to him, but was not going to throw herself at someone she barely knew... not yet anyway.

They both agreed that it was now too hot on the roof and retired to the bar, where Helmut was busy with a dozen or so customers.

"Where in England are you from originally, Emily? Maybe near London?" Lionel asked.

"Just outside. A place called Essex," she replied. "My parents were both Northerners, though. So, I'm not a true Essex girl. My memories of growing up were not too sad. I made a few close friends, though have lost touch with them, sadly."

"What about you, Lionel? What's your story?" Emily asked.

Lionel thought to himself, "Just tell her the barest details. Don't open up too much," but, before he knew it, he was opening up and, by the time he'd finished, she knew what size shoe he took!

"Wow," she said, "that's quite a story. What was it like growing up in Glasgow, then?"

"Probably what you'd expect really.... Tough, unforgiving, mostly cold. That's probably why I love it here so much. Anyway, enough about me. Could we have dinner together tonight? Would that be okay with you?"

Emily smiled. "As long as we go Dutch..."

He smiled, reluctantly agreed, and booked a table for 8:30. Then they both retired for a siesta.

Emily decided to call Sam before her nap. She was curious to find out about the message in the paper and said as much to Sam, who encouraged her to follow up the article as soon as she returned.

After the meal, Emily and Lionel found themselves back on the roof. It was a lovely evening, the sky was clear, the moon was full. The view was stunning, and Emily thought to herself how romantic it was. Lionel went to the bar to refresh the drinks. Emily's mind drifted. Life was good. She was extremely happy, and yet she felt a barrier coming down when it came to Lionel. "Not just yet," she told herself, "you really need to keep it platonic just for a while, maybe exchange numbers and meet up another time." Lionel returned from the bar and within seconds they were kissing.

Lucy…. Home to Roost

Barry was in the aviary, busy as usual with the chicks. Angie called him on the intercom to tell him Lucy was there.

"Okay, I'm just coming up for a sprinkle anyway, Doll!"

Angie smiled and said to Lucy, "He'll be up in a minute. We want to thank you for doing this. It'll be nice to get mum away for a short break. Thank you so much."

"It's not a problem. I'm not confident I'll be very good at it, but I'll do my best."

"I'm sure you'll be fine, Lucy." Angie smiled as Barry came into the kitchen.

"See Ange, told ya she wouldn't let us down. Thanks for agreeing to this Lucy. It's really good of you."

"I just said to Angie, I'm not confident…." Barry butted in.

"You'll be fine. We'll have a cuppa and then I'll show you the ropes, so to speak."

Lucy smiled. They were a lovely couple. Yet….

Barry went to the bathroom, messed about with what hair he had left and had a swig of mouthwash. "You bloody idiot," he thought to himself, 'who are you kidding?'

"Okay, let's go," Barry said. "You coming, Ange?" Angie was busy in the bedroom and shouted, "No, I'm busy here and I've got to pop over to mum's. You can start dinner if you like." By the time she said it, Barry and Lucy were halfway to the bottom of the garden.

He opened the door and Lucy gasped.

"Twenty-nine pairs, Lucy. Only eleven chicks at the moment, but we think there's more on the way." Barry spent the next hour showing Lucy what he wanted her to do.

At first it seemed a daunting task but, by the time Barry had finished, she felt a lot more confident.

"Well, what do you think Lucy?" Barry asked.

Lucy nodded her head. "Yes," she said with a smile on her face, "Yes, I think I'll be okay!"

Barry gave her a big cuddle. "That's my girl. I knew you'd be okay with it."

Lucy felt her face go red as they were now very close. For a second, she was tempted to kiss him but changed her mind. At that same time, Barry kissed her on the cheek. "You're an angel." He smiled and pulled away. "Will you be alright here for a minute? I've just got to go to the shed and get some more seed. Can't have you struggling, can we?"

Barry made his way to the shed, not realising that Lucy was following him. He opened the shed door and turned on the light. As the door naturally closed, Lucy opened it and turned the light off.

"What you doing, Lucy?" he exclaimed.

She walked over to him, stood on tip-toe and kissed him on the lips. This was it, she thought. This was going to go one way or the other. To her surprise, Barry kissed her back, gently at first, then more passionately till she pulled away. Neither of them said anything for a few seconds. Then Lucy turned, said sorry and headed towards the door. Barry put his hand on her shoulder and pushed the door shut.

Aaron's Secret

Percy was baffled. Was it something at Jack Fleet? He considered everything, every possibility, but was unable to come up with an explanation.

"I don't know, Ada. This has me puzzled. In a way, we have to understand why the hospital did what they did, but I can't think of anything that would cause this. Yes, two of the boys are ill, but what about the others? They're all fine."

He sat down at the kitchen table. Ada didn't say anything. She was as baffled as he was. He thought of Barry. Yes, Barry would have some idea. He jumped up. "I won't be long, Ada. Gonna see Barry." Before Ada could say anything, he was out the door. "Silly ol' fool," she whispered, "he's not at home. Oh well, he'll find out soon enough." Ada had remembered Barry and Angie had taken Connie, Angie's mum, away for the weekend.

Jamie and Aaron were in the same four-bed ward. The doctors were no nearer to finding the problem. They were both 'nil by mouth', both bored stiff and both keeping quiet about their secret.

When the lights went out, Aaron would walk over to Jamie's bed, still attached to his drip stand, and would warn Jamie of the consequences of spilling the beans. "Yes, Aaron is still a bully," Jamie thought to himself.

****

Lucy was in the kitchen. She loved Barry's house. It was beautiful, even more beautiful now.

Lucy was coping brilliantly with the chicks. "Barry will be so pleased with me," she thought to herself.

There were no new additions to the chick count, but there was still plenty to do. She made herself a hot drink.

She heard a knock at the door. "Hello," she said as she opened the door.

"Hello, pet. Can I see Barry, please? It's really important I..."

Lucy put her hand up in front of her. "I'm really sorry, but he's away for the weekend." She went on to explain and told him when he would be home.

Percy shrugged his shoulders and walked back to his car. He was on his way home and was approaching Ronnie's pub and decided to speak to him about the problem.

He pulled into the car park just as Jock McBride was shaking hands with the crook himself, Terry Watson. He had heard that the two were as thick as thieves and it made his blood boil, but he sat motionless in his car till they had gone their separate ways.

He entered the lounge bar and almost knocked a tray out of Barbara's hand. "Oops, sorry Barb, I'm a clumsy old fool, aren't I?"

That brought a smile to her face. "Percy, don't be silly. You're fine. I wouldn't want you any other way. Is it a drink or Ronnie you're wanting...or both?"

Percy thought for a second. "Maybe just a half Barb, please. Is he about?"

"Yes, love. I'll give him a shout," Barb replied.

A couple of minutes later, Ronnie joined him. "Hi, Percy. Is it another session you're after?" Ronnie said jokingly.

"Yeah, that would be all I need. No, just this half while I bend your ear, Ron."

"Okay, Ronnie said as he sat down. "Bend away."

Percy went on to explain what had happened and Ronnie, too, was baffled. It didn't make any sense.

"So, have the environmental people been round yet?" Ronnie questioned.

"No, we haven't heard anything yet." The two of them just stared, not knowing what to say.

"Hey," Percy said, "I see the Kray twins were here again, then. I'd love to have been a fly on the wall there, Ron."

For a second Ronnie was confused.

Percy continued, "They're here quite a lot, ain't they? Or so Barry said."

Ronnie then realised he was talking about the Mayor and the plumber. "Oh, sorry Percy. I didn't know. I've been in the cellar all morning. Anyway, yeah, you're right. Two or three times a week. They never stay long, though, and never sit near anybody either."

"Yeah, bloody scumbags," Percy murmured. After a few minutes, Percy finished his drink, shook Ronnie's hand and said goodbye to Barb as he left. It was only a five-minute drive through the lanes. He didn't notice Terry Watson's car parked behind the Mayor's off-duty vehicle.

"Jock, do you think he knows?" Terry asked uneasily.

Jock gave him a grin. "He knows nothing, not a thing. Don't worry about it." Things were warming up. Jock was super confident that nothing was going to derail his plans. "He knows nothing."

Bon Voyage

Emily kissed Lionel on the cheek. She was sad to watch him leave, but felt good about the way they were with each other.

They decided to get together in a few months in Lima. When Emily suggested he stay with her, he declined. "I want to say yes. But I believe it's for the best if I stay at a hotel."

Emily was okay with that. She said she understood.

When they had their first real chat, Emily was surprised to find out that he was a practicing solicitor and, by the sound of it, a very successful one, too. His father had his own company and they covered all types of fields: criminal, property, and just about everything else.

"Why didn't you stay in the business?" Emily enquired.

Lionel had been asked this question so many times before, it was like pressing the button on a tape recorder when he answered. "Basically, I wanted to work for myself, to do my own thing. If I'd been working in the same company without my dad being there, I may have stayed. So, I looked for something different. Don't get me wrong, though. I do miss the game. It can give you a real buzz."

Emily could envision him in a courtroom. She'd believe anything he said. He was so smooth and confident. She couldn't imagine him losing a case.

She returned from her daydream. "Ah well, what's a few months?" She went to the bar, ordered her usual and said, "I'm going, Helmut. See you in the morning. Did you book my taxi?"

"Yes, 10:30 on the pot, Emily."

"Dot Helmut, dot." She laughed.

Emily sat in the lounge looking out the window, but she wasn't really seeing anything other than Lionel. Consequently, she nearly jumped out of her skin when Helmut approached her.

"Your taxi awaits, madam."

She really wasn't focused at all. "Thank you, Helmut, and it's been a wonderful few days. Thank you so much."

Helmut gave her a hug and walked her out to the waiting taxi.

As she pulled away from the hotel, she wound her window down. "Take care, Helmut. See you next year." She wasn't sure if he heard, but she would call him when she arrived home safely. She arrived at the station with twenty minutes to spare before the train arrived. Her mind was still on Lionel. "If it's meant to be, we will see each other again," she thought to herself. She dozed off just a few minutes into the long journey back to Lima, woken only by a dog owned by an old couple who joined her in the carriage. They exchanged pleasantries, then she fell asleep again. The journey definitely felt quicker and soon she was in another taxi to her home. Home. It felt good…. Lionel….

Lucy's Love

"Lucy!" She hadn't heard them arrive. It was good to see him.

"How's it been? Any problems?" Barry asked

Was she going red? Get a grip. "No, everything's been fine. Well, I think it has. You'd better check."

Barry replied, "We'll have a look in a bit. I'll make a cuppa. Coffee, Doll?"

Angie had just collapsed on the settee. "Love one Baz. I'm worn out."

"How did your mum enjoy it, Angie?" Lucy asked, trying to sound interested.

"She loved every minute of it. Drove me up the wall though, I don't mind telling you. Shopping, shopping and more shopping. Ordinarily I love it, but she knows how to wind me up like a spring. Bloody nightmare."

Lucy laughed. "Oh, Percy from Jack Fleet called round. He seemed really disappointed when I told him you were away for the weekend."

"Silly old sausage. I told Ada we were away. Don't they talk to each other? I'll give him a bell in a while." Barry smiled shaking his head. "Don't suppose there's any news on Emily Fleet, Lucy?"

"Sadly, nothing yet. But we are placing the ad weekly now, which hopefully will get a response. I don't know what else we can do." Lucy was getting more proactive regarding the campaign to save Jack Fleet House, even though she was related to Jock McBride.

She was pleased to see Barry, but had hoped that Angie had decided to stay a while longer. Oh well, never mind.

"Right, let's see if I've got any birds left," Barry laughed.

"Barry, don't be horrible. I'm sure they're fine." chided Angie.

Lucy went red again as they walked towards the Aviary. She watched Barry checking each cage carefully. He was handsome. He was…. somebody else's.

"Lucy," Barry called. "did you check each cage this morning?"

"Of course. 8:30 as usual. Why what's up?" she worriedly asked.

"It's alright, love. These things happen." Barry had found one of the parrots dead.

Lucy started crying and ran out towards the gate. Barry shouted after her, but she was in her car and gone.

"Poor girl," Angie commented when Barry told her. "She's taken it to heart."

Barry felt for her. The bird was still warm. He'd get it to the vet's to establish the cause to make sure it was a one off. Tomorrow would do. "I'm gonna go see Lucy, Doll."

"Okay," Angie replied. "Don't forget her present!"

"Oh yeah. I don't want her to worry about this. Put her mind at rest, you know…." At that, he was off.

Angie wheeled her small case into the kitchen, took out the washing, then went to the bedroom and sat on the bed for a minute. Then she lay down and drifted away.

Barry had stopped at a T-junction when a car behind him tooted. Barry saw it was Percy. They stopped in a lay-by.

Percy explained about Jamie and Aaron both being in hospital and the problem the doctors were having in finding out what was the cause of their illness.

"It's a worry," said Barry. "Leave it with me, Percy. I'll go and see them tomorrow and try to find out what's going on."

It was nearly nine o'clock by the time he got to Lucy's and he wasn't sure she would open the door. He knocked at the door. Nothing. So he knocked again, still getting no answer. He had taken a few steps down the stairs when he heard the door open. "Lucy, my pet, you okay?" At that Lucy started crying again. "Lucy, you didn't cause the bird to die. It's one of them things that happen now and again. It's not the first bird I've lost, honestly." By this time, he was cuddling her at her front door. "Come on, get the kettle on, I'll make us a cuppa."

She led him to the kitchen and they were soon sitting at her breakfast bar dipping digestives.

"I love digestives, don't you?" he said, trying to cheer her up, but she was still very down. "Lucy, liven up girl. There's nothing you could have done. You did nothing wrong. So, nice little place you've got here. Nice area too. Neighbours okay?" Barry was winning his battle to bring her out of it.

"Yeah, I like it. Neighbours aren't too bad. A couple from Poland, but mostly British. Most of the time I don't see anybody," she replied.

"How's work? He keeps you busy, don't he... Ronnie?"

"He really does. He's a slave driver alright," she agreed. "I've not had a chance to catch up on my emails while I've been staying at yours."

He looked at her. She'll be okay. She was beautiful, so young. And beautiful. They looked at each other and hoped they knew what the other was thinking.

"I guess I'd better be off now, love." Barry seemed to regret what he had said.

Before she knew it, Lucy asked, "Would you like a beer?" A few seconds elapsed, and Barry said, "No thank you, love."

Lucy stood up, thinking Barry was leaving as he said, "But I'll have one of these." He put his hands on her shoulders and kissed her, gently on the lips. She responded for a few seconds. Then the magic flowed. They were together. Lucy's mind was fine now. Oh yes, she was fine. She was with her man. Her man!

Barry crept quietly in the front door. It was 11:30. Angie was in bed, still in her clothes. Barry's mind was racing. What had he done? He didn't regret it, no sir. It was fantastic, absolutely fantastic.

He took his tablets and had a glass of the hard stuff. Sitting in his armchair, he relived the evening that had just gone. Wow, he thought.

The Plan

Four times today. Still he has not picked up her calls. He must be busy. "I'll ring him again," she thought. "But what if Angie answers it before Barry. Do nothing. Be patient." Besides, it was always a busy day.

She hated Wednesdays. The Gazette always came out on a Thursday, but it was always dated for the Friday. It was the third week of the ad for Emily Fleet, too. There was still no response. She doubted they would hear anything now. They had printed three monthly ads and now three weekly ones. There was no way she would stop the ad as long as there was a chance. It would make Barry so happy if there was news. No, we must continue. Her phone rang.

"Hello." It was Jock.

"Oh hi, Uncle Jock. How are you?"

She listened to her dad's brother. He was nothing like her dad. If she was honest, she just tolerated him, kept him at a distance. Jock wanted to get some information on advertising and asked if she could send him some prices, etc. There followed a little small talk. He said he'd see her soon.

"Okay, bye for now." Lucy sighed, glad the phone call was over. Her mind went straight back to Barry. She picked up the phone to ring him again as her door opened.

"Lucy!" She blushed. "You look gorgeous. Come here."

"Barry! Ronnie might come in," she grinned.

Barry put his finger on her lips, "Shh, he's just gone out. Told me to come up."

She relaxed, and their lips met in a long passionate embrace.

"I've called you several times today, Barry," Lucy admitted.

Barry sighed, "Yes I know pet. I've had my phone on 'silent'. Can't be too careful."

Oh, so that's why. "Okay, that's fine," she thought to herself.

"How are you, Lucy? I'm all over the place. My mind is struggling to focus on anything. Well I say anything…. I can't stop thinking about you."

"I'm the same. I don't know how I get any work done. I daydream, and a few times Ronnie has caught me staring into space." She blushed again. "Can we meet up soon?"

"Too right," Barry nodded. "That's why I'm here. Can you get away for a weekend, only…."

She stopped him. "Yes, yes of course I can. Just say when. But how will you get away?"

"I've an old friend who lives in Norfolk. Angie knows of him, but she has never met him. I can sort something for this weekend if you're free."

"Oh, yes." Her heart was racing. A weekend together where nobody knew them. She couldn't wait.

Changing the subject, Barry enquired about the ad and already knew that no news wasn't good news as regards Emily Fleet.

"We'll keep posting the ad," Lucy reassured him.

"Thanks, pet. I'll call you Friday lunchtime. What time do you finish work?"

"I can be ready just after six. Is that okay?" Lucy replied.

Barry said that was fine and that he would pick her up from home.

Friday couldn't come quick enough for Lucy and she was sure Barry felt the same way. In no time it was Friday. Approaching six o'clock, her buzzer went.

"I'm coming down. Just a minute." Lucy grabbed her small suitcase and her coat and made her way downstairs.

From a distance, it was difficult to make out who it was he was helping into the passenger seat of his car. It's okay, he thought. I'll follow them and will soon find out.

A couple of hours later, Jock McBride's phone rang. "Hello…. Uh huh. Yes, you've done well. Thank you." He put the phone down. "Got him!" he smirked.

Time To Read

Sam wasn't feeling too well but he made himself get up out of bed. After all, his best friend was coming around this morning and he hadn't seen her for nearly a week. He tidied up though, to be fair, he wasn't a messy person. He'd always been the type of man who had kept his home clean and tidy. He assembled all the Gazettes and left the one with the ad about Emily on the top of the pile. He sat down in his armchair and soon fell asleep, only to be awoken by a football crashing through the window. By the time he got to the front door, his neighbour's son Alex was already there.

"Mr. Sam, Mr. Sam, I'm sorry. I was showing Paco my ball juggling and lost control. I'm so sorry, Mr. Sam." He was almost crying.

"Alex, don't worry. It's only a pane of glass. Don't worry." Sam remembered a similar thing happening to him when he was a boy in Sunderland.

Alex calmed down, but continued to apologise. Sam again told him it was okay. He saw the funny side of it.

While he was sweeping up the glass, Emily arrived, "Oh, have you had an accident, Sam? You okay?"

Sam laughed and told Emily the story of what had happened. "Would you like a cup of tea, Emily?"

"Most definitely, Sam. You make the best tea." She sat down and noticed the papers on the coffee table.

Sam was pouring the milk into the mugs.

"Sam, are these the papers you were talking about on the coffee table?"

"Yes, love." He placed Emily's tea on the side table. "You still don't take sugar, do you?"

"No thanks, Sam," Emily replied. She was scanning the ad section of the paper. It read, "Does anyone know Emily Fleet or anyone in the Fleet family? If so, please get in touch with The Thurrock Gazette, etc, etc." Emily was intrigued. Curious too. She wondered what it could be. She asked Sam what he thought.

"I don't know, love. Wouldn't hurt to drop them a line though, would it? I wouldn't phone. It'd cost you a fortune. No, I'd write to that person, Lucy somebody, isn't it?"

Emily looked at the ad again. "Yes, Lucy. I'll do that Sam."

She went on to tell him about her little break up north. She never mentioned Lionel, though, and if she was honest, she wondered why she didn't tell Sam about him. She loved Sam. He was such a softly spoken man, but you could still tell he was a Geordie. No sorry, a Mackem. Sam had told her that before. Newcastle was where Geordies came from. If you came from Sunderland, you were a Mackem.

Underage Poison

Jamie found his way to the dayroom, turned the radio on and listened through his headphones. Aaron sat watching him for quite a while. A part of him felt sorry for Jamie. It must be horrible not being able to see. No, not nice at all. But he had to know that Jamie would not tell anyone. They had both done it, anyway. He'd lost count of how many times they'd been in Percy's cocktail cabinet and yes, it was probably the alcohol that had put them both in hospital. Aaron was sure he would never drink again. Although Jamie didn't know what he was drinking, as Aaron had mixed lemonade with his drink, he did know that he was in the wrong for doing it. Aaron had even put whisky in Jamie's bedtime drinks in hospital. The staff never worked out that these two young boys had alcohol poisoning. Why would they?

On the day the hospital discovered that this was the problem, Aaron had been rough all night and the night sister smelt alcohol on his breath when she tucked him in. When Aaron finally went to sleep, she searched his cupboard and belongings but found nothing. She then searched Jamie's. "Gotcha!" she said to herself quietly. One empty bottle of vodka and half a small bottle of whiskey. The sister on the early shift called Percy and asked him and Ada to come in as they had got to the root of the problem.

Soon after, Percy and Ada were sitting in the matron's office. They were in shock.

"I can't believe it! And you say it was in Jamie's cupboard? No, that can't be." Ada would never believe it of Jamie.

"My wife is right, Sister. This is all Aaron's doing. He's the one responsible," Percy said with total confidence.

"Well," the Sister replied, "at least we should see some improvement in them, and pretty quick too." Part of her wanted to laugh, but she stopped herself.

"I bet I know where he got it from," Percy said angrily. "My cabinet. I haven't touched a drop of the hard stuff for months, since I got stopped for..."

Ada cut in. "Does this mean they can come home today, Sister?" She hoped that was the case.

"I'm afraid not. We will need to keep an eye on them for maybe another day or two, but they should be fine by then."

"So how do we let them know that we know, if you know what I mean? I mean it's not going to be easy for them. I mean..." Percy was unsure what to do or even what to say.

The Sister asked both of them to wait in her office for a few moments while she spoke to Matron, who was on another ward. A quarter of an hour passed, and Sister returned with a social worker who, when she introduced herself, was aware of a hostile glance from Ada.

"Mrs. Herbert, don't worry. I'm not here to judge you and your husband. I'm going to talk to the boys on their own, initially. Then I would like you to join us. Is that okay with you?" she asked them politely.

Percy and Ada both nodded their heads and said that they didn't mind.

"Bloody Aaron. I could kill him." Percy was fuming. Ada was angry too, but she was more concerned about possible consequences. It could give more ammunition to McBride and his cronies.

After the meeting, the social worker motioned to Ada and Percy to remain seated. Sister and a nurse took the boys back to their beds and rather sheepishly they went too.

"I just want you to know that this meeting, this whole incident, stays in this room," the social worker said reassuringly. "I am aware of the situation you are facing at Jack Fleet House and I want you to know you have an ally in me. I've been following the goings on and am quite disgusted with the Scottish mafia running this council."

Percy and Ada smiled and gave a huge sigh of relief. "Thank you so much," they chorused together.

"We really appreciate it. Thank you. Sorry, we don't know your name," Ada asked.

"Oh, sorry," she said. "It's Annie O'Reilly. And I want you to know if there is anything I can do, let me know." She smiled and passed them her business card.

"Thank you again. We will," Ada said, nodding.

They both decided to go straight home. The boy's looked stunned at the end of the meeting. Jamie was dumbstruck. He didn't have a clue what Aaron had been doing. Okay, he knew they were having secret drinks, but he didn't realise the drinks were laced with alcohol. He did feel funny when he had drunk them, but he just put it down to something he had eaten.

When Percy and Ada got home, they quickly notified all the important people: Barry and Angela, Bill and Tricia. Soon, everyone was feeling much happier about the situation. Some of them even had a little chuckle to themselves, while realising it could have been much more serious.

Crossed Paths

Emily decided to write to the Thurrock Gazette. Phoning would be quicker and probably more informative but, sadly, too expensive. Not that she couldn't afford it, but she had been brought up to be frugal first. Curiosity got to her as each day went by. Maybe it was an old school friend, or even somebody from her past that she had courted. Yes, she was very curious.

Once the letter was posted, her thoughts turned to Lionel. Where was he? Was he thinking about her? She remembered he had said that he would or should be back in Peru within a couple of months and, as she had been home for just over one month, it wouldn't be long, not long at all.

Lionel checked into the hotel. He hated the cold. He was in Glasgow for a family funeral. He felt duty bound, although he hardly knew his reclusive uncle. Still, like most funerals, it was, though sad, an opportunity to catch up with friends as well as family. Lionel saw quite a few unknown faces and, though he kept his thoughts to himself, there were a few dodgy characters he declined to strike up conversations with.

"Lionel!" He heard it from behind him as a gentle hand grabbed his shoulder. It was his Aunt Jenny, probably the only non-Scot at the wake.

"Jenny, you don't look a day older." He tried to sound convincing; she wasn't taken in.

"You're 'avin a laugh. Always been good at flannel, aint ya!" she laughed.

It was true and probably one of the reasons for his success. Talking a good game with confidence and backing it up with good looks and a type of smartness rarely seen.

"So, Jenny, did you manage to drag Bertie down south then?" Her husband, Bertie, always said he hated England, especially 'bloody cockneys'. Then he fell head over heels for one.

"What do you think, eh? It was no contest, Lionel. He always says he wants to come back, but deep down he loves it and, let's be honest, the southeast has the best weather. So, what you been up to? Brazil or somewhere, ain't it? Bet that was hot there. Did ya get any out there? The Brazil birds look a bit tarty to me, especially with a good-looking fella like you."

There was a slight pause, then she was off again. "Is that a glint in your eye? Touched a nerve then, didn't I? Well, was she Brazilian? What was she like? Tanned? Skinny?" she questioned.

"She was English actually," he butted in, "and she was from Essex."

"You're kidding. An Essex girl? No, I don't believe it. A super smoothie like you falling for an Essex girl. I've 'eard it all now!"

Lionel just wanted her to stop now. "Please shut up" he thought, but Jenny was off telling everyone and Lionel couldn't hide. After all, they hadn't seen him for almost a year and family ties are very strong in Scotland, especially Glasgow.

He ducked out of the lounge bar, going through swing doors like the ones from the old west that you see in films. The public bar was much quieter, so he ordered a pint of Guinness and sat at the bar.

The waitress was quite attractive. Nice figure too, and talkative as well.

"Why do you not stay next door?" she asked. "Drinks are free, and your family I presume."

He tried hard not to start a conversation with her, but she was cute and not too pushy, so they did talk for some time in between her serving and clearing tables.

Her name was Lisa. She was twenty-eight, single and the impression Lionel got was that she was looking for something, but didn't quite know how to go about it, or even what she wanted.

When she asked him about his job and where he had been recently, she was spellbound. "He's a catch," she thought to herself. "Would you like to take me out tonight honey? I finish at six. I could meet you back here at seven-ish, if you like?"

She wasn't backwards in coming forwards this one, he thought. But straight away he thought about Emily. "I'm afraid I'm away to the airport, Lisa. I'm flying to London tonight, then Peru midday tomorrow. It's been nice chatting to you though, Lisa. There's a big old world out there, sweetheart, and it doesn't hurt to dream. Grab hold of your life and make changes while you can."

She was hooked on him.

He leant over the bar and kissed her on the cheek. "You take care of yourself and don't wait for something to drop into your lap. Go get it yourself."

He went back into the lounge bar where he saw an old school friend, Jimmy Mahoney. "Jimmy, you old fox, how are you?"

Jimmy was surprised to see him. "Blimey, look at you. It must be twenty years or more, Lionel. You're looking a bit dapper, mate."

Before Lionel started working for his dad, Jimmy and he were like brothers. They did everything together, absolutely everything.

"Do you remember Jill?" Jimmy sniggered. "Jill, she was a handful, wasn't she?"

Jimmy was sitting with one of the people Lionel had thought of earlier as 'dodgy'.

"Sorry, Lionel. This is Jock. I went to school with his son. I used to be round his house all the time," Jimmy stated.

Jock smiled. "Ah, but that was nothing to do with my niece Lucy though, was it?"

An hour-and-a-half later, Lionel made his apologies. After getting Jimmy's contact details, he bade him farewell, promising to catch up on his next visit. He felt a little worse for wear and was out like a light in no time. It seemed like he'd only just gone to bed when the alarm went off. He laid there for a minute or two to get his bearings. He had a shower and now was in the 'Lionel time for business' mode. Well, time for Emily. He looked in the mirror, imagining he was looking at her. "Not long now, Em, not long."

His flight was on time. Pretty soon he was at Heathrow Terminal One. He'd arranged the connecting flight well. He had time for a couple of glasses, hair of the dog so to speak. Then some lunch. Hopefully, take-off would be on time and he'd have a nice sleep.

"Emily, I'm coming, sweetheart."

Jack's Story

Jack Fleet held on. "Bloody Japs!"

He didn't know how long he'd been in the water - 4, 5, 6 hours, he didn't know. He was alone, alone in the Indian Ocean. He couldn't feel his arms or his legs. He didn't know how he had stayed afloat. God knows, there were so many that hadn't. He was scanning the horizon every which way. Turning north, then south, just hoping for a miracle.

Jack was a Chief Petty Officer in the boiler room on the Hermes. Sorry, the 'Happy Hermes'. He didn't get that. He'd had a few misdemeanours on his way to this post, but his superiors had enough faith in him to overlook some, although not all of them. He recalled getting a 48-hour leave with the understanding that he could not leave Pompey. Yeah right! Before the train pulled out of the station, he was underneath the long six-seater seat and only came out when given the all clear by a kind-hearted civilian.

"It's okay," the civilian whispered. "The red caps have gone. They've got off the train."

"Thank you so much," he said, shaking the man's hand. "I've got to see me girl. I can't stay here, no duties to do."

The civilian smiled. "No harm in it is there? No harm at all."

The train pulled into Waterloo. He had time, but not a great deal. He had to get around to Fenchurch Street and catch another train to meet her. Maybe eight or nine hours later, he'd be back at Waterloo. It hardly seemed worth it. Nevertheless, it had to be done. After all, she would come back to London with him.

The time spent together raced by. Before he knew it, they were a couple of steps away from Fenchurch. "Give us a kiss then, girl."

He didn't know how long he'd passed out for and how he had stayed afloat. Then he heard someone shouting, then nothing.

Suddenly, there was chaos, splashing around, shouting and then laughter. Can you believe it? Laughter.

When the Japanese dive bombers called their base to report a successful mission, the Japanese government got in touch with the government of Ceylon to inform them that they had just sunk a British aircraft carrier and another smaller ship, and that there would be survivors in the water if they were quickly to hand.

Jack had only learnt of this many years later and was always struck with the same thought.

The stories you hear about Japanese P.O.W camps were terrible. So how come the same race of people were capable of showing this much compassion?

His wife, Bessie, cried unstoppable tears when she heard that he'd survived. Her neighbours were baffled at first, thinking the worst. "No, he's okay," Bessie had wailed.

"Then why you bloody crying, you silly cow?" said her closest neighbour, Eileen.

Bessie started laughing. "Shut up." They all laughed together.

One week's leave, that's all. One week.

Jack was a pillar of the community in every conceivable way. If the council were causing grief, Jack sorted it. Crime? Well there wasn't any. The police even came to Jack for advice. Everybody knew Jack, his wife Bessie and the children.

Frankie was the eldest, not quite 17. He wanted to join the Navy, but his dad put him wise. Peter was 15. Then there was Emily, just two years old. Two years old and gorgeous.

They lived in a huge house, left for Jack by his father. It was much too big for Jack and his family, but he realised its value would increase and it was mortgage free. Oh yes, he was staying right where he was.

Jack's next ship was his last. They had left Portsmouth as an escort for some merchant ships traveling to the Mediterranean. A German U-boat put an end to all their dreams just before the straits of Gibraltar. Jack didn't stand a chance.

Bessie never remarried. Frank joined up just as the war ended. He died in a car accident while holidaying in Cairo.

Peter left for Australia in 1947 and was never heard of again.

All the love that Bessie had was now poured into Emily. She was a beautiful child. She had her father's eyes and sense of humour as it turned out, often dreaming up something to make her mum laugh.

The loss of Jack had left a huge hole in Bessie's life. What would become of her? What would become of Emily? Where was Peter? So many questions unanswered. She had to sort herself out. She had responsibilities and she was Mrs. Jack Fleet, a woman of substance. "The buggers won't grind me down," she said to herself, and they never did.

She started a women's welfare group, not just for women though. Children were under the same umbrella. Pretty soon, their home had become a safe haven for battered and abused wives and orphaned children. The war had marked the community badly. There were so many lost and lonely souls out there. Bessie was on her feet up to sixteen hours a day, never thinking of herself and, although she didn't mean to, she found it hard to find time for Emily.

Adverse conditions don't always have an adverse effect, even as children. Yes, children were vulnerable, but they also had a sense of belonging to a community, where everyone you knew was doing their bit to help others. That can't help but rub off on those who witness these conditions on a daily basis.

Emily found she had managed herself very well. She was an achiever at school. In most subjects she was among the best in class, but in Physical Education she was the best in the school. Every discipline in the gymnasium came so easily to Emily. She was slight in build, but so adept in this category. The school had high hopes for her. The district sports day was the highlight of the sporting year and Emily didn't disappoint - three gold medals, plus a shield for 'all-rounder of the day'.

She, relatively speaking of course, was a star. Bessie was proud of her. She could imagine Jack's face if he were there. He would be beaming.

'What will become of us?' Bessie thought, as Emily walked towards her.

Love Returns

Emily was awake. She checked the time. It was too early to get up just yet. Although she was usually an early riser, she felt like having a lie in. She didn't have much to do. She did want to have a tidy up before Lionel turned up and thought what a messy way to exist. Lionel…. It was still another couple of weeks before he was due. Her thoughts turned to England. There was still no news from the Gazette.

She had written more than a week ago. Perhaps they hadn't received it yet. Sometimes the mail could take a week just to leave South America. The locals were not the quickest. She stayed in bed, drifting in and out of sleep, until hunger got the better of her. She decided to make herself a little breakfast. "I know," she thought to herself. "toast and marmalade, mmm, lovely." Sam had given her a couple of jars of marmalade from the parcel he'd had sent over from the UK.

Lionel went down to reception and showed the clerk Emily's address, "Ah yes, Senor, very nice place." Lionel smiled, "How long in a taxi?"

"It's market day, Senor. It may take twice as long, maybe one hour. If you leave it until the afternoon, it will be quicker for you."

Lionel thanked him and asked for a taxi to pick him up around eleven. He walked into the restaurant, sat down for breakfast, and wondered about Emily. Was she 'the one'? Was she right for him? He was positive on both counts, as positive as anybody could be. They really clicked from the first time they met. Similar likes and dislikes, but not totally agreeing on everything. Emily was quite headstrong on certain things and it was not easy to turn her opinion on something. She knew her own mind and she was nobody's fool. He went back to his room, freshened up, grabbed his gift bag and made his way to reception.

The taxi was already there. It was an interesting drive through the city. Yes, it was very busy as they had said it would be on market day. There seemed to be stalls everywhere, with no real pattern to them. It took around forty-five minutes before the driver pulled over.

"Senor, the road you want is just the other side of these villas. Here, go between them and the next road is the one you want."

Lionel thanked the man and gave him a tip the size of which he'd probably never had before. He was so grateful, he offered to wait to do the return journey.

"Sorry, my friend. I'm not sure how long I'll be here for," Lionel smiled.

The driver gave him the number of the office. "Ask for Pablo, Senor. I come straight away."

"Okay, Pablo, thank you." Lionel laughed to himself. It was not surprising. The locals were mostly in the 'not too well off' category and were very helpful, when it could be argued the opposite may be expected more.

He walked between two villas. It was cooler in the shade. Soon, too soon, he was back in the sun and looked up and down the street. He remembered Emily saying she lived at the top of a long road, so off he went, getting hotter and hotter. The area was one of the more salubrious areas of Lima. Emily was only renting her property, but it was quite expensive, relatively. She lived just off Avenue Angelica Gammara in a road called Calle Sonomoro. Lionel stood outside Emily's home and hesitated. Suddenly he became nervous. What if she had changed her mind. Maybe it was just a holiday romance. After all, they'd only known each other, what was it, six days!

It Hits The Fan

Lucy arrived at the office earlier than usual, picked up the mail and put it on Ronnie's desk. She was about to walk away when she noticed the Air Mail 'Par Avion' sticker on the top letter.

She picked up the envelope; it was stamped Peru. She thought straight away of Emily Fleet. Could this be what she was waiting for? It was addressed to her as her name had been the contact on the advert. She went through to her office, put the letter on her desk and did nothing for what seemed like an eternity.

She was really excited, but also apprehensive. It might not be what she hoped it was. She thought about Barry. If it was good news, he'd be thrilled. She picked up the letter, contemplating what to do. A voice inside her said "just open it" and, with that, she picked up her letter opener and slid the end into the envelope. "Oh my god, it's from her, it's from Emily!" She was ecstatic. She read the letter.

Emily Fleet was alive, living in Lima, the capital of Peru, and she had seen the ad in the Thurrock Gazette. "Unbelievable, absolutely unbelievable," Lucy thought, her hands shaking. Emily had written her contact details; the phone number, everything. She had to phone Barry. He would be so happy with her.

****

Lucy couldn't wait to tell Barry about the letter from Emily Fleet. She had tried to call him a few times but was unable to get hold of him.

Meanwhile Barry was trying to deal with a problem with Angela.

Barry felt he had been careful enough to hide his affair with Lucy, but Angela had been in this situation before with her first relationship and knew the signs. She was convinced there was something going on, and she finally decided to confront him.

Barry had always been faithful to Angela. The problem he had was that, unlike some people he knew, he didn't know how to deceive his wife and get away with it. In the end, he confessed.

"I'm so sorry, Ange. It was just a one of. It meant nothing." he exclaimed.

"Next you're gonna tell me it won't happen again!" Angie screamed. "I want to know who it is who has loused up our marriage. Who is it? I want to know, or you can get out!"

Barry sat down, near to tears. He told Angie it was someone he met on a weekend with the lads. He didn't even know or remember her name. They had both been drunk. He was mortified.

"You're just sad and pissed off that I've found out, aren't you. You were never going to tell me, were you? WERE YOU!" She screamed again.

There was a pause. Barry was trying to think of something to say, then the phone rang. Barry got up to answer it.

"Leave it!" Angie bellowed. Barry sat down again.

You can sleep on the settee or go to hers if you prefer!" Angie shrieked sarcastically. "I don't want you near me. I'm done with you!" Angie stormed out of the lounge into her bedroom and slammed the door. Barry could hear her tears for what seemed like an eternity.

Morning came at the Wilson household. There was silence as they met face to face. Not a word was spoken. Barry couldn't think of anything that he could say that wouldn't lead to another row, so he decided to keep a low profile. He dropped into his routine with the birds and took his time He was dreading going back into the house only to have more arguments and bad feelings thrown about. No, it was time to let her make the first move, although he wasn't sure he wanted to know what the first move would be. He was still at home, he thought. She hasn't said I should leave. Maybe time will sort it.

He had been in with the birds probably twice as long as usual, so he decided to go into the house. When he walked into the kitchen, he felt an eerie silence, so much so that he called out "Angie?" But no reply came. He quickly checked around. She wasn't anywhere to be found. The last room he checked was the bedroom. He didn't see the envelope on the dresser until he returned to the bedroom an hour or so later.

When he read that Angie had gone to her mother's, he just sat on the bed and started crying.

The phone rang. It was a reflex action. "Ange?" he gasped.

"No Barry, its Lucy, I..."

Barry cut her short. "I can't talk, Lucy. I'll phone you tomorrow. Please understand." He ended the call, not giving Lucy a chance to explain about the letter from Emily Fleet.

Lucy wondered what was wrong. He sounded upset. She hoped he was alright. A part of her hoped that Angie had found out about them and then they would be able to be together. Curiosity got the better of her and she called him again.

Barry answered the call. "Lucy, I'm really sorry. This has to stop. I can't do it anymore. Angie has left me. She knows I've been with someone. She doesn't know it's you, but I... We must finish it. I'm sorry." He didn't wait for a reply. He just ended the call.

Lucy was crestfallen. "He can't do this. We love each other. How can he just end it like that? I'll find Angie and tell her it was me, that's what I'll do." Who was she kidding? She wouldn't tell Angie. What was she going to do, though? At that moment there was a knock at her door. "Barry," she thought. She rushed to the door and opened it. She was never very happy to see her Uncle Jock and today was no exception.

"Oh, it's you," she sighed unexcitedly. "What do you want?"

Jock grinned, "Aw, that's a nice welcome for your Uncle Jock. I thought I'd come and see if you're okay, that's all honey."

Lucy gestured for him to come in.

"Aren't you going to put the kettle on then?" he asked as he sat down.

"I suppose," Lucy vacantly replied.

They talked about nothing really for the next hour or so, until he said he had somewhere to be. "Aye, it's time I was away. Are you sure you're okay, Lucy?"

Lucy knew he had sensed she was not in the best of form, but she couldn't tell him why, could she? He would love to have something over Barry.

As he was about to leave, he said, "Oh by the way, a friend of mine said he saw you at a hotel in Norfolk a couple of weeks ago with an old man. He presumed it was your dad. I told him it couldn't have been your dad. He's long gone."

"Norfolk? I've not been to Norfolk for years. He must be mistaken." Lucy's head dropped. She wasn't very convincing, and Jock seemed sure of himself. How did he know? "I bet he had him followed," she thought.

Jock carried on smugly. "When he described the car you arrived in, I thought to myself, the only person I know that has an XJR is Barry Wilson." He said no more but looked at Lucy and she couldn't hide her feelings anymore.

Jock came back into the room and Lucy just broke down. Jock put his arms around her and smiled to himself. "Don't you worry about Mr. Birdman, Lucy. He won't get a chance to hurt you again, the old bastard."

"I love him, Uncle Jock, but he's told me we can't go on. Now I hate him!" Lucy cried.

"Lucy, I told you. I'll sort him out. He won't get away with hurting one of my family. I'll get even, don't you worry about that!"

Lucy just kept crying. Jock hugged his niece, but couldn't stop smiling, "Oh yes, Mr. Barry Wilson. I've got you where I want you. Your life is about to start sinking. You mess with my family, you take the consequences."

Bully Boy

Things were very quiet at Jack Fleet these days. There were lots of empty rooms. Percy was still busy doing maintenance to keep standards at an acceptable level, but he doubted if these sometimes tedious jobs were actually worth doing. After all, it was still highly likely the council would win the battle and claim the land for the profiteers. The likes of the Scottish midget would win the day and it was making Percy's blood boil.

As he walked past Jamie's room, he noticed the door was ajar. He opened it further. "Aaron, what are you doing?" Aaron was pushing Jamie around.

"We're only playing, Percy, ain't we, Jamie?" Aaron said unconvincingly. Jamie's face was flushed.

Percy wasn't happy. "Go back to your own room and stay there till I come to see you," he demanded. Aaron tried to continue his version of events, but Percy was unmoved. "Just go to your room, I said."

At this, Aaron decided he was not getting anywhere so did as he was told.

Jamie was very quiet. Percy tried to get him to talk. "Would you like some refreshments, Jamie? I can get Ada to rustle up some cake or biscuits for you, or do you want to tell me what that was all about?" Silence. Percy waited. He was ninety percent sure Aaron was up to no good, given his history with the drinking problem. He was certain that Jamie feared Aaron and this was the reason he was reluctant to reveal what Percy needed to hear.

"I'll have some cake, if that's okay," Jamie finally replied gingerly. He just would not open up.

"Okay, son. I'll get it sorted. Do you want to come down to the kitchen or shall I bring it up to you? What do you think?" There was a prolonged silence. Percy stated, "I'll bring it up to you, okay?" Jamie nodded.

Percy made his way to Aaron's room. He didn't bother knocking and just walked in and said coldly, "Just stay here. I'll be back."

Aaron was sure Jamie hadn't told him anything and knew that the old git couldn't do anything to hurt him. He just sat on his bed and replied, "Okay."

Percy made his way to the kitchen, where Ada was busy as usual. He wondered to himself how she did it, keeping everybody happy and everything ticking over. She was his rock.

"Hello, lovey," she smiled. "I've just made a lovely Victoria sponge. Do you want a taste?"

Percy loved her cooking. "Only if you make a cuppa with it, too!" Percy said cheekily. "I'll take some up for Jamie and Harry as well."

Ada asked why not Aaron. When Percy explained what had just happened, Ada was not amused. "That boy! Jesus, I don't know what his problem is, Percy." They were unable to turn this problem child into a decent human being. God knows they had tried everything, but nothing seemed to work.

Jamie smiled at his delicious, rather large piece of Victoria sponge. "I can't eat all that," he gasped, as he wrapped both hands around to pick the cake up.

"Course you can't," smiled Percy.

Percy left him to it. Now for Aaron. He sat with Aaron for around half an hour, but Aaron would not divulge anything or any wrongdoing on his part. It was hopeless. As he left Aaron's room, Harry came walking round the corner at the top of the stairs.

"Harry, just the one I wanted to see. Percy smiled. Harry looked concerned. "Don't worry, I just want to chat. Shall we go to your room?"

Harry was a shy lad. He had been here for three years now. Percy noticed when he first arrived that he was a little slower than average, but his manner was that of a good soul.

"Harry, what does Aaron have on Jamie?" He was very subtle, our Percy.

"What do you mean?" Harry replied sheepishly.

Percy thought for a second. "Well …. I think Jamie is being bullied by Aaron, but he won't say he is, as if Aaron has some sort of hold over him." Percy sighed.

Harry said nothing for a few seconds. Then he exploded. "He's a bully. It's not more than that! He's been that way since I've been here. I've hardly seen him any different than that, but he's devious and always seems to wriggle his way out of it!" The frustration in Harry's tone was clear. He was being bullied too, it was obvious.

Percy reassured him. "We need to get to the bottom of this, Harry. I can't be having a bully getting away with causing so much misery, okay? Thanks for telling me. I promise I will sort this problem once and for all."

He thought for a moment. "I need to resolve this, even if it means the removal, yes, the removal of Aaron. Aaron has a brother. I'll try to get his brother in the picture. We'll see then.

Happy Days In Lima

Emily was doing the dishes, not really with any thoughts of the domestic chores. She had promised herself she'd clean up before Lionel arrived later in the week. She had just taken the rubbish bag out of the bin and opened the door to put it outside when she was surprised by Lionel standing at the door about to ring the bell.

"Oh, Lionel. You're early. It's lovely to see you." Before she could say any more, Lionel's lips met hers. She was ecstatic. He was early. He was here. All her doubts disappeared. He was actually here. "You should have told me you were going to be early. I'd have met you." Emily was so excited.

Lionel just smiled, put his hands on her shoulders and took in her beauty. "Wow! You're just as beautiful as I remember. I've really missed you." He was genuine. He was also really pleased with himself for arriving early.

Emily ran her fingers through her hair. She was positive she didn't smell very nice as she had been doing the housework. Lionel didn't seem to mind though, as he broke away from their third embrace in as many minutes.

"Would you like a coffee?" Emily asked.

Lionel just stared and said, "Aren't you going to show me around? I mean, where's the bedroom?"

The pair of them smiled in unison and, in no time, were wrapped, naked, in each other's arms. Emily was in heaven. There were no second thoughts, no doubts, just total bliss like she had never experienced before. Yes, this was heaven.

It must have been the excess heat that made them fall asleep, added with the sexual energy they had used up. Emily woke first and stared at her lover. He was handsome, she thought, really handsome, and he was here with her. He came early to be with her. How long would he stay, she wondered, still smiling.

She went to the kitchen and put the kettle on. As she was stirring his mug, he kissed her neck. "You are so beautiful. I've missed you so much."

He sounded really genuine, Emily thought. "So, how long are you here for then?" she asked, hoping he would say forever. "Not sure, but I'm yours for at least two weeks, maybe longer. I have some business to attend to in Rio, maybe a month from now, but maybe earlier. Let's not think about that for now. I'm here with the most beautiful woman...the most beautiful woman I know. I'm... "

Emily stopped his words and touched his lips with her forefinger, then kissed him.

This time they were asleep so long after, it was dark when Lionel woke up. He kissed Emily to waken her and they lay there together, not needing to say or do anything. They were totally immersed in each other.

The day was gone. She was with her man. She looked at her clock; it was 6am. She thought to herself that they had wasted a day, but she just laughed. Wasted? No way. It was a fantastic day and the best thing of all was there were lots more days ahead. She just lay there staring at her man. Sometime later, Lionel woke her with a cup of tea.

Whenever Emily had a cup of tea, she always compared it to Sam's tea. "Sorry, Lionel. In future, I'll make the tea. There's a right way and a wrong way to make it. No offence, but I'll make a fresh cup."

Lionel laughed. "A recipe for a cup of tea? Emily, please."

Emily laughed too but, when Lionel tasted Emily's tea, he conceded the point and they laughed together.

"What's for breakfast, then? I can't think what I've done to work up such an appetite," Lionel said cheekily, and they both giggled together.

Emily suggested they go to town and have a continental breakfast. Lionel was fine with that, saying he needed to sort out his lighter clothes. It had been a while since he'd been in the sun. They walked into town together, arm in arm, neither of them with a care in the world. Emily ordered; Lionel insisted that he would pay. They sat on the terrace and watched the world go by. By the time they finished, the sun was high and the temperature was, too. Emily suggested they head for the coast for the day. Lionel was only too happy to concur, so they headed back to Emily's to pack a picnic and a few drinks, of course.

While they were sorting themselves out, there was a knock at the door.

Lionel, being the nearest, opened the door to see an old man standing there. "Yes, can I help you?" he asked. It was Sam. "Hello Sam," he said shaking Sam's hand. "Emily has told me so much about you. My name is Lionel." If he was honest, Lionel felt a little uncomfortable. He knew Sam was like Emily's father figure.

Emily arrived at the door. "Sam, it's lovely to see you. Come in. Do you want a cuppa?" Emily could see Sam needed something. It was very hot out there.

"Aye pet, I'll have a cuppa. Do you want me to make it?" Sam replied.

Lionel said, "I think you should let Sam make it, Emily. After all, doesn't he make the best cuppa in South America?"

Sam had a puzzled look on his face.

Emily smiled. "It's my fault, Sam. I told Lionel that you make the best cup of tea and I guess he just wants to taste one for himself."

Sam chuckled, "Oh, okay then, I'll make it. Let the dog see the rabbit then girl, out of the way." Sam went over to the kitchen and set about making the best cup of tea Lionel had ever tasted.

"Wow!" Lionel said. "I know it's only tea, but what is it that you do? That really was the nicest cup of tea I've ever tasted. Unbelievable." Lionel was indeed surprised.

Sam smiled. Emily smiled. They were all smiling. And when they realised this, they all burst into laughter.

Lionel wanted to know Sam better and, before too long, the two of them were engrossed in conversation, leaving Emily to sit and listen to two people, who really should be worlds apart, get on like a house on fire.

Maybe an hour had gone by when Emily suggested, "I think we'll give the beach a miss today, Lionel." Lionel just nodded his head. Sam had him hook, line and sinker, talking about the old days in the northeast, all the same stories that had the same effect on Emily. Sam had another friend and Emily loved it.

Hell Hath No Fury

Lucy couldn't sleep. How, why would he finish it? She'd been awake for hours. It was nearly time to get up for work. "Ah stupid," she thought. It was Sunday morning. She would get even. Don't you worry about that. She finally drifted off to sleep.

Jock was an early riser, always had been. He loved Sundays. He could take his dogs for a proper walk and usually came home shattered. He gave a lot of thought to Lucy. She was a good kid and now the plumber had dumped her. He was sure she would be a useful ally in the Jack Fleet area. Oh yes, Jock knew the Gazette was against the decision to close the home down and having Lucy on the inside was a real bonus. His thoughts turned to Terry, who had assured him this project was the first of many planned in the area. He knew the value of Jock and his control of the council. Jock could and, providing he was rewarded financially, would rubber stamp any projects that Terry put his way. It was looking extremely good for the pair of them. Jock smiled to himself. Life was sweet and getting sweeter all the time. He decided to give Lucy a call. His efforts to reach her came to nothing, so he left it with a plan to try again later.

Lucy woke around noon, still tired and still angry. The light was flashing on the phone.

Jock answered straight away. "Hi, Lucy. How are you?" He could tell by the tone in her voice that she wasn't in a good place.

"Uncle Jock, I need to see you. I have something you'll be interested to hear." She begged him to come and see her today.

"Okay, pet. I'll be about an hour, okay?" he replied curiously.

"That's fine," Lucy replied. She decided to have a shower to try and wake herself up.

Jock arrived just under an hour later.

"Come up, Uncle Jock," Lucy said through her intercom. She ushered her uncle into the living room. "Do you want a drink or anything?" she offered.

Jock declined. "It's too near me Sunday lunch, you know. Don't want to spoil me first pint." Jock would always be found in the pub Sunday lunchtime. He never missed. "Now Lucy, what's on your mind?" he asked, eager to hear the answer.

"Well," Lucy started, "Do you know the Fleet family? I mean have you heard of the Fleet family at all?" Lucy looked at Jock quizzically.

"I've heard of them but, as far as I know, they're all gone. Why?" he asked.

"Well, what if I told you that one of them has contacted me at the office. Barry had an ad put in the paper asking for the whereabouts of any of the Fleet family, and one of them has just written to me. You'd never guess where from." Lucy paused. Jock looked baffled and just shook his head. "Peru, Uncle Jock. She lives in Peru."

Jock's face turned to concern. "Does she know about Jack Fleet, then?" he asked.

"Well, Mr. Barry Wilson would have been told by now but, seeing as he doesn't want to know me, I don't think I'll be telling him now, do you?" Lucy said sarcastically.

A smile came to Jock's face. "What did she put in this letter, then?"

Lucy replied, "She just wants to know why the Gazette wants to speak to her, but I've not replied to her. What should I do?"

Jock thought for a minute. "Lucy, sit on it for the minute. I'm going to do some digging. That's it. Just hold fire and put the letter somewhere safe, or do you want to give it to me?"

"It's up to you. I don't think anyone will see it. I can bring it home with me when I finish work tomorrow," she said.

"That's alright then, pet. That'll do. I'll have a think for a few days and see what I can sort out. Lucy, you've made my day. Thank you, sweetheart."

Half an hour later, Jock walked into his local with a huge grin on his face. Beautiful, just beautiful. He was soon joined by his regular crew. Sunday lunch consisted of a few beers and a game of cards. Not surprisingly, he usually won, being a canny Scot. He didn't give much away. He drank more on this occurrence than usual and his playing partner made sure he didn't drive, though it was challenging work getting his keys off him. He was trying to sing. He was extremely happy. Everyone just laughed.

Broken Man

Barry was finding it hard to motivate himself. He was a shadow of the man he was before. The bungalow was a mess. Empty bottles of wine and beer lay strewn all over the place. Angie wouldn't answer his calls. He'd screwed up big time and couldn't see things getting better in the near future. Yes, he'd screwed up alright.

The phone rang. "Hello, Angie?" Barry was wishful thinking.

"Hello, Barry. It's me Percy. You okay? We haven't seen or heard from you in weeks. What's going on?"

"I'm alright, Percy. Don't you worry about me. I'm okay," Barry sighed.

Percy sensed there wasn't a lot of truth in that statement. "I'll come round and see you. Be there in ten." With that, Percy rang off.

Barry looked around the place. "God, what a mess!" he thought to himself. He set about tidying up before Percy arrived and he did manage to neaten the place so it wasn't too bad. Trouble was he didn't have time to sort himself out. He was unshaven, wearing tracksuit bottoms and a wrinkled T-shirt. He heard Percy's car pull onto the drive. Barry got to the door before Percy rang the doorbell.

"Percy, how are you? Come in. Do you want a cuppa?" Barry tried to sound cheerful.

Percy nodded. He looked at Barry. He'd never seen him looking so dishevelled. He was a real mess. Percy and Barry were good friends and, consequently, they were usually honest with each other.

"Okay Baz, what's up?" Percy asked in a way that friends do.

Barry didn't respond straight away but, just as Percy was going to speak again, Barry said "She's left me, Percy. My Doll, she's left me." Barry was close to tears.

Percy was lost for words. He thought Barry might be ill, but Angie had left him. Why?

Percy confronted him. "Why?"

Barry sighed, "Because I couldn't keep my cock in my trousers, Percy. I thought I was a youngster, a teenager or something. Fucking idiot more like. I've screwed up, literally. What a fucking idiot." That was it. He sat down and burst into tears.

Percy walked over, put his arm around his friend and patted his upper back. "Barry, you bloody old fool."

Aye, thought Barry, an old fool is about right.

Percy decided to stay a while and help his best friend. He didn't have a clue how he was going to do that, but he was sure it'd be better with him there. Barry tried hard, so hard, not to break down in front of Percy, but the pain and the guilt combined were too much to bear. He knew he had to shake himself out of it and get back to sorting things with the business. The business! Christ, what about the business! Tom, his assistant, was a real asset but could only do so much. Barry was sure he would need to at least go to the shop and put some hours in. Then he realised he'd been lax in taking care of the birds, so much so that he jumped up and went to the kitchen where Percy was making a brew.

"Percy, can you give me a hand for an hour or two? It's just that I need to sort Polly and the gang out down the bottom of the garden," Barry asked.

Percy looked puzzled.

Barry said, "Sorry mate. I need to clean and feed the parrots... Polly... you know."

Percy smiled. His friend had lifted his head up and was ready to get himself back on track. "No problem, Baz. I'd love to."

They decided to take their cuppas with them. It was quite a chore. The birds took a lot of sorting but, with two people at it, it was done in half the time.

"Right," Barry said positively. "Right, now Percy, I have to go to the shop and straighten that out as well. I'll give you a bell later and Percy, thanks so much for everything. I really appreciate your friendship."

Percy smiled," Oh, so you wouldn't have done the same for me then?"

Now it was Barry's turn to smile. "Point taken, Percy. Thanks again anyway, though."

Barry watched Percy walk to his car and drive off. His electric gates were just swinging shut, when a car pulled into the drive. He couldn't quite see who was in the car, not until they got out. It was Lucy. This was the last thing he needed. Didn't he tell her it was over? Surely she'd got the message by now.

He reluctantly opened the door. He'd forgotten how beautiful she was. Oh dear. "Lucy, I'm sorry sweetheart. You can't be here. It's over. It's not right. I'm not right for you."

Lucy was stony faced. "Don't flatter yourself, Barry. I don't want anything from you. Why would I? After all, you only broke my heart. Wasn't nothing really was it, eh, Mr. Barry Wilson!"

The venom in her voice was powerful. Barry was taken aback. "Lucy, Lucy, I'm sorry."

Lucy stopped him mid-sentence. "We're finished. You're obviously happy with that. Well, it's fine by me too. I've just come to tell you that Emily Fleet has written to me. How's that for news, then!" Lucy still wasn't smiling, though she continued. "The trouble is, though, I'm afraid I can't seem to remember any details of the letter, or even where it is now. Ain't that a shame? Your big chance to keep Jack Fleet House open has disappeared!"

Barry was shocked. "Lucy, you can't do that. You know you agreed with us when we were talking about the home, how wrong it was that the council were trying to close it down!" Barry thought for a minute. "Oh, I get it. Blood is thicker than water, isn't it Lucy? Your twisted Uncle Jock is behind this. How could you do that to the kids, to Percy and Ada? How could you?"

Lucy was silent. Barry had hit a nerve, but she wasn't going to change her mind. "You should have thought about that before you dumped me then, shouldn't you?"

Barry wasn't going to let her out the door. "You…. I can't believe this of you. Your uncle has something on you and he is making you do this."

Lucy by now was at the door. "Let me go… PLEASE!"

Barry realised there was no point in saying any more "Okay girl, off you go. Hope you sleep alright. Oh and say a prayer for Jamie and the other kids tonight, won't you?"

Lucy felt that and almost stopped in her tracks. At that moment, she showed a stubborn side just like her father and his brother, Jock; Scottish, stubborn, mean too sometimes. She got into her car and waited for the gate to open, then drove home. Sadly, she couldn't help thinking about what Barry said as she left.

Barry stood at the door. It was getting dark. He wondered what Angie was doing. God, he missed her. What could he do about it? Nothing. She never returned his calls. Her mum always answered the phone, saying things like, "She's in the bath" or "She's out at a friend's house". All he knew was that he wanted her back and was determined to get her back somehow. He closed the door behind him.

He decided to have a couple of beers. He went to the fridge. Empty, not just of beer but of food too. Only one thing for it, he thought to himself. He picked up the phone. "Ronnie, is it too late for Barb to cook me a meal? I know it's just gone nine, but I could eat a scabby horse."

Ronnie shouted to Barb, who was cleaning the kitchen after a busy night of pool and darts matches. "Yeah Baz, she'll knock something up for you. See you in a bit."

Barry smiled to himself. He'd drive there and get a cab back, or even walk. It wasn't far.

Ronnie went into the kitchen. "Barb, don't dish him up anything yet. Just get it prepared. I've got a feeling he's up for a chat."

"I've got some steak and a few homemade chips already prepared. If he's too late, you'll have to cook for him, though. I'm knackered. I hate pool nights," she complained.

Ronnie gave her a kiss on the cheek. "Thanks, darling." Ronnie was on the customer side of the bar when Barry walked in. "Alright, Baz." Ronnie shook his hand. "You okay? What's up with Angie? She not well?"

Ronnie was genuinely shocked when Barry told him what had happened. They had found a quiet area of the bar. After almost an hour and four beers each, Ronnie said, "You want some grub then, Baz?"

Barry sighed, "If I'm honest Ron, I've lost me appetite." At that Carol, Ronnie's best barmaid, came walking past with a tray of left-over sandwiches and pork pies from the pool match. "Oh, they'll do me, Carol. Is that alright, Ron?"

"Of course it is," he replied. "Do you want some crisps or pickled onions with it?"

Barry was chewing on a sandwich and just shook his head.

The two of them had a right old natter. Barry finally stood up and said, "I'd better be off, Ron. I'll see you in the week."

"Okay. Baz, you ain't driving are ya?" Ronnie asked. Barry looked guilty. Ronnie sighed, "Oh no, give us your keys. Wait a minute, wait right there." Ronnie ran to the back of the pub to the car park where the visiting pool team were about to leave. He then went back to the bar. "C'mon Baz, I've got you a lift." Only when Barry was in the minibus did he give Barry his keys back. "What a mess," Ronnie thought to himself as the minibus drove away. Who would have thought it? Barry and Angie, solid as a rock. Midlife crisis came to mind. Lucy was an attractive kid, but she was a kid all the same.

When Ronnie reached the bar, he shouted, "Last orders were half an hour ago people. You might not wanna go to bed, but I do."

Some of the regulars mumbled, complaining. One of them, another Ronnie, shouted "You on a promise then, Ron?" They all started laughing.

It even brought a smile to Ronnie's face. He replied, "I got two chances of that happening and slim has just left town." More laughter erupted as they left, with the words "See you tomorrow lunchtime, Ron" echoing in his ears.

Ronnie poured himself a small beer and sat at the bar, mulling things over. Life in general was good. He and Barb were doing a fantastic job with the pub. Barb especially was pulling in so much business on the restaurant side that they were quite often turning people away at weekends with their Sunday roast. Everything fresh, no frozen veg. That was the difference. He looked around. Did the place need a face lift? No, not just yet, he thought. His thoughts then turned back to Barry. He hadn't mentioned the closure of Jack Fleet House, which was most unusual. Prior meetings about it had been intense on Barry's part, and Ronnie thought at the time that Barry would be the main reason the home actually might get a reprieve. Ronnie sighed, locked up and went upstairs. Barbara was reading. "Thought you were tired, Barb," he said.

"I was, Ron, but couldn't get to sleep. So, I'm trying to make my eyes tired," she responded.

Ronnie stopped her. "Barb, you know what will make you sleep?" He smiled at her.

She smiled back, "Make it quick, then" and started laughing.

"Ha ha," Ronnie said as he kissed her.

It was usually quick anyway. Quarter of an hour later, the pub was in darkness.

Destiny

Around twenty years ago, a young lad was growing up in the Falls Road area of Belfast. He had just started work and was a good worker too. He took to his job really well and was soon being asked to do the more difficult tasks that his co-workers were not able to.

David McCallister was a tiler, working for a large company based in Northern Ireland. Matchless Tiles were expanding. They had just won a contract on the mainland, in Liverpool. They were looking for volunteers from their Belfast depot to relocate to Liverpool as the contract was expected to last nearly two years.

David was asked to go and see the boss. He walked into Paddy Maloney's office. He liked Paddy and the feeling was mutual. David was only twenty but was far better at his job than most of the people on the payroll, except Paddy himself, of course.

"Morning, young Davey boy. How're you doing?" Paddy asked him, joyful as always.

"I'm good thanks," David replied.

Paddy thought for a moment. "Davey, have you thought about the Liverpool job? Do you fancy it?"

David had thought about putting his name down for it but hadn't yet. "Yeah, I was thinking I'd like to be on that job. It would make a change."

Paddy smiled. "That's what I wanted to hear, Davey boy. How do you fancy running it then?"

David was stunned. Run the job? Was he serious? "I don't... I mean I'm..."

Paddy motioned for David to take a seat. "Right, listen. You, as far as I'm concerned, are streets ahead of the rest of that lot out there. I don't have anyone more qualified than you for this job. Your work is outstanding and I'm confident that this is right up your alley. Run the job for me, Davey boy. There'll be a significant pay rise for you obviously." Paddy smiled and continued. "In five years' time, you'll be known all over the UK. I see big things for you, Davey. This is the first step in what, I believe, is going to be a fantastic journey for you." He paused. "I'm going to be honest with you. I can't give you more time to make a decision. I need you on board. The job will involve long hours initially and I'll be there to start with, going through the drawings with the technical guys. So I'm afraid I need to know by the end of the day."

David didn't respond at first. It seemed like ages. Paddy didn't speak. David was thinking, then he said, "Okay, Paddy, I'll do it."

Paddy jumped out of his seat, put a hand on David's shoulder and shook his hand.

"You little star. You won't regret it, Davey boy. When you come in tomorrow, can you be here by 6am?" David nodded. Paddy continued excitedly, "Great. Oh, and wear your suit and pack a bag. We're going to England for a couple of days. Pack a bag. In fact, it's two o'clock now. Have the rest of the day off and sort yourself out, okay?"

David replied, "Thanks that will help. I don't have a suit."

Paddy laughed "Well, when you get one, get a receipt and I'll take care of it, okay?"

David was over the moon. This had all happened so fast. His life was about to change and little did he know how much. His life would never be the same again.

John Lennon Airport was extremely busy for a Thursday. Okay, it was the tail end of rush hour. But, all the same, having to wait thirty-five minutes for Paddy's bag to come through seemed excessively long. They arrived at their destination just after ten. Paddy insisted on paying for breakfast, an Irish breakfast at that. Neither of them was surprised. Many people had said that Liverpool is the 'Capital of Ireland'.

Paddy started to explain in detail the job ahead of them. There were three buildings in Hope Street, all three storeys and all being totally refurbished. It was, as Paddy said, a 'cracking little earner'. David was in awe of the size of the job, thinking to himself, "Wow! I'm in charge of this effing job?" Wow indeed. After meeting 'the suits', as Paddy called them, Paddy exclaimed, "That's enough business talk today, Davey boy. Let's go into town. They checked into the Hard Day's Night

Hotel in North John Street. David was chuffed. He had his own room and it was luxurious. Paddy smiled and said that he would meet him downstairs in an hour.

Davey unpacked his toiletries and, after shaving, decided to phone his mum. "Mum, it's a cracking hotel, you should see it!"

His mum, Sarah, was so proud of her youngest child. Twenty years old and already running the job. She was thrilled to bits. "Dead on, David, dead on." she beamed.

Davey went downstairs and ordered himself a beer. It wasn't quite an hour since he'd left Paddy, but he wanted to be ready.

They spent the evening in The Grapes and ordered some food just before they closed the restaurant. Consequently, they were virtually alone by the time they finished their meal. Paddy took his napkin and cleaned around his lips, looking at his protege. He'd taken Davey on because he knew his father and was confident he would fit the bill. Davey's father, Patrick, was a self-made man. He called it as he saw it and, most of all, would not ask his employees to do something he wouldn't do himself. Paddy was sure Davey was the same. He really was onto a winner with this one.

The next day was mostly spent taking in the sights that Liverpool had to offer, from Anfield to Penny Lane, the walk across Stanley Park. They saw the funny side when, outside Anfield, anybody who parked their vehicle was quickly approached by kids no more than ten years old who offered their 'services' to look after their cars for a fiver, saying they would stop the older boys from nicking their wheels.

Paddy asked Davey what he wanted to do on their last night. Davey said he was okay with whatever, so the pair of them went back to The Grapes and started drinking. It was about four in the afternoon and Davey was to regret starting so early. At around eight-thirty, Paddy managed to get his little star up to his room and laughed when he was about to turn off the light. Davey looked at him and groaned, "Paddy, can you stop the room from spinning, please?"

Paddy gave a huge chuckle and said, "See you at breakfast, Davey boy."

Unsettled

At Jack Fleet House, there was an oppressive mood. A cloud was hanging over the home, the staff and the children. They were, each and every one of them, totally consumed by the possibility that, despite everyone's efforts, there really was nothing anyone could do. Aaron was as unclear as anybody and was clearly troubled. He had even started treating Harry and Jamie like he should and, in trying to start conversations with the two of them, it only sufficed to confuse them both. He was like some kind of Jekyll and Hyde character.

Harry said to Jamie, "How do we deal with him, one minute bullying us, the next almost pleading with us to join his company?" It was difficult to deal with. A part of him really didn't want to be his friend, but Aaron was so erratic in his moods, he decided to just leave it alone.

As he walked past the kitchen, he overheard Percy talking to Ada. "I'm not looking forward to this love," he heard Percy say.

Ada replied, "Well, you brought this on yourself, didn't you! You shouldn't drink and drive, so just be a man and take the consequences."

"Aye, you're right pet, only myself to blame. We'll have to get taxis everywhere we go," he sighed.

Ada understood his frustration and, although she would never tell him, she did feel sorry for him. He was to be at the courthouse for ten, though that didn't mean he would be seen at ten. Everyone at court that day would have been told to arrive at ten. Ada asked, "Are you sure you don't want me to come with you, love? I don't mind. You'll be glad for someone to talk to if it takes all day, won't you?"

Percy just didn't want Ada there. It was down to him and he had decided he would rather be on his own when the worst happened.

When he arrived at the local magistrate's court, he looked around to see if there was anybody he recognised. He was quite pleased that he didn't know any faces. What a relief. Around three hours after he arrived, he was finally called to court number 2. The three magistrates, two women and one quite old gentleman, were at the bar.

"Mr. Herbert, before we start, is there anything you wish to say, any mitigating circumstances?" Percy was ready for this question and declined not to prolong the proceedings.

"Very well, then. I believe there is somebody who wishes to speak about you and this prosecution," the elderly man said. "Mr. McBride, would you please stand and say what you have indicated in this letter I have before me."

Percy was speechless. The instigator of all the misery that was about to fall on Jack Fleet House was here to speak on Percy's behalf!

Percy could not restrain himself. "Your honour, I'm sorry but I don't want this man saying anything about me. I don't respect...."

"Mr. Herbert," the magistrate interrupted. "Mr. Herbert, this gentleman has something to say on your behalf and I have to insist that he WILL speak, so will you please sit down and not interrupt." Percy sat down. "Thank you, Mr. McBride. The floor is yours."

Percy sat and listened. You'd have thought they were brothers. The Scottish dwarf told lie after lie and Percy had to listen. "Unbelievable," Percy thought. "Totally unbelievable."

"Thank you, Mr. McBride. We appreciate your kind words. You may be seated." The magistrate gestured.

Jock stayed standing and said, "Your honour, I have somewhere I need to be. So, if you'll excuse me, I must go." He turned to Percy, winked and mouthed 'good luck' and was gone.

Percy was stunned. The taxi pulled up outside Jack Fleet and Percy didn't realise he was home. He finally came to his senses and got out, only to forget to pay the driver. It was only the driver sounding his horn that made him realise what he had done. "Sorry John. There mate, keep the change. Thank you."

Ada opened the door, "Well?" Percy looked down.

"Well, what did you get?" Ada was annoyed at having to wait for an answer.

"You won't believe what happened, Ada. You just won't believe it." Percy was still in shock.

"Percy, if you don't tell me what happened, I'll clobber you with me frying pan. Now tell me." Ada was getting worried.

"Okay, okay," Percy said. "I got off."

Ada was astonished. "What! What do you mean you got off?"

"Basically, I've got a suspended sentence for three years," Percy explained.

Ada's frown turned to a smile. "Percy, that's great. Why are you so down then? That's good news. Come on, snap out of it." She was so happy, but she was confused too. Why was Percy so down?

When the two of them reached the kitchen, Percy started to explain what had happened.

Ada was just as bewildered now as Percy. "Jock McBride spoke up for you. I don't understand, Percy. Why? Is it because he feels guilty or is he now going to ask you for a favour. He has helped you blah blah, now you can do something for him?"

Percy just sat on the kitchen unit. "Ada, as I was leaving the court, there was an old fella by the door. He came over to me and whispered something like "It pays to be a mason, don't it mate?' I just looked at him and told him I was no mason and left the court. I reckon the elderly magistrate is a mason and I know the dwarf is too. I just don't understand why he would do something like this." Percy was struggling to come to terms with it.

Ada reassured him. "Percy, just let it go, let it go, love." She gave him a cuddle.

Where Are We Going?

Emily was in love. She felt as if she was dreaming. She and Lionel were in love. Although they hadn't said the words, they were indeed in love. She was a little worried though. He had told her that he had to go to Brazil on business and he couldn't be sure how long it would take. He was doing deals all over the place and it got her thinking. So, this is what it would be like if they were indeed an item. She would only see him now and then and it was slowly dawning on her that was the case. Could she really throw herself into that kind of relationship? She was starting to realise the consequences of having this kind of affair. No, that's wrong, she thought to herself. This is the real thing. But she was sceptical about being apart so much.

Emily sat watching her lover in the ocean. He was so attractive. She loved him, no doubt about that. She loved him so much that her concerns about their relationship had to be, must be, resolved. She knew that now, and it was time to get her feelings out there and to await his response. She would do it after dinner tonight, definitely.

The two of them stayed on the beach almost until the sun went down. Lionel indicated he would like a beer on the way back home, but Emily steered him away from that by mentioning the time and adding that there was beer in the fridge back home. They walked up the hill, passing bars as they went and, at each bar they passed, Lionel tried to steer her into it for that beer and each time she got her own way. The question was, would she get her way after dinner? She wasn't sure. Lionel was a very successful businessman. He'd carved out a very rewarding way to do his business, and Emily wasn't sure he'd be willing to change it for her. Lionel volunteered to wash up after dinner, which surprised Emily to the extent that she joked, "Are you sure you want to, I mean keep in touch with your feminine side? You can if you like, Lionel. I don't mind. Honest." She started laughing.

After dinner, they sat in the garden. It was a warm evening. They'd had a couple of glasses of vino with and after dinner and they were both chilling. Emily was ready to dive in and test the water, so to speak. She stood up and asked Lionel, "Would you like a brandy? I have an unopened bottle of Napoleon, if you like." She looked at him and he smiled.

"I will if you will, Em." She nodded and a couple of minutes later, she returned and sat across the garden table from her man. She felt nervous. Was the impending chat going to cause a problem? How would he react? She had never been in this position with anyone before. Not a surprise really; she'd never loved anyone like this before. He was the one. She was sure of that. It was a clear night. The stars were crystal clear in the sky. Okay, she thought to herself. This is it. She used her foot to move the footstool over so she could relax and stretch out.

"Lionel," she said quietly.

"Yes, my love," he replied.

She paused for a moment. "Where are we going?" she whispered.

Lionel smiled, "Well, I'm kinda hoping the next move is to your bedroom."

She couldn't help but smile too. The statement made her think of them, lying naked on the bed. No sheets; it was too warm for sheets. Then she repeated her enquiry, "Where are WE going?" There, she had opened the door to the future. How would he respond?

Lionel himself hadn't given much thought to the situation, other than the fact that he'd fallen head over heels in love with a beautiful, beautiful woman. His answer came after a short pause. "I'd love to spend the rest of my life with the most beautiful woman I've ever had the pleasure to know, Emily. I don't, I mean I hope that's what you wanted me to say. I love you so much. When I'm not here it hurts so much. I can't bear to be away from you. You are my everything." So, there it was. He had laid his cards on the table. Now it was her turn.

"So, how is this going to work then, with me being here and you globe-trotting? Is that our future, Lionel?" Emily had said it. She had laid her cards down too.

Lionel was taken aback a little. He admitted to himself he wasn't too concerned about their different careers, presuming that they would just continue with their jobs. After all, lots of people did it, didn't they? Surely she wouldn't expect him to give up his job, bearing in mind that he wouldn't find anything that paid anywhere near what he earned. No, it would have to stay as it was. Lionel didn't speak. He sensed that this situation was turning into a problem. He didn't want that. He wanted Emily.

Emily loved her job and certainly didn't think about leaving. On the contrary, she was mulling over signing a new contract that would keep her in Lima for another four years. No, she wasn't going anywhere. So here they were then. The proverbial rock and a hard place had appeared. Would either of them compromise? They certainly both appeared set in their ways. Unfortunately, it seemed like love was going to be the loser.

There was an uneasy silence. The only words said before they retired were trivial. In the bedroom, they lay down with their backs touching. Emily could not sleep. Lionel got up after about an hour or so and sat in the garden and eventually fell asleep there.

The consequences of the heart-to-heart were still not resolved. They were going through their routine after breakfast without too much conversation, so much so that they were both pleased to see Sam walking up the hill.

Lionel tried to break the ice. "I'll put the kettle on, shall I?"

Emily nodded.

The next couple of hours were much more bearable. Lionel enjoyed the stories Sam told. Emily had heard most of them before, but they still made her smile. Sam, although he noticed there was an atmosphere, never mentioned it. He was his normal jovial self.

On his walk home, Sam was reflective. Something was wrong. He had enjoyed his afternoon with Emily, but there was definitely an atmosphere. It was quite obvious. He realised it wasn't his place to ask questions and hoped it would be resolved promptly. He thought the world of Emily. He'd also forgotten to ask her if she had heard anything from the Thurrock Gazette. It had been a couple of months since Emily responded to the ad. Oh well, it'll sort itself out. He continued down the hill, promising himself he would get in touch with Emily tomorrow just in case. You know, just in case.

Emily woke first. Lionel was snoring. She made herself some tea and toast and sat in the garden. She was determined to sort this situation out. Where did she stand? She presumed Lionel wasn't interested in changing his way of life for anyone. He was very successful. It seemed like Emily had to change her life or accept the occasional visit from her lover. Right at this moment in time, she wasn't prepared to do that.

"Any more coffee going, sweetie?" Lionel appeared in his blue speedos.

"No, I'll make a fresh one," Emily replied.

Lionel said kindly. "No, you sit right there. I'll get it. Would you like some breakfast, love?"

Emily smiled, "No, it's alright thanks. I've already eaten."

A few minutes later Lionel joined her. They both tried to forget the atmosphere from the night before. Conversation was very matter of fact and Emily wasn't having that. She decided to re-light the fire.

"So, Lionel, when do you go to Brazil? And for how long will you be gone?" She tried not to, but there was some venom in her voice. "Well?"

Lionel was a little shocked at her tone. "Emily, what is your problem? You knew from day one my situation with work. It's impossible for me to work nine-to-five. I've created my income by being ready to go where I need to at a moment's notice and, I have to say, I don't intend to change. I know it's not ideal but, ironically, we wouldn't have met if I had a nine-to-five job, now would we?"

Emily nodded. She knew he was right, but only right for him. She just couldn't see herself in limbo, not knowing when she would have her man at home.

"Emily." He leant across and took her hand. "Emily, I know you have your career. I was thinking you could travel with me."

Emily let go of his hand. "I don't think so Lionel, not a chance. Honestly, I love my job and have just received an extension offer so no is my response to that. I'm afraid we seem to have reached an impasse, haven't we?"

They both sighed. It really seemed as if their brief relationship was doomed to fail.

Lionel took the empty cups into the kitchen and called out to Emily, "I'm going for a walk, Em."

Emily replied, "Okay," and sighed again. This was it then. There was no way to solve the problem. She needed to talk to someone, to bounce her thoughts and concerns off, get a second opinion. Sam, she mumbled to herself. She hurriedly wrote a note and left it on the kitchen unit, saying she was going to see her friend. In half an hour or so she arrived at Sam's and knocked at the door. Sadly, there was no answer.

She was about to leave when Sam called out, "Hello, who's there?" He was on the roof, tending his plants.

"Sam, it's me, Emily. Shall I come up?"

"Aye lass, the door's open. Come on up. Oh Em, bring us a glass of squash each will you? It's roasting up here!"

Emily had told Sam on numerous occasions about leaving his door unlocked, but he never seemed to bother.

"Morning, lass." Sam gave her a big cuddle, bigger than usual she thought. Sam was sure that something was up, but waited for Emily to raise the subject.

It was small talk for ten minutes or so, then Emily told Sam of her predicament. Sam listened intently and could see Emily was upset. She must really love this man, he thought, and he wanted to cuddle her and tell her everything would sort itself out. But he felt that, with everything she was saying, it seemed obvious that she was leaning towards ending the relationship as soon as possible. Bless her. He really felt for his friend.

"Emily, I think you want me to give my opinion as to what you just told me. To be honest, pet, I don't think you need any help. By what you've just told me..." He paused. "By what you've just told me, unless Lionel is willing to lay down some roots and make a commitment, then this will be the end. That's what you're saying, I think."

Emily's head dropped. When she looked up, Sam noticed a tear. "Emily, sweetheart, don't cry." Emily was sobbing now, and Sam was doing his best to comfort her. But she was falling apart in front of him. It almost brought a tear to his eye as well. He loved Emily like a daughter and this was hurting him too.

Eventually, Emily calmed down and, as they made their way down from the roof, she gave a little chuckle as Sam missed the last step. "Bloody stairs; they'll be the death of me." He turned to look at Emily and laughed himself when he saw her laughing. The mood lightened as Sam made his famous cup of tea. Emily was in a better place by the time she said goodbye to Sam and started her walk home.

She needn't have bothered worrying about how to tell Lionel because, by the time she got home, he had gone. Packed his case and gone. Just like that!

She was numb. "The coward," she thought to herself, "the bloody coward." She set about doing some housework. She changed the sheets to get rid of his smell. She had the radio on and was slowly snapping out of it. "He's showed his true colours, hasn't he?" she said to no one. "Bastard!" She lifted a box that was on the table near the window and knocked a newspaper on to the floor. It was the Gazette "Hmm..." she thought to herself, "I think it's time I gave them a ring and found out what they want from me. I'll ring them tomorrow from the call cabin in town." She spent the afternoon tidying up and eventually sat in the garden and took in some late sun, which, as Sam always said, was the best sun to get. It's less harmful and gives you a better tan. Sam said it; it must be right.

She opened a bottle of rosé while cooking her dinner and had drunk most of it by the time she finished her meal. She tried really hard to forget. She didn't understand Lionel, not for digging his heels in about his career, but why just leave, without so much as a note or a goodbye? This was not the Lionel she knew. It really surprised her. She was feeling sleepy and drained. The day had been an emotional one, so she decided to have an early night.

It was five in the morning when Emily woke. "Damn," she thought. 'Why did I go to bed so early?" She tried for an hour to go back to sleep, before giving up and going downstairs. It was only six fifteen, far too early. What could she do? She opened the curtains. It looked like it was going to be another scorcher. After breakfast, she had a shower and searched around for some change for the call cabin. She had used them before, but not much. They always said they didn't have any change so, when you paid with notes, they usually made extra money from your call.

****

Lucy called in sick. She was burning up and aching all over. Her boss Ronnie was okay without her, but it did create a few problems for him. It was a Monday, so it was relatively quiet in the office.

At around one thirty, the phone rang. Ronnie answered, "Hello, Thurrock Gazette. How can I help?" It was a poor line, so he had to ask again when the caller identified herself.

"Hello, my name is Emily Fleet!"

"Oh, my god!" Ronnie gasped. "I'm sorry. It's just that we've been trying to contact you for so long. We'd just about given up." Ronnie was sweating.

Emily tried to speak clearly. "I'm calling from a call cabin and I'm fast running out of change. Is it possible that you can call my home number?"

Ronnie replied, "Of course, no problem. What is your number and I'll call you tomorrow, around this time. Will that be okay?"

Emily responded, "No, I'd rather it be a little bit later, if that's okay." With that the line went dead.

"Wow," he thought to himself. She had finally gotten in touch, after months of trying. He couldn't wait to tell Barry. He was about to give Barry a call, then decided he would do it later and just ask Barry to be at the office tomorrow when he called her and Barry himself could speak to her. He found it hard to contain his excitement. He did realise that, although they had found her, there was no guarantee that she would be the answer they were looking for. He realised that, but he was a positive thinker and the glass was definitely more than half full.

****

Barry was at the shop, getting ready to lock up, when he heard the buzzer go by the showroom front door. He poked his head around the corner to see who it was and Ronnie Dexter jumped out from behind a display cabinet and said "Boo!"

Barry jumped out of his skin. "You bastard! You scared the shit out of me there," he said as he started laughing. "How are you, Ronnie? What can I do for you? You know if you're buying, the price just went up after scaring me like that."

Ronnie smiled, trying to contain his excitement again. He couldn't wait to see Barry's face when he finally got to speak to Emily Fleet tomorrow. "No, I'm not buying. I was thinking of putting an editorial in this week's edition, and was wondering if you'd join me and a few others at the office tomorrow, about two o'clock?"

Barry was already nodding his head, "Of course, Ron. Who else will be there? Have you asked Percy?"

Ronnie nodded. "So far, Percy said yes. Ron J has said yes. It's just you to confirm and we can bang our heads together, see if we can make Mr. Mayor squirm on his throne." Ronnie hated the Scottish dwarf as much as any of them, but he had to be careful what he put in print.

Barry locked up five minutes after Ronnie left and decided to pick up fish and chips on his way home. A treat. Why not? He'd still had no contact with Angie. Countless calls went unanswered, but he couldn't give up, wouldn't give up. When he pulled into his drive, he was shocked to see Angie's car already there. He parked the car, sat for a moment and thought about what he was going to say. He couldn't cock it up again. He had to eat the proverbial 'humble pie', no question about it.

Angie was sitting in the kitchen, perched on the stool by the island. She had a glass of wine in her hand, but no smile appeared. For a few moments, neither of them said anything. Then, as if on cue, they both spoke at the same time. Barry laughed. Half a smile from Angie was more than Barry could hope for, but he got it. "You first, Ange."

Barry went over to the oven, switched it on and placed his fish and chips in there. "Sorry, I didn't know you were here." There was another half smile from her. He continued, "Do you want me to go and get you some? I don't mind." He was almost begging.

Angie walked over to the sink unit, opened the drawer and took out a knife and fork. "I don't mind them out of the paper. If you want some, you'd better go back, hadn't you? Oh, and bring me a couple of pickled onions, please."

Barry was gobsmacked. "Okay, right, I'll go back then. See you in a bit." He couldn't believe it. She was back. His Angie, his Doll was back. Then he thought about it. Wait a minute, was she really back? "You'll just have to wait and see Barry boy," he exclaimed to himself. He drove faster than he should have, but managed to get back in one piece. This time when he walked in, Angie was sitting on the sofa listening to music. He noticed she had dimmed the lights. Barry didn't say anything, went to the kitchen, brought Angie her pickled onions, then joined her on the other end of the sofa. It was an eerie silence between tracks, but they occasionally looked at each other, without any words. Then, when Angie finished her meal, Barry said, "Leave your dishes on the side. I'll sort the dishwasher out."

Angie just nodded and waited till Barry had finished his food. "Well," she said as she stretched her arms, "I think I'll have an early night."

Barry just said "Okay." He didn't want to say what he was thinking. She was here, and she was going to bed, and that's all that mattered.

"Night, then," Angie muttered.

Barry turned as he was walking towards the kitchen. "Night Doll." He loaded the dishwasher and turned the music down a bit, kicked off his shoes and stretched out on the sofa.

A few minutes later, Angie came back into the living room in her negligee, and said, "Aren't you coming to bed, Baz?"

They were naked in no time and Barry was over the moon. A couple of times during their love-making, he started apologising, only for Angie to tell him to "shut up and concentrate." He was in heaven. Angie, too, was happy to be home. She was a little concerned about the two of them getting it on, but they had always, until recently, had a good sex life. Angie was determined her man would not feel the need to stray ever again. She didn't give him much rest till the morning, when she phoned the shop and told them he wouldn't be in.

They slept till around ten. Angie was first up and made tea and toast for them both, in bed of course.

They spent the rest of the morning catching up on the time they were apart. Barry told Angie about the meeting that afternoon. The problems at Jack Fleet were their biggest joint priority and Angie was right behind anything that would help keep the place open.

"What time do you have to be there?" Angie asked.

"Half past two, I think. What time is it now, Ange?"

Angie stood up, walked over, grabbed her man by the hand and said. "It's bedtime, I think!" She giggled and, surprisingly, Barry didn't complain.

My Name Is Emily Fleet

Ronnie Dexter sat in his office. No Lucy again. Poor girl, he thought. She must be rough. It was the first time in over a year she had gone sick. By the time Barry arrived, Ronnie J and Percy were already there. It was just after two-thirty.

"Percy said you were going to do an editorial about the home?" Ronnie J asked.

"Yes, that was my original thought but, I must confess, I have another reason for getting you all here. First, I must just ask you all to go into Lucy's office for a few minutes while I make a personal call. Is that okay?"

The three of them nodded and entered Lucy's office.

Ronnie opened his diary and picked up the phone; it was 09:45 in Lima. When Emily answered, it was as clear as a bell. "Ms. Fleet, I'm so grateful to you for responding to the ad, and I can't believe that, after all this time, we can finally talk to each other."

The excitement in Ronnie's voice was puzzling Emily, "Did you not get my letter then? I posted it nearly two months ago," she said.

"That's a strange one. No, I don't believe we did. Anyway, can I put you on hold and my good friend Mr. Wilson will speak to you?" She said that was fine. Ronnie put her on hold and went and got the three amigos back into his office.

Ronnie invited them in and asked Barry to sit at his desk and pick up the phone. Barry had a confused look on his face but did as he was asked and didn't query it. As he put the phone to his ear, Ronnie pressed the hold button.

Barry stammered a little, then said. "Hello, this is Barry Wilson. Who am I talking to?"

A female voice replied, "Hello, my name is Emily, Emily Fleet."

"Oh, my god, you're Jack Fleet's daughter?" He was shaking.

"Yes, Mr. Wilson. I'm his daughter."

Barry was mumbling. He seemed to have lost the thread of what this was all about. Ronnie, sensing his loss for words, took the phone from Barry and proceeded to tell Emily the reason for their desire to contact her.

Ronnie was finding it hard to hear what Emily was saying. All he could hear was the other three asking questions, like where was she, is she going to help, etc. Ronnie asked Emily if she minded being put on hold again for a second and she said it wasn't a problem.

"Guys," Ronnie shouted, "I can't hear or think straight. Go back into Lucy's office, so I can at least have a conversation with Emily." They grumbled and reluctantly retired to Lucy's office.

About twenty minutes later, Ronnie called them back in. All three of them were off at once. "Where is she? Is she going to help? Does she own the land?"

Ronnie understood, but it was time to grab hold of the situation. "Listen to yourselves, just LISTEN," he yelled. They finally were silent. "Okay, now one at a time."

Eventually they heard the details of the conversation that Ronnie had with Emily. He told them she lived in Lima, the capital of Peru. She was surprised to see the ad in the paper and said that she wrote a letter over two months ago, which he had no record of.

Barry thought to himself, "Two months ago.... About the time I finished with Lucy... I wonder."

Ronnie continued, "Emily doesn't think there are any family in the UK anymore. Her brother, Peter, lives in Australia and, if anyone knows about the land on which Jack Fleet House is built, it will be him. So that's the good news."

"What's the bad news then, Ronnie?" Percy asked.

Ronnie answered his question. "Well, she hasn't been in touch with him for about eighteen months."

They all frowned. It seemed they were no better off.

****

Lionel was miserable, as miserable as sin. How had this happened? He loved Emily so much. Yet he was in the departure lounge of the Jorge Chavez Airport and had already missed one flight. He was drunk, seriously drunk, yet he knew no airline would allow him to board a plane in the condition he was in. He needed to get to a hotel and sober up. He made his way to the taxi rank and asked for the nearest hotel. A few minutes later, he was checking in at the Delfines Hotel and, in no time, was asleep in his room. Around seven or eight hours later, he was ready for something to eat and made his way to the restaurant.

It was four o'clock in the afternoon. He fancied a drink, but something stopped him. "I need to get to Glasgow," he said to himself. "Got to get this woman out of my head. Who does she think she is, trying to get me to settle down? Next thing, she'll be wanting kids and all the trimmings. No way."

It was going to be a long trip home, Lima to Amsterdam with no immediate connection to Glasgow. Not till eighteen hours later. Brilliant! Now he definitely needed a drink and duly found his way to the bar. Like most airport bars, it was busy, and it wasn't long before he was on his fourth drink. He loved Guinness; he'd been brought up on it, first by his father, who used to top it with a small bottle of tonic. He mulled over the events of the last weeks and found himself almost continuously thinking about Emily. Was there a way for them to work out their problems? They loved each other, that was a fact. It was simply the actuality that they were both committed to their careers and neither of them would compromise. It was a stalemate situation. Before long, Lionel was considering cancelling his flights and returning to Emily. What would she do? He had another drink.

Emily was not with Lionel but, emotionally, she was in the same place: miserable, not doing anything. She even called in sick for the first time since she had been living in Lima. She had never experienced love like this. She'd been with a few men. One was, for her, quite a long relationship, a year or so, until he screwed her best friend. So that was goodbye to him, and her for that matter. A friend indeed.

Emily had not lifted a finger. There were dirty dishes and dirty clothing lying around her home. This was just not like her; she was quite house-proud. Love was never meant to be like this. These two people were desperate to be together, but it was proving almost impossible to find a way to make it happen. It was now approaching her bedtime. She looked around her living room and just sighed. What a mess.

She was about to go upstairs, when there was a knock at the door. Who's calling at this time of night, she thought. She walked over to the front door and asked, "Who is it?"

She heard muffled sounds and decided to go against her better judgement and open the door. Lionel was sitting on the ground.

"Lionel!" she gasped. "What are you doing here?"

Lionel looked up at her and gave a huge grin and said, "I've come home to the lady I love, and you ask me what I'm doing here? Emily, I can't be without you. We have to work this out."

Emily smiled too. "Yes, Lionel. We have to find a way, you're right."

Lionel got to his feet and they kissed passionately for a few moments until Emily took his hand, let him in, locked the door and led him upstairs, where, try as she may, he would not wake up after a brief cuddle. She looked at him while he slept. "We must find a way," she thought. Emily herself was asleep a few minutes later.

Emily was up bright as a button at about six-thirty, back into her routine. She woke Lionel at eight-fifteen with tea and toast and said, "I'll be home around four, love. We can go to the beach if you like?"

Lionel sat up "Yeah, that'll be great." They seemed to be on the same page at least. Time will tell, Emily thought, as she shut the front door and headed off to work. Lionel didn't get out of bed straight away but, when he did, he decided to have a bit of a tidy up. When Emily comes home she won't recognise the place, he thought. She was house-proud and yet, he understood the dishevelled look as a consequence of how she was feeling. Hadn't he been the same? They had to find a way. Lionel was ready to play his part.

Emily didn't recognise the place when she got home. There wasn't a thing out of place. Not only that, Lionel had lit the barbeque and had been to the local butcher's, and the display of meat all prepared was quite impressive.

"So, I take it we're not going to the beach, then?" Emily said with a smile.

"Love, I think, or I thought, I should say... What I'm trying to say is, I wanted to do something special for the most amazing woman I have ever known, and I'm not going to apologise for that. So, if Madam would like to take a seat." He gestured to the sunbed that wasn't far from the shaded area of the garden. "Now, what would Madam like to drink? I have rose, chardonnay, maybe a spritzer?" He was smiling his smile.

She was already starting to giggle. "Rosé, please." She continued to giggle. Lionel poured her a full glass and handed it to her. "Lionel," she said. He sat down with his glass of beer. "Lionel, I just wanted to say, I don't want a life where I don't have you. I need you so much."

Lionel smiled, "Emily, I want the same thing but, until we can find a solution, we must continue as we have been. Yes, being apart is a bind, but it's not going to be forever, is it?"

He had said the last two words on a definitive question.

Emily appreciated the emphasis he put on these two words. "Exactly, Lionel," she said, "I think I was wrong to expect anything so early in our relationship. I'm sorry for that. The truth is, I want to grow old with you."

He moved closer and kissed her on the cheek. "So do I," he replied. "So do I!"

They sat in the late afternoon sun and Emily was amazed at Lionel's culinary skills. He told her later, "Alright, so I know that when the barbie comes out, the man of the house springs into life. But I looked into it deeper and really made an effort to create special food, rather than just throwing it on there and leaving it."

Emily smiled. He was an excellent chef, no question. She was quite full by the time they'd eaten. She had drunk almost a bottle and a half of rosé. Lionel noticed and suggested she retire while he cleaned up. She didn't argue and was in her PJ's before long but insisted on helping tidy up. Just before they went up to bed, Lionel said, "I'm thinking of going home for a week or so. So you want to come? You could pop down to London to sort out the business with the local paper if you wanted."

Emily replied, "That's a nice thought, but I honestly can't afford it. Even if I could, I'm not sure I could get the time off."

Lionel smiled again. "Emily, it's not going to cost you a bean. I don't work the hours I do for nothing. I do it because it gives me a good living. So, I won't hear of you using money as a reason for not going."

Emily didn't respond. She just thought for a minute.

Lionel challenged her, "Em, just do it. We'd be together most of the time. What do you say?"

It was a promising idea, she thought to herself, and yes. She could go back to Essex and see the people who had been so keen to speak to her. "Okay then, but I'll have to tell a fib or two to the school, but it'll only be a white lie, won't it?"

Lionel nodded his head. "Of course it will. Listen, I'll sort it in the morning."

Emily was so full. Not with food and wine, but full of love. This man was everything to her and there was no way she was going to let him be with anyone else but her. When they walked into her living room, the song on the radio was just finishing...... Yes, true love's a many splendored thing. They both smiled. It truly was.

Solid

Barry and Angie. They were the real deal. Those who knew them knew that anyone who tried to come between them would not succeed in driving a wedge between them. Of course, everyone goes through tough times. They had their blips but, generally speaking, Barry and Angie were solid as a rock. Yes, they had just encountered their first real problem, but their love for each other had won the day. Nobody would doubt the two of them. They were busy with the birds at the moment and Barry, although he said he'd be okay with the extra load because of the chicks, was chuffed that Angie went out of her way to help him when it was extra busy.

"Do you remember, Doll?" he laughed. "Do you remember when we first got the birds, how stressed we used to get? Look at us now; it's a breeze, ain't it?"

Angie did see the funny side. They did indeed find it difficult at first but, as time went on, they got into a routine. After all, didn't the birds sell well? On average, around £550 each. Sometimes it worked out to one or two sales a week in the best times. Added to that, the shop was doing nicely, thank you very much. Yes indeed, they were more than comfortable, and Barry was determined he wouldn't ruin what was a lucrative business. But most of all, he loved Angie. She was his rock and, in the past few weeks, he realised how close he was to losing her. No, that couldn't happen again.

Angie shared most of Barry's ideas and was also in a confident mood regarding their relationship. She was obviously hurt by Barry's behaviour, and considered breaking it off completely, but there was only one man in her life and she had been offish with him for a few months and sort of understood why it had happened. No, it would not happen again; he was the only man for her. Something inside her spoke out. "Dare he try this again." She'd kill him. She couldn't really believe that he would ever do something like this again. Yes, she was confident it was not going to happen. They would be fine now, she was sure.

There was no misplaced confidence in that thought, not a chance. They had known each other most of their lives. They had lived in the same street, which was a mix of council flats and privately owned semi-detached houses. Barry's mum and dad were quite well off and had bought their house the year they got married. Angie's parents weren't quite so well off and lived in a three-bedroom low-rise flat. The kids on the street mixed as kids do. There was no divide between the so-called posh side of the street and the council flats on the other side. They'd all played together and even had street parties for royal occasions when they occurred. It was a good place to live and bring up children.

Whenever Angie was around, he made a bee-line for her.

"Go on Baz, go play with the girlies!" They would taunt him every time he got close to Angie. In later years, when Angie started courting, Barry got really upset if he heard of Angie going on a date. She was his 'bird', alright! Not officially, but something inside him told him that they would end up together. And so they did. And here they were having just been through their biggest test as a couple. They had, to no one's surprise, come through it. True love. Simple.

New Start

The new position suited David. He took to the demands of the job like he'd been doing it all his life. Already his boss had glowing reports from the technical guys and the promise of bigger contracts was just around the corner. When he passed these compliments on to Davey, he couldn't hide his feelings. He was doing the right things and the right people were noticing.

One possible contract caught Davey's eye. It was just outside London. It would involve all the floor and wall tiling in a brand new shopping centre, reckoned to be the biggest in the UK. It would take years and he'd fancied delving into the southeast, not just because of London, but because he always felt that was where the money could be made. The weather was always better, too. As time went by, his boss, Paddy, was doing less and less and the opposite was happening to Davey.

As the Liverpool job was drawing to a close, Paddy flew to Liverpool to meet his protégé. The main reason was to introduce Davey to thè engineers and draughtsmen for the new shopping centre and also the 'suits' with the cash, as Paddy put it.

After a successful couple of days of meetings, all that was left was for all parties involved to meet on site in three days' time.

Davey was gushing; it was a huge task.

Paddy said to him, "Choose your crew carefully. Get yourself a right-hand man, someone to push away the trivial stuff so you don't get distracted. You're going to need total dedication, Davey boy, that's for sure."

Davey already had a name for his right-hand man, Scouse Andy, who was a country mile above anyone else. He thought to himself, "I've already got one Paddy. Can he come with us?"

Paddy nodded his head and said, "I kinda knew you would say that son. Is it Scouse Andy?"

Davey smiled, "Yes, of course it is. He's a grafter and he's just the man to keep the petty stuff away from me. He's the man alright."

When Davey finished work, he asked Scouse Andy to stay behind because he needed to have a chat with him. Davey was in his office. It was just before six when Scouse walked in. Davey told him to let him speak and not interrupt him, just to listen and then tell him what he thought when he'd finished.

"I'm in," was all Andy said.

Davey smiled. "We'd better go and have a few to celebrate, what do you think?"

Andy smiled too and said, "Sound," and ten minutes later they were in The Grapes.

To be honest, it could have been any night. The Grapes was their local and they were there most nights for dinner anyway. Tonight, though, was different. They were about to set out on an adventure that could end up leading them to... who knows. It was an exciting time for the pair of them.

Davey had decided, even before he finished work that day, that as he had the day off tomorrow, he would take the opportunity to nip across the Irish Sea and see his mum and dad. He couldn't wait to tell them the news.

Scouse Andy too was very happy and felt good about himself. When your boss goes out of his way like Davey had, it made you feel proud and he loved feeling that way.

He'd been in the tiling game a few years but, like most contracting jobs, it wasn't always possible to be in work non-stop. Contracts ended and everybody was looking for the next one. Sometimes it could be a couple of months before you got picked up again so, being spotted by Davey eighteen months ago was a good day and the good day had just got even better.

London was going to be great. The pair of them sat on stools at the bar after their meal. There were a few silent moments. Presumably, they were both wondering what lay ahead for them.

"One thing is certain," Andy thought to himself, 'Davey boy is going places and I'm going right along with him."

They were on the verge of leaving, when Andy noticed a couple of girls sitting near the pool table. He didn't said anything to Davey, but walked over and chatted for a couple of minutes. He came back and said, "Davey boy, we're in here. Go on over. I'll get some more drinks."

Davey seemed reluctant at first but, by the time Andy got to the table, he was in full flow. "Cheers, Andy. This is Maureen and her friend, Brenda."

The girls were giggling. It turned out they'd been on a bit of a pub crawl and hadn't been home from work yet. A couple of hours later, Davey closed the door of his hotel room and heard Andy making the girls laugh as they waited for the lift.

Davey couldn't sleep. Home tomorrow. Then on to London.

Back Home

Emily sat on her bed. She'd never been so happy. She had found her man, her soul mate. They laughed about the first time they met and Lionel making out he needed physio. Sometimes things are just meant to be and so it turned out for these two young people, miles from home. Fate must have lent a hand in crossing their paths for, since they met, it had, other than one small hiccup, been pure bliss for both of them.

Today they were preparing for a trip back 'home', although Emily classed Lima as home now. Lionel was the proverbial gypsy, 'wherever I lay my hat' etc. Anyhow, the itinerary was all arranged and Lionel, true to his word, wouldn't let Emily pay for anything. Lima to London. There they would go their separate ways. Lionel to Glasgow for a few days at least, and Emily had contacted an old school friend, Maureen, who lived about three miles from Emily's hometown. She could stay with her and meet the supporters of Jack Fleet House.

Lionel was downtown, sorting out a few last-minute details of his trip to Glasgow. He too was excited, not so much about going home, but the idea of spending quality time with Emily, secretly hoping that he would get a chance to take her up to Glasgow to meet his family and friends. He really wanted to show her off. They were due at the airport check in at eight o'clock in the evening. Three hours later they would be on their way.

Emily didn't know what to pack. She didn't own much heavy type clothing so, when Lionel got home, she asked, "What's the weather like in the UK?" It was early March.

Lionel assured her, "It'll be none too warm, but don't worry. I've sorted you some clothing. I've got a friend who lives in London and she is going to bring a small suitcase and meet us at Heathrow."

Emily smiled, though she did feel a little uncomfortable about the idea.

"Em, don't worry, she is a lovely lady and has perfect dress sense. She'll kit you out just fine. Anyway if you're not happy, I'll come with you and you can buy your own. It's no big deal." That was it then. All sorted.

On the way to the airport, he asked her, "When you have done your visit home, would you come up to Glasgow? I'd like you to meet my family and friends."

She smiled, "Of course, I'd love to." They arrived at the airport.

They had time for a couple of drinks at the bar, the same bar where Lionel bad been so drunk a few days earlier, and Emily noticed one of the bar staff giving Lionel a strange look. "Do you know that waiter?" she asked inquisitively.

Lionel shook his head, "No, but I was here a couple of days ago, wasn't I? I did tell you, didn't I?" He wasn't sure.

Yes, Emily did recall that conversation. For somebody who was always flying somewhere, Lionel surprised Emily when he said, "I hate flying, especially long-haul flights. This will be nearly a twelve-hour flight, Em... Twelve hours!"

Emily laughed. "You'll be asleep if you have a couple more of those." He'd almost finished his third Manhattan. She was probably right, too.

Their flight was called earlier than expected and they made their way to the departure gate. Emily always adopted the theory that yes, she was flying on this plane. She had her ticket and she was at the departure gate. "This plane will not leave until I'm in my seat, so the mindless procession of people who stand up and queue for half an hour, when they could be sitting down relaxing, will not be joined by me," she thought. So, when they opened the gate and Lionel jumped up, she just grabbed his hand and beckoned him to sit down. And sit down he did.

The flight wasn't full by any means. They'd booked with Air Canada, where drinks were free, and they both used that facility in the hope that they would sleep for most of the journey. In fact, it was less than ninety minutes before they both fell asleep. Two and a half hours from Heathrow, they were both woken up by the worst turbulence that Lionel had ever experienced. Emily was petrified. Lionel put his arm round her as they both buckled up their seat belts. "We'll be fine, Em. We'll be fine."

Almost four hours later, they came out of baggage reclaim through to the meeting area, when, suddenly, Emily was almost knocked over by a large man in an incredible hurry.

"Hey, do you mind!" Lionel shouted.

Emily not wanting any fuss said, "It's okay Lionel, I'm okay.

As they cleared the meeting area, Lionel spotted his friend, Penny. He waved. She waved back and made her way over to them.

They found a quiet table. Lionel went to the bar. Emily could sense Penny's sideways glance at her. Emily wondered if Penny was thinking something like "so this is the one, then.' Emily blushed as Lionel returned to the table. "There you are, Em, and orange juice for you, Pen. Is that okay?"

Penny nodded, "Of course, you know I don't drink and drive. Where is it you want me to take you Emily? Lionel did tell me, but I've forgotten."

Emily looked at Lionel with a puzzled face. He reassured her, "It's alright, Em, Penny is going to run you home to Essex. Saves you getting I don't know how many trains or how many stops. You will check the clothes Penny has bought for you. You did get some clothes for her didn't you, Pen?"

Penny smiled. "Of course I did, and you were right. I think we are the same size, so it was quite easy to sort it.

Emily found herself looking at Penny. That was probably why Penny looked at her the way she did when they first met. She was a very attractive woman, and classy with it. She was very well dressed and Emily guessed she was no pushover when it came to business. It made perfect sense for Lionel to have somebody like her at his beck and call. They spent maybe an hour in the bar before Lionel got up and said, "Right, it's time. My flight to Glasgow leaves from Terminal 1, so I must be away. Look after Em for me Pen, won't you?" He smiled that smile.

Penny reassured him. "We'll be fine. Essex here we come."

Before Lionel left, he gave Emily a long, lingering kiss. "Now you take care, Em, and I'll see you soon." He then gave her a peck on the cheek. "See you. Thanks again Pen," and with that he was gone.

Old Friends

Emily was looking forward to seeing her old friend, Maureen. It must have been 12 years or more since she last saw her. They were close, almost inseparable at school. 'Me and my shadow' was about them for sure.

She glanced at Penny while they were travelling from Heathrow. It was raining. "Rain," Emily said to herself. She couldn't remember the last time she saw rain. "How long have you known Lionel for then, Penny?" she asked, not expecting the answer that she gave.

"Only nine months, that's all. We met through a mutual friend who I used to work for and Lionel made me a better offer. Simple as that really," she replied.

Emily smiled. That was Lionel, always looking for an improvement, something that would benefit him and his business. If something was in front of him, he would shift heaven and earth to get it. Penny was a classy lady. She dressed beautifully, Emily thought, and her posture was that of a person who had been schooled to perfection.

Penny sighed. "Bloody weather. I hate it. It's bloody cats and dogs out there now!" It was hammering down. Not the best driving conditions, but Emily found herself struggling to keep her eyes open. "How much longer, Penny?" Emily asked.

Penny noticed she sounded tired. "You've got time for a nap, Em. I'll wake you when I need directions, okay?"

Emily thanked her and laid the seat back. Jet lag was a pain, but an hour wouldn't hurt. "I'll still sleep tonight," she thought. Ten minutes later, she was asleep. Penny glanced at Emily when the traffic had virtually stopped. She was very attractive and could see why Lionel had fallen for her. She herself fancied Lionel, but had never become involved with anybody she worked with or for. It was a no-no. The traffic wasn't getting any better, but eventually they were on the A13. Penny patted Emily's leg four or five times before she woke up. "Come on love, the A13 is your territory. You're my pilot now," she laughed.

Emily put the seat upright and started giving Penny directions. Twenty minutes later, they pulled up outside Maureen's bungalow. It was in a cul-de-sac, a very nice area too. It had now stopped raining. Maureen was delighted to see Emily and, after hugging for a minute or so, she asked Penny if she would like a drink before heading back. Penny declined, said her goodbyes and set off back to London.

She was pleased for Lionel. Emily was made for him and surely she was the one who would be his long-time lady. Yes. She was sure that, in the brief time she had known him, she thought she understood him and his needs. Emily had obviously struck a nerve with Lionel and he had virtually talked about nothing else with her prior to today. She was genuinely happy for him. He had been a great person to work for. Her life had changed for the better in the last year, not only financially either. Lionel had a way about him. He would ask advice and had taken notice, indeed acted on her opinions and rewarded her for the ideas too. He was, she thought, a touch of 'old school' but with a modern twist. He was clued up on today, but the lessons from the past were never forgotten. As she made her way home, she recalled part of the conversation she had with Emily and promised, at the time, that she was available for advice should she need it.

Emily and Maureen were totally immersed in the past, laughing with and at each other. Taking the mickey out of each other, too. School days were way back but, as we all know, lots of memories are triggered by the mention of a name or situation. They laughed until they both cried at one stage. Emily sat cross-legged, while Maureen replenished their glasses.

"Do you remember Smudger Smith, Maur?" Emily asked her friend.

Maureen giggled, "Oh my god, Smudger Smith. What a plum he was. Didn't he ask you out too?"

Emily chuckled, "Didn't he ask everybody out in our year? I'm sure he held some kind of record, and yet he never, I mean, I never saw him with anyone, did you?"

Maureen thought for a moment. "Do you know what, I think I did. Now who was it?" She touched her lips while trying to remember. "Oh, you've done me now, Em. I'll not sleep till I think of her name." At that they both started giggling again.

Maureen eventually sat down with more drinks. Then Emily started to explain about the children's home and what or maybe what could happen. Emily explained that she wasn't sure she would be able to help in any way, but if there was anything she could do, she would be pleased to do it. Maureen offered her services if required. "All hands to the pump," she said.

Work In Progress

Davey and Andy arrived in London and they both seemed in awe of the pace of the city. It could be the start of something, but it had a reputation for all sorts of things that could, and quite often did, lead people astray.

"You look after yourself down there," Davey's father had said, and Davey was not about to forget those words. They stayed at the Tower Hotel, both in the same room.

Paddy had told them, "Sorry boys, but it's too expensive to do otherwise." They both understood. When they got to their room, the pair of them just burst out laughing. The room was enormous. It overlooked the river and it was just getting dark. The realisation was laughable, that these two tilers were at a top London hotel and had never experienced the finer things in life... ever. And here they were hobnobbing with the rich and famous.

'What a ride we're going to have,' Andy thought.

"Well, we'd better hit the bar then," Davey laughed. Andy hesitated. "What's up?" Davey asked him.

"I'm not carrying much cash, Davey, I'm not." Andy replied.

Davey reached into his pocket and pulled out an envelope. "Here, Paddy gave me this. It's your expenses." He offered the envelope to Andy. "C'mon, take it."

Andy reluctantly took the envelope and began to open it. "Fucking hell!" Andy shouted. "There's two weeks wages here, Davey."

Davey laughed, "I know. I put it in there. Paddy told me how much to give you and he also said if you run out of money, you'll have to go busking."

The two of them rolled up with laughter. Ten minutes later, they were having words with the barman when they didn't like the price of the beer they were drinking.

"Andy, let's get out of here. It's too fucking pricey for me," Davey moaned.

"Aye, it is that," Andy agreed.

They flagged a taxi down and asked for a good boozer. The driver grasped the opportunity with both hands and took them to the South Bank. They walked to the river's edge. To their left was the Founders Arms and so that was it for the rest of the evening. Although they were far from impressed with the price of everything, they still managed to have an enjoyable time. By the time they got back to the hotel, it was coming up to 2am. "Andy," Davey said, "we're up at six. Shit."

Davey was awake. It was 5:30. He didn't need an alarm clock; he had never needed one. He found the cups and tried to make some tea without waking Andy, but he woke around ten minutes later.

"I'm shattered," Andy yawned.

Davey laughed, "So am I. I've been for a run." He couldn't hide the grin.

"Fuck off. No you haven't." Andy himself laughed.

They were meeting the suits at nine o'clock on site, so they quickly ate breakfast and made their way to Fenchurch Street. Fortunately, most of the rush hour traffic was coming into London, so there was plenty of room on the train. The pair of them nearly missed their stop as they both had a cat nap.

As they got off the train at Purfleet, they looked around. "I don't believe it. No taxi rank," Davey commented.

They scanned the area. Davey noticed a shop and said, "Wait here Andy," and walked over to get the number of a taxi. The taxi turned up a quarter of an hour later and, after a short journey, they arrived at their destination.

The site offices looked down on the whole building site. Davey and Andy looked at the view in front of them and, for a few moments, neither them said anything. When they did speak, the expletives were many. "Jesus Christ, fucking hell" etc. It was an eye opener alright. The site was huge. They'd seen artists' impressions of what the finished article would be like and yes, they were expecting it to be a big job. But this, this in front of them was massive.

They were still taking it all in when they heard a familiar voice from behind them. "Davey boy, what about this?" It was Paddy. "Andy, you look like you've seen a ghost," Paddy laughed.

"Paddy, it's fucking massive!" Andy gasped.

"Aye lad, and it's your home for the foreseeable future." Paddy stretched his arms around the two of them. "C'mon now, let's go and see the suits."

There followed lots of discussions and they even went for a liquid lunch, but mainly it was business all day long. The whole picture was unfolding in front of them now and the size of the task ahead excited Davey. This was made for him. He had so many dreams he needed to fulfil, and this project was the perfect vehicle to get his dream started. Was he ready? Davey McCallister was born ready.

The Meeting

Emily asked Maureen if she would take her to the Gazette office in the morning and, of course, Maureen said no problem. Emily woke to find a cup of tea on the bedside table and, to top that, she could smell that smell. She got up, slipped on her dressing gown and found Maureen in the kitchen. "Maureen, do you know how long it is since I've smelt that smell?"

Maureen laughed, "Can't you get bacon in Peru?"

Emily said, "Well you can, but only streaky. I've tried it, but it's not the same really."

Fifteen minutes later, after adding some brown sauce, Emily was full. "That was something special, Maur. Thank you."

"All I say is, don't be expecting it every morning, Em."

They laughed together. Maureen loved having her best school friend with her. They'd kept in touch, but it had been so long since they'd been able to spend some time together. They set off for Grays town centre and couldn't find a parking space near the Gazette office, so they had to walk for five minutes or so. Once inside the office, there was a young, blonde girl in reception. "Hello, can I help you?"

Emily replied, "Hello, I have an appointment with Mr Dexter. I'm a few minutes early though, sorry."

The young lady said, "That's okay. I'll see if he's ready for you. Who shall I say is here to see him?"

"My name is Fleet... Emily Fleet."

Well, the young lady almost passed out. Lucy was in shock. "Oh my god, how did she? Why? Get a grip," she thought to herself. She felt herself blush and she also realised that she didn't seem to be handling this situation very well.

Eventually Ronnie Dexter came out of his office and invited them in. "Take a seat, Ms. Fleet and..."

Emily quickly introduced her friend, "Maureen. This is Maureen."

Ronnie shook her hand, "Hi Maureen. Lucy, would you make some tea for our guests?"

Lucy was all over the place, but did as she was asked, all the while thinking about the event. "How did this happen? I never replied to her letter. How is she here? Uncle Jock will be fuming when he finds out." She really was in a state, and Ronnie even asked her if she was alright when she brought the tea in. "Lucy, you okay? You're shaking."

"Ron, it's the crockery. You only buy cheap stuff." She forced a smile.

She then sat at her desk. This was a real shock. Did Barry know she'd been found? If he didn't, it wouldn't be long before he did. She had to tell her Uncle Jock after work. He'd be furious, but he had to be told. Next thing she heard was the bell on the front door. As she looked up, she felt herself blush again.

"Morning, Lucy. Ronnie's expecting us. We'll just go through, shall we?"

Lucy was dumb-struck as Barry, Angie and Percy all filed into Ronnie's office.

"Oh dear. What am I gonna do?" she thought.

Then Ronnie called her on the intercom with an order for more drinks.

"Okay, Ronnie." Her whole body was shaking now, but she managed to pull herself together by the time the drinks were ready. She placed the drinks on the office table adjacent to the people concerned but she never looked up at anyone, least of all Barry. She wondered what was going on. Was this Emily Fleet going to cause her uncle problems? There was nothing she could do but hope that Ronnie would tell her something after they had gone.

The meeting lasted nearly two hours and, when Lucy heard the noise of chairs moving on the floor, she positioned herself in front of a filing cabinet so she didn't have to look at anyone as they left. Every one of them said bye and thanked her for the drink. Ronnie saw them all to the front door of the office and she heard him say, "What time did you say, Barry?" But she didn't hear his reply. As Ronnie was about to enter his office he said "Lucy, can you come into my abode?"

Lucy said "Of course," and, as a matter of habit, picked up her writing pad.

"Take a seat Lucy, will you," Ronnie gestured with his hand for her to sit down.

Lucy nervously sat down.

"Do you remember getting a letter from Ms. Fleet, Lucy?" Ronnie asked.

Lucy didn't hesitate. "No, I saw no letter. Why? Did she write one then?"

Ronnie was rolling his pen through his fingers, "Well, yes. She claims she wrote ages ago, maybe two months or more. I guess it must have got lost in the post. These things happen. If it turns up, save it for me, will you?"

Lucy nodded her head, then asked, "What was the meeting about then, Ronnie?" knowing full well what was covered.

Ronnie replied, "Oh sweetie, nothing to worry your little head about. Are you on schedule for print this week?"

She nodded. She was worried.

Moving House

Davey and Scouse Andy had settled down in Riverside. It'd been eighteen months since they started in Essex, and there were still maybe another two years before they would be moving on. They were both renting property locally and, surprisingly, were both dating local girls. They were regulars at the local night club and soon got to know the local crowd.

Davey spent his Sunday mornings playing football, egged on by Scouse Andy and their two lady friends. Davey took his football seriously and, if things had been different, he maybe could have played the game at a professional level. Scouse Andy was a professional. At weekends, he was a professional party goer and was eager to go to parties whenever the opportunity arose. That got them involved with the two girls. When they first met their partners, they would often laugh with each other over the 'Essex Girl' tag they would both be landed with. But it didn't bother either of them. Davey was head-over-heels in love. From the moment he met Tricia, he knew she was the one, and it was only in the last week that he had asked the question, to which the answer was an emphatic 'YES'. Tricia moved into Davey's three bed house only a few days ago.

Andy wasn't against moving his lady into his flat. Allison did stay with him most weekends, so it didn't seem it would be long before she moved in with him. Davey, over the last few months, had seemed distracted. When Andy asked if he was okay, he just shrugged his shoulders and said, "I'm fine." Davey kept his own counsel. There were opportunities to expand and grow, but his concern was Paddy. He felt loyal to Paddy, which was understandable, considering the chance to grow that Paddy had given him. The truth was that Davey felt he couldn't miss these possibilities that had appeared in front of him. Sadly, he didn't want to tell Paddy. In fact, Davey had to form his own company and it was this that was causing him to be somewhat distant when Andy asked the question. Davey knew what he had to do. He just wasn't looking forward to doing it. Okay, Paddy had been good to him, but he only gave him a start because Paddy knew Davey's dad, Patrick. Nevertheless, he was a natural. He was now a qualified stone mason, as well as being excellent at laying tiles with a craftsmanship Paddy had rarely seen. Davey owed so much to Paddy and that was the problem that was giving him sleepless nights.

Davey had made a name for himself and his stock was rising. So many of the 'suits' were making him offers, unbelievable offers, and each time it was getting harder and harder to turn them down.

One such offer dropped into Davey's lap due to a decision on Andy's part to have a quick pint at a country pub called the King's Arms. It wasn't the first time they had been there, but they'd seen this fella in there before and, out of curiosity, had struck up a conversation with him.

His name was Archie Divers. Archie was known locally as Mr. Fix It. He could sort any problem almost any time. The governor of the pub, Ronnie, had told Andy and Davey about Archie and that if they wanted to know what was happening in the building trade in the southeast, Archie was a fountain of knowledge. True enough, on the day they called in, the lads started talking to Archie, who seemed to take to them straight away. At times during their conversation, Andy seemed lost and would take a back seat. Davey, on the other hand, pushed and pushed Archie to open up and let go of the cards close to his chest. Davey was close to making a discovery that would be instrumental in changing his life forever.

Archie had heard from a source that Transport for London were looking for a new contractor to refurbish and expand over one hundred tube stations. Once Davey heard this, he was hooked. He remembered one of the civil engineers, Chris… something, he couldn't remember, mentioning that the underground contract was massive and if anybody could land that deal, it would be life changing. Davey was, as usual, ready. He knew what he had to do. He just wasn't looking forward to doing it.

Six or seven times that day, he had tried to contact Chrissy Earland. He'd left messages at his office but had no reply.

Paddy was on site more and more lately and, given the way things were at the moment, it made Davey uncomfortable. Paddy would quite often walk in to find Davey and the architects having a meeting and would ask why he wasn't asked to attend. It was all a bit embarrassing for Davey, but

Paddy was thick skinned and would generally just sit in and listen and, more often than not, agree with everything that was said, especially if it was said by his little star employee, Davey boy. He was so proud of what he had achieved in the last two years. So much so that, one afternoon, Paddy was in the site office when Davey entered the room and sat down opposite Paddy.

Paddy looked at him and said, "Davey," he paused, "Davey boy, I'm knackered. I've been thinking." Davey was reading a newspaper, but he put it down to listen. "What I'm trying to say. I.... I'm gonna retire Davey. It's time. It won't change anything for you. I've been to my solicitor's and transferred the business and all its assets over to you. Is that okay with you?"

Davey was dumb-struck. For a minute he didn't say anything.

Paddy asked again, "Is that alright. I mean you're ready. I know it, you know it. It's yours if you want it. We'll need to sort out some financial stuff with my legal team, but that's just a formality. I'm sorry but I've got to ask you again. Is it okay with you, Davey?"

Davey choked up. "Paddy... Paddy, of course it's okay, but are you sure? You'll be lost without this, you know you will."

Paddy nodded his head, "Of course I will, but it'll be her indoors who will get me through it, Davey. She's got it all planned. Weekends away, clubs for this, clubs for that. I'll probably be busier that I've ever been, if I'm honest. I'll be really chuffed if you'd take hold of the reins. I told you some time ago that this is what you were put on this planet for. This is and probably was always the way to go. And Davey, I wish you good luck and don't take no shit."

Lucy Bites Back

Barry was deep in thought. Angie was busy doing the housework. Now and again, she looked over at Barry as he sat motionless on the sofa. She knew what he was thinking about.

The meeting with Emily Fleet wasn't as fruitful as they'd hoped. Hope was, in fact, the one thing they could all do. Emily had informed then that the land that Jack Fleet House was built on was owned by the Fleet family, but the documentation needed to prove this was not available to her. She believed that her brother was the likely holder of such information, but said his whereabouts were unknown. The last she'd heard, he was somewhere in Western Australia.

Barry was trying to be philosophical about their current predicament, but was unable to shift the thought that they would soon be in a position where they had done all they could.

"Cheer up, Baz," Angie said as she switched the Hoover off. "We're not done yet, are we?"

The last two words of her statement were not meant as a question, but it seemed that way to Barry.

"I just can't see a way out of this, Doll," he sighed.

"Baz, something will turn up. We all have to believe it, we do." She was trying but she, too, could see the logic in what her husband was saying. "Maybe we should look at the situation from a different viewpoint, Baz. Maybe we're missing something. The Scottish dwarf must have some dirty linen in his cupboard. We just need to make everyone aware of it."

"I'm not saying you're not right, Doll, but he's got so many people in his pocket because of stuff they've done wrong in the past. None of them would grass him up, even if they knew anything," Barry said hopelessly.

"What about his niece, Lucy? She seems like a nice kid. Wouldn't she help? She loves the kids, you know she does," Angie asked innocently.

Barry felt his face redden. "She won't help. Family comes first. Not a chance."

Angie sensed some anger. "It was just a thought, Baz."

"I know, Doll, I know you're only trying to help. One thing you said has given me an idea, though. Maybe we should look at the problem from another angle," he said thoughtfully.

Angie smiled and carried on with her chores. Barry got up and went to have a chat with the parrots.

Meanwhile, Lucy had told her Uncle Jock of the arrival of Emily Fleet. He'd not seemed too bothered, but did thank Lucy for her useful information. What to do about it, though. He still had the shake on Mr. Goody Two Shoes Wilson. He was confident that his wife Angie didn't know that it was Lucy who her darling husband had the affair with. No, that would keep. He wondered where this Ms. Fleet was staying. He'd love to know if she was going to be a problem or not. He thought about asking Lucy's boss, Ronnie, straight up. Don't beat about the bush, you know. Just ask the bloody question. But he thought better of it and decided that the situation regarding Jack Fleet House was as good as sorted and there was nothing anyone could do about it. He never considered for a moment any other outcome than the one that he favoured. No way was this deal not going to happen.

Lucy was out in the town for lunch in a local pie and mash shop, when Ada came in and sat next to her.

"Hello, pet," Ada greeted her. "How are you? Haven't seen you up at ours for ages. Jamie was asking after you, you know. He thinks the world of you." Ada liked Lucy, even though she was related to a horrible man.

Lucy found herself talking about everything but the kids. She did genuinely like all the children, although most of them had since left. As for Jamie, he was still a special young boy. She thought a great deal of him. Ada talked of nothing else, saying how sad everyone was and that their hopes of Emily Fleet being some sort of saviour had been false hopes.

Lucy had mixed feelings later when she returned to work. She did feel for the kids and Percy and Ada, but she couldn't do anything about that. It was their problem. When the home closed, wouldn't the kids just go to a new home. What was the big deal? Her Uncle Jock had promised her a reward for keeping him informed about the goings on at the Gazette, providing the home was closed down eventually. She was happy about that, wasn't she?

Far Away

Lionel was missing Emily. He had spoken to her a couple of times at Maureen's and all it did was make him miss her more. He was smitten. He hoped that she would be able to come up to Glasgow to meet his family. He had told them all about her. They were amazed because he had never been this excited about a woman before.

There were other women, one special one, many years ago who, sadly, got cancer and passed away. It all happened so quickly. From the initial diagnosis to losing her took less than three months. Lionel was devastated. For a while afterwards, he stayed away from the fairer sex. He was hurt and felt he would be better on his own.

Emily, though, was good for him. She brought the best out in him. His family ribbed him about getting it off with an Essex girl, and he managed to laugh about it too. He decided to call her around ten in the evening and, sure enough, Emily was there.

"Lionel, how are you? Is it cold up there?" She was ecstatic to hear from him.

"No, it's not cold and, in any case, my family will give you a warm welcome. They're really looking forward to seeing you. Have you sorted out your bit of business yet, love?" He couldn't wait to see her.

Emily loved hearing his voice. "Well, sort of," she said. "There's not much I can do for them. It's a bit sad really. I want to help them. I'm going to see the children's home in the morning. It sounds so lovely. Apparently, the local Mayor is as bent as a nine-bob note. That's what one of the supporters said anyway. It all hinges on my brother, who I've lost contact with. He's somewhere in Australia. It's so sad. They were all hoping that I would be the one to save the building from being demolished by having the necessary documents for the ownership of the estate. I don't know what else I can do. Do you have any ideas, Lionel?"

Lionel replied, "Well, I'm not going to say I have, but I do know some people who might have. Leave it with me. I'll make some calls. When do you think you'll be able to come up here then?" Lionel crossed his fingers. He was being presumptuous.

"Well, I suppose I could come up in a couple of days. Shall we say Friday?" She smiled at Maureen.

"That's great. Friday it is. I'll sort your flight out and get back to you. Bye love." Lionel was happy with that.

"Bye, Lionel." She put the phone down. "Well, Maur. It looks like I'm off to Scotland!" Maureen hugged her. She was genuinely happy for her best friend.

Wonder Of You

Angie was finding it difficult to forgive Barry for his infidelities, so much so that they had only slept together once since she had come back from her mum's. All she could think of was her man 'doing it' with another woman. No matter how hard she tried, she was unable to get that thought out of her mind. Sure, Barry was leaning over backwards, offering all sorts of things to try to make everything okay and get things back to normal. But, deep-down, Angie knew that it was never going to happen. She wasn't sure what Barry was thinking but, surely, he couldn't ever expect things to be the way they were. No, he wasn't that much of a fool, though he'd had a good try at ruining everything they had spent their lives working for.

There, that was the reason Angie came back. She had never stopped loving him and never would. It was just heart-breaking what he had done. She often wondered who it was, but she never pushed him to tell her who nearly fucked up their marriage. It was, Angie thought, better not to know. He assured her it wasn't anybody she knew and, in a way, that was some sort of consolation. She couldn't bear it if it was somebody she knew.

She found herself spending more and more time with the parrots, so much so that she mentioned to Barry that it was taking a lot of time out of her day. She knew he would understand, but he had been extremely busy at the shop for the last couple of months and the days were getting longer.

She phoned the shop to ask if he would be home at the normal time or whether he would be later.

"Doll, at the moment it's looking good. I should be in for six at the latest. What delights am I coming home to, Doll?"

Angie hadn't really thought about dinner. "Not sure, Baz. What do you fancy? I've some mince; can do you shepherd's pie, if you like. How's that sound?" She knew he would be smiling; he loved shepherd's pie.

"Doll, you spoil me. That'll do me just fine." He was beaming.

"Alright," Angie said, "make sure you're home on time then. I'll aim to dish up around six-thirty, okay?"

"Okay, love. See you in a bit," Barry replied.

The time was approaching three o'clock and Angie picked up her current novel and settled down on the sofa for an hour's read. She loved reading, especially on holiday, laying in the sun. Then the thought hit her. A holiday may be just what we need.

Barry left the shop at around ten to six. Plenty of time, he thought to himself. Sure enough, he was in good time for his favourite dinner. Angie, unlike a lot of people, actually did roast potatoes with the shepherd's pie, plus all the usual vegetables of course, and she had to admit it was a lovely meal.

He had walked in to find Angie cooking away, listening to Elvis on the radio. It was some kind of special show, non-stop Elvis till eight o'clock. Barry didn't mind a bit of Elvis.

"So, you had a good day girl? On the wine as well, eh? I think I'll have a beer. I've got time, ain't I?" Barry asked.

"Just the one, Baz. I'm dishing up in about fifteen minutes."

Barry went to the fridge and poured himself a beer. At that moment, they both went to speak. Barry stopped. "You first, Doll."

Angie smiled, "Baz, I was thinking..." She wasn't sure how he would react to her suggestion. "I was thinking we should get away for a week or so. I think it would do us good, I mean..."

Barry cut in and said, "Angie, you've been so good about everything, I can't turn you down. In fact, it's a great idea. We'll need somebody to look after the birds, though. Lucy told me she wouldn't have time when I bumped into her last week, not that I was thinking of going away. It was just to give you a hand as I've been so busy. I couldn't expect you to take on the extra load. No, give me a couple of days and I'll sound out someone. I've got a couple of ideas, okay?"

Angie just smiled and finished her glass of wine.

Barry asked her if she wanted a refill. Angie was not usually a drinker, but she nodded and said, "Yeah okay. I'll slow dinner down a bit if you want another beer."

"Okay Doll, let's get on it!" She laughed, and Barry looked at her. She didn't smile much since... well you know, and she had a beautiful face. When she smiled, she looked stunning. How could he have been unfaithful to her. What a pillock he was. He liked the idea of a holiday, too. Where should they go, though? More to the point, who could he get to look after the birds? Something will turn up, he thought to himself. They sat together on the sofa, listening to The King. When he held Angie, he felt like a king. Then he started singing, "That's the wonder, the wonder of you." Angie just laughed and put her fingers in her ears. He was tone deaf, but it never stopped him from trying to sing, using a bottle of beer as a microphone. It was terrible.

Angie sat there laughing as he shook his body when a faster track came on. Then he lost his balance and fell on Angie, nearly knocking her drink out of her hand. As he tried to get up, she put her arm around his neck and pulled him towards her, then surprised Barry by giving him a long, sexy kiss. When she stopped the kiss, he tried to carry it on but Angie stopped him, stood up and went to the kitchen. Barry followed her and said, "Sorry Doll.... I thought..."

Angie touched his lips with her finger and whispered, "You better get in the bedroom. I'll turn dinner off. I'm suddenly not hungry. Well, hurry up then."

Barry ran to the bedroom like an excited school boy.

When they finally came out to the kitchen, the dinner was virtually ruined. "Oh shit!" Angie cursed. "Baz, shall we have a takeaway?" Barry nodded. Angie carried on. "Get it delivered. I fancy another drink and you've got a couple left as well. Might as well make the most of it, what do you reckon, Baz?"

"I've got absolutely no problem with that suggestion, Doll," he replied.

The Elvis special was coming to a close and Angie went to the side unit underneath the stereo. "I fancy chilling out, Baz. What shall we put on now?"

They had a fabulous collection of vinyl albums, in mint condition too. Barry just laid back on the sofa and said, "Whatever you fancy, Doll. Put what you like on."

Angie was fingering the edges of the LPs and decided on the acoustic side of the Crosby Stills Nash and Young album, Four Way Street. The pair of them sat on the sofa cuddling, Angie occasionally gently punching her hubby when he tried to sing along. It had been a good day. They were both extremely happy. Angie didn't reflect on the bedroom antics, but she was pleased she was able to manage what for her had almost seemed an impossibility. They had slept together and she surprised herself by being dominant for a change.

Barry was just happy. Oh yes, it had been a good day. Angie was relieved she had been able to please her man again.

Mystery Caller

Lionel phoned Emily at 8am the next day. "Emily, I can get you a flight this afternoon, if you'd like, or an early one tomorrow morning. What do you think?"

Emily thought for a second. "No, tomorrow will be fine, Lionel. Besides, I promised Sam I'd look in on his brother while I'm here. I should have sorted that already, but I haven't so I'm afraid it'll have to be tomorrow morning love, okay?"

Lionel was a little disappointed but understood and said he would call her that evening with the flight details. Emily put the phone down and went straight to her handbag and found Sam's brother's address. Sam had talked about his brother, George, quite a lot. He'd lived in Tilbury since he was in his early twenties.

George and Emily had five children and every one of them, except Bessie, had the travel bug. George, Jr. was in New Zealand. Mary was the first to emigrate. She went to Canada by boat from Tilbury. And Linda, the youngest, went to New York. Jack was in the army and had lived in Singapore. He was now stationed in Tripoli in Libya. Bessie also lived in Tilbury.

Emily (Fleet) asked Maureen if she would take her to see Sam's brother, George. Just half an hour later, Emily was sitting having a cup of tea with George and Emily.

She was staggered at how much alike Sam and George were. Even their accents were rooted in the northeast brogue. Emily thanked George for sending Sam the local paper and explained why she had to come and meet these supporters of Jack Fleet House.

George was a quiet man and, after a while, Emily realised that it was George's wife Emily who was the dominant one. She was very opinionated and not the type of person who would change her mind easily.

George told the same stories about the coal from Roker Beach that Sam had mentioned. Emily was smiling at the stories, especially when Emily took control of the story that George was trying to tell. They were a lovely couple.

After an hour or so, Emily said her goodbyes, accepting their good will comments to give to Sam when she returned to Peru. When she left the flat, Maureen hadn't yet arrived, so she sat on a bench. This was a nice area. The old folks seem to be well looked after.

Maureen arrived five minutes later and, as Emily opened the door, she laughed. Sitting on her seat was a bulging, white paper bag.

Emily's eyes were wide open. "It's chips, Maureen, isn't it?"

Maureen laughed again, "Yes, Em. You'd better open them. We'll eat them as we drive home."

Emily hadn't tasted chips from a bag like this for years, and she loved them. "Aw, thanks Maur," she said gratefully.

The pair of them didn't speak until the last chip was eaten. "They sure fill you up, Em, don't they?"

Emily finished eating the last chip and licked her fingers. "They certainly do. We should have an English chippy in Lima, but it'll never happen."

The afternoon snack had filled both of them up and they decided to give the evening meal a miss. They were settling down to watch the TV when the phone rang. Maureen said, "That'll be your Lionel, won't it?" and motioned for Emily to answer it.

Emily picked up the phone. "Hello." She could hear somebody breathing. "Hello," she said again.

Then a deep Scottish accent replied. "This is a friendly message. Is your name Emily Fleet?"

Emily looked startled but said, "Yes, it is."

The caller then said, "If you know what's good for you, don't get involved with Jack Fleet House." Before she could reply, the caller hung up.

Maureen could see Emily was upset "What's the matter Em? Who was it?"

Emily told Maureen what was said.

"Oh dear!" Maureen didn't know what to say.

Emily was worried. "It was a really deep Scottish accent, Maur.... It... I must.... It unnerved me a bit, to tell you the truth."

Maureen put her arm around her. "Don't get yourself worked up Em, probably nothing."

Emily struggled to forget about it, though. When the phone rang again, Maureen answered it. "Hello" she said in a stern voice.

"Hello, can I speak to Em please? It's Lionel."

Maureen smiled, "Of course, hold on... It's Lionel," she whispered to Emily.

"Hello, love." Emily said with a touch of relief. "All sorted?" Emily listened. "Right, what time?" she said loudly. "Eight thirty from Luton? But that's too early, Lionel, ... Yes .... No, I don't want to get up at half past four in the morning. Maureen and I are going to the pub tonight, you'll ...." She waited.

Lionel sighed, "Okay, leave it with me, I'll sort it. You go and have a drink. Think of me though, won't you!" They made kissing noises over the phone and hung up.

Maureen questioned, "'So... We're going to the pub, then?"

Emily laughed, "Yes, Maureen, and all of the supporters of Jack Fleet House are going to be there."

"Oh, okay then. In that case, we'd better get our skates on," she replied.

At that, they rushed around, booked a taxi, got themselves dolled up and were both surprised that they were actually ready when the cab turned up.

Barry and Angela, Percy, Ronnie Dexter and the landlord of the King's Arms, Ronnie J, were sitting in the now closed restaurant. Thursday night was pool night, so the pub was busy. Ronnie, in his wisdom, had built an extension on the back of the pub to house two pool tables, so the bar area wasn't too busy.

"I mentioned to Emily that we would be here tonight, lads. I don't know if she's still in the area. I know she's supposed to be heading for Scotland at the weekend so I'm not sure," Barry told the others.

Do you reckon she gives a toss?" Ronnie J asked. "I mean, she lives in South America and this business about her brother in Aussie land... I mean, it's not looking good is it?" He sounded very low and there didn't seem to be much positivity around.

They sat talking about nothing really until Angie noticed two women entering the bar and, yes, one of them was Emily.

Ronnie J jumped up. "Hello ladies. What can I get you? Ms. Fleet, for you?"

"It's Ron, isn't it? You're the landlord, aren't you?" Emily smiled.

"That's right. Now what would you like?" he asked again.

"We'll have two JD and cokes and make them doubles, please," Maureen said.

"Doubles it is" replied Ronnie and started to mix the drinks.

"Maureen.... Doubles?" Emily frowned.

"Go for it, girl," Maureen replied with a smile.

At that, Barry came over and showed the ladies to the table. "You know everyone here don't you Emily, and your friend is?"

Emily introduced Maureen. "Sorry, this is Maureen. A very old friend. Well, not too old. I mean we have been friends a long time."

"I know what you meant, Emily. How have you enjoyed your visit. You're off to Scotland soon as well, aren't you?" Barry enquired.

Emily's face beamed. "Oh yes, I've loved it. It's just a shame I can't do much about the kids, though. It's just so sad, isn't it?"

Ronnie returned with another round of drinks and the mood had lightened quite a bit. Maureen and Angie were getting to know each other, while Emily was glued to a conversation with Barry. Percy and the two Ronnies were having a chat about golf.

"Baz, Baz!" Angie called out.

"Yes Doll," he replied.

"Baz, listen to what Maureen just told me. Go on Maur. Tell them."

"Well really, it should be Em telling you or do you want me to tell them, Em?"

Emily regretted not asking Maureen not to say anything about the nasty phone call she had received. But she had said it now. Oh well, she thought. "Well, I answered the phone expecting it to be my boyfriend who is in Scotland. Instead it was this man. Funnily enough he had a Scottish accent, a deep Scottish accent. He just said that if I knew what was good for me, I wouldn't get involved in Jack Fleet House. Then he put the phone down."

They were all shocked. Then Barry and Percy both said simultaneously, "Jock McBride!"

Ronnie J swore. "I'll kill the wanker. Sorry ladies. He's breathing somebody else's air. I mean, he's bent. He's a scumbag!" He was fuming.

"We don't know for sure it was him, but I think most of us would put money on it, wouldn't we?" Percy said and those that knew him nodded their heads. "What do we do, then?" Percy cried. "We can't prove anything, can we?"

They were all trying to come up with a solution, anything.

"We need to get something on him, play him at his own game," Ronnie Dexter suggested. He had hated the man for as long as he could remember.

The mood quietened and, as the evening was drawing to a close, Emily stated, "I'm going to help as much as I can. I don't know how. I know I need to get in touch with my brother. At home I have all his letters in a cardboard box. I'll go through them to see if I can get any names and addresses of people he knew over there."

They all agreed that would be a good place to start.

Emily and Maureen phoned for a taxi as Ronnie J put two more doubles in front of them. Maureen just got a fit of the giggles, quickly followed by Emily, and half an hour later they were still giggling as they got into the taxi.

The Villain And The Tragedy

Being Jock McBride's 'go to' man when he needed something sorting was not getting any easier. Jimmy Miller had been in the Mayor's pocket for about five years now. When Jock asked him to jump, well, you know the rest. This, though, was too much. When asked by the Mayor to do his latest task, he refused. Jock would not take no for an answer, though, threatening to tell all that he knew about Jimmy. Oh yes, he would, Jimmy thought after initially doubting him.

He'd been outside the bungalow in his van for about ninety minutes. He wasn't visible from the road when they had eventually left the place in a taxi. It was dark, quiet and there was a moonless sky.

Jimmy got out of the van, carrying a small canvas roll with tools in it. He emerged from the bushes, looked both ways and crossed the road into the drive. He threw down a couple of black bags from his pocket and lay down on them next to her car. He switched his torch on and did the deed. "Never again, Jock," he thought to himself, "never again!" He crossed the road, got into his van and drove off with no lights on. He was feeling sick. What if? He tried not to think of the possible consequences of what he had just done. It was impossible.

A couple of hours later, Maureen and Emily arrived home after what Maureen called 'a squiffy night'. They had both had too much to drink and went straight to bed. Emily woke around 3am and chuckled to herself when she passed Maureen's room. Maureen hadn't even taken her coat off. She went in to try and remove the coat without waking her. She almost managed it, but suddenly Maureen grabbed her and pulled her toward her and tried to kiss Emily on the lips. Emily's reaction was slow, due to her surprise, and their lips touched briefly. "What are you doing, Maur?" Emily shouted.

Maureen sat up. "I'm sorry Em. I'm really sorry. I didn't... I...... Oh shit!" Maureen started crying.

Emily was shocked. Her friend, her lifelong friend, fancied her. Was she a lesbian? She didn't understand. "Maureen, just go to sleep. It's alright."

Maureen tried to get up, but she was so drunk, she couldn't manage it. Emily pulled the door to, but looked through the crack. When she saw Maureen finally lay down and that she seemed okay, she left her to it. Emily was confused. Was she just blind drunk or what? She decided to let the matter drop and not bring the subject up in the morning. Emily readied herself for bed, but had trouble sleeping. Lionel. She would be in his arms later tonight, but Maureen... What was that all about? Eventually she drifted off to sleep.

When her eyes opened next, it was light. She thought she had only been asleep for a few minutes but it was now light. It was seven-thirty. She lay there for a while until she heard noise from the kitchen. She got out of bed, put on her dressing gown and walked into the kitchen. And there it was. That smell again. Bacon.

"Morning, Em. I'm giving you one last treat. Aren't I the best?" Maureen smiled and laughed.

Emily joined her in laughter. "Thank you, Madam. You're so kind." Nothing was mentioned about the kiss, so Emily ignored what her conscience was saying.

Maureen asked, "So what time do we have to be at Luton, then?"

Emily sighed. "Three-ish is okay." She had mixed feelings. Of course she wanted to be with Lionel, but she had enjoyed seeing Maureen. They were like sisters.

"How do you fancy a run out? We could go to the riverside, either Coalhouse Fort or Tilbury Fort. And there's a pub near both forts. We could grab some lunch. What do ya reckon?" Maureen asked.

Emily nodded her head. "No drinks though, Maur. I'm a bit hungover, to be honest."

"No, definitely no drink," Maureen agreed.

After breakfast, they quickly got ready and walked out to the car.

"Well, which one?" Maureen asked. "Which fort would you like to see, Em?"

Emily replied, "Tilbury Fort. Is the pub still there? The World's End, isn't it?"

Maureen nodded. "That's the one. Come on then."

They drove through the lanes. As they approached a T-junction, Emily heard a noise from Maureen. "What is it, Maur?" she asked.

Maureen explained the brakes were a bit spongey, but the same had happened before and were quickly back to normal after pumping them a few times. They got to Gun Hill and, as they started down the hill, Maureen pressed the brake pedal. Nothing. It went right down to the floor. "Oh my god," Maureen cried, "I've... We've got no brakes!" They were gathering speed. There was a gentle curve at the bottom of the hill, followed by a sharp right-hand bend. Maureen was pumping away like mad. She grabbed the hand brake and it just pulled straight up. "What the hell!"

By this time, Emily was screaming. They were hitting sixty and were just yards from the sharp bend. Maureen looked at her and said, "Sorry, Em." As they hit the bend, Maureen tried to steer, but the momentum took over and the car rolled once, then a second time. They ended up in a ditch. They both lay upside down, motionless.

A HGV lorry was the first vehicle to come along. After checking their car, he returned to his vehicle and used the radio to call for an ambulance.

Half an hour later the police, fire brigade and ambulance were all in attendance. Emily was conscious, but Maureen wasn't. Emily was hysterical and proving very difficult to calm down. The fire brigade used their cutting equipment to assist in the rescue. Emily found she was not too badly injured, but Maureen was still unconscious. "Please hurry. Help her!" she screamed.

A police woman put her arm around Emily and walked her away from the scene. By this time, a paramedic was there too. Emily was trying to see what was going on, but the officer was forcing her gently to come away. The three paramedics were doing their best but, after around twenty minutes or so, they had to concede that they had failed to resuscitate Maureen.

As they were walking back to the ambulance, a senior officer approached Emily and said, "I'm really sorry but..."

"Oh no, no, no. She can't be. No! No!" The woman P.C. and the senior officers tried to console her, but she was inconsolable. "Why? Why did the brakes fail?" Emily wailed.

The senior officer went to his car and asked for SOCO to come to the scene and somebody from the car squad too. While he was doing this, one of the fire team came over and whispered in the senior officer's ear. They both walked back to the car. Emily was informed that, as the car was upside down, it showed clearly that a brake pipe and the handbrake cable had been cut.

Emily phoned Lionel, who immediately said he would come straight away, asking if there was anybody she could sit with. Emily said she'd be okay. She was in shock, though, and the woman PC didn't leave her side. She told Emily she would stay until her Lionel arrived.

After an hour or two, she decided to phone Barry, who came straight away. They hadn't known each other for long but, as soon as Barry walked in the room, Emily rushed over to him in hysterics. Barry threw his arms around her till she calmed down. Barry asked the police officer what caused the accident. She replied, "I'm not really supposed to say, but it does seem like foul play, sir." Barry was fuming. He said nothing out loud, but he knew who was behind this tragic incident.

Emily was pleased to see Barry but, as pleased as she was, she couldn't stop herself from crying. She'd be okay for a few minutes but here she was, in her best friend's bungalow, and her best friend was dead. Worse than that, somebody, it seemed, wanted this to happen. She didn't, couldn't understand. She accepted Barry's offer of a cup of tea. She wished Lionel was there. She sat, head in hands, as Barry placed a mug on the coffee table in front of her.

"Emily," Barry struggled with this sort of situation, but felt he had to try to help. "Emily, drink your tea, love."

Emily picked up the mug and forced a smile, but when she looked at it, she realised it was Maureen's mug with 'I'm the boss' written in large pink letters. "She was my boss, Barry. She's always been the dominant one. Of course, if I didn't agree, we'd debate the point and usually she won the day.... I...." Emily's eyes filled with tears. "I can't believe she's gone. Why? Why did this happen? I don't understand." She burst into tears again.

Barry moved from the armchair to sit next to her and put his arm around her. Suddenly, the doorbell rang. Barry got up and went to the front door. There were two plain clothed policemen standing there. "We'd like a word with Ms. Fleet, sir, if that's okay. We understand it's a tragic time for her, but we need answers to a few questions as soon as possible.

Barry replied, "I understand, officers. Let me just make sure she's up to it. Won't keep you a moment." Barry left the door ajar. "Emily, there's a couple of officers who'd like a quick word. You don't have to see them if you don't want to. I'll get rid of them, if you like."

Emily stood up. "No, Barry, let them in please." She sat down again.

Barry brought the officers in. They introduced themselves. "Hello, Emily. Thank you for agreeing to speak to us. My name is Detective Sergeant Graham Carter, and this is Detective David Buxton." Emily nodded her head. Barry sat next to her. "We do understand this is a very tragic time for you and may we offer our deepest sympathy. We would just like to ask a couple of questions. Is that okay?" Emily didn't speak. She just nodded her head.

"What it is Emily, is... Well, I'll be honest with you. It does seem like Maureen's car was tampered with. As the car was upside down, one of the fire crew noticed that both the handbrake cable and the brake pipe to the slave cylinder seem to have been cut."

Emily broke down. Barry's efforts to comfort her were not making any difference. She was inconsolable. She only stopped crying after Barry suggested that the two officers give her more time.

"It's okay, Barry," she said still sobbing. "It's okay. I'm sorry, officers, I just can't believe that someone would do such a thing. It doesn't make sense." She broke down again.

The officers looked at each other. Detective Buxton just raised his eyebrows. D S Carter pressed on with the questions. "Did either of you notice anyone hanging around this morning or last night? When did you last go out in the car?" Emily answered each question as more tears were falling. D S Carter continued, "Emily, just one more if you don't mind. Can you show me where the car was parked when you left this morning?"

Emily nodded and proceeded to show the officers where it had been.

"Thank you. I think that will be all for now. If you remember anything relevant, please call me." He gave her his card. As they left the garden, they walked over to a police van that was parked across the road. A young female officer got out of the car. On the side of the vehicle the word 'Forensic' caught Barry's and Emily's eyes. The Detective brought the young officer to the position where the car had been parked. She put her black plastic briefcase down right next to the place where the car was parked. She took a roll of barrier tape from the case and cordoned off the area. At that, a second forensic van arrived, this time with two male officers. It seemed that this was a very serious matter and they were not treating it lightly.

D S Carter waved to Barry and Emily as he got into his vehicle and left. Barry ushered Emily inside and sat for a few minutes and then said, "Emily, would you like something to eat? I could do you something, if you'd like." Emily just broke down again. Barry thought for a second, "Em, do you... I mean, would you like to come and stay at my house?" He thought it couldn't be easy for her. Everywhere she looked, she was reminded of Maureen.

Emily was pleased at this suggestion and agreed that it would be a good idea. She gathered her things together and went into the bedroom. She started sobbing again, but quickly gained control and soon she was locking the front door.

Barry asked, "What about Maureen's family, pet?"

Emily shook her head. "Other than her brother, she has no family Barry. It's a long story, but no, she was a bit of a loner, bless her."

Barry felt himself choking up. It was a terrible tragedy and, to know that it was down to somebody, somebody who did this on purpose, was just so hard to comprehend. Barry put Emily's suitcase in the boot of the Jag, and they set off. Pretty much as soon as they were away from Maureen's, Emily seemed to find relief at being out of her best friend's home. It helped her to at least be able to talk and have a conversation with Barry without sobbing.

"When the officer said it was done deliberately, Barry, you seemed to be… well, not just surprised… but thought you knew who might have done this. Is that right?" Emily questioned.

Barry was sure it would be the Scottish dwarf who had done this. Maybe he didn't do it himself, but got somebody to do his dirty work for him. He didn't want to let Emily know just yet, so he said, "I don't know, Emily. I can't believe it would be the Mayor. Surely not. Maybe it was, though. Maybe it was done to scare you, not to cause the death of anybody. Just to make you forget about why you came here."

As Barry approached his drive, he pressed the button on his gate fob.

Emily just said, "Wow, Mr. Wilson. Is this your house? I mean, it's beautiful."

Barry popped the boot as he got out. "We like it, Emily. It's a shadow of what it was like when we first moved in, but the conversion has improved it no end." Barry opened the front door as Angie was about to do it from inside. "Angie, love. I said Emily could stay with us for a bit. It's too…. Well, you know."

Angie just said "Of course," and hugged Emily when she entered. She honestly didn't know what to say. "Emily, come on. I'll show you your room." Emily followed her into a large room with a double four poster bed in it.

Emily gasped, "Wow, Angie. It's a beautiful room. Thank you so much for letting me stay. It's so kind of you."

Angie smiled, "Don't mention it, Emily. You're welcome to stay as long as you need to."

Emily had cheered up somewhat compared to a couple of hours before. Then she had a thought. Lionel. She'd given him Maureen's address. He wouldn't know how to find her. When she mentioned this to Angie, she went and got Barry.

Barry listened to Emily. "That's okay, Emily. I'll pop back to Maureen's and leave a note for Lenny."

Emily laughed, "Lionel, Barry. His name is Lionel." The pair of them laughed.

He went to a drawer in his office, wrote a short note, put it in a clear plastic wallet and drove back to Maureen's to tape it to the front door.

When he arrived, the SOCO people were still scanning the area where the car was parked. There was another car there and a good-looking man in a suit was standing by a five series BMW. Barry presumed he was a senior officer and approached him. "Hello, officer. How's it going?"

The man turned to Barry and said, "I'm not police. My name is Lionel."

Before he could say anything else, Barry said, "Ah, you're Emily's fella. She's round at mine. It was too traumatic for her to stay here. If you follow me, I'll take you to see her."

Lionel remarked, "As soon as she told me what happened, I knew I had to get here as soon as possible, so I hired this and drove down overnight. Then, once I got into Essex, I got lost. Then I got a puncture and got the AA to come out. Two bloody hours it took them. Oh well, let's go and see my lady."

He followed Barry through the lanes and he, too, was impressed by Barry's home. "Nice," he commented.

Angie opened the door. Emily looked and was absolutely shocked to see Lionel standing there. Within ten seconds, the emotion poured out and they stood by the front door for a couple of minutes while Lionel tried to console her. After a while, Emily settled down. She was so glad to see her Lionel. Angie and Emily were sitting at the bar in the snooker room. Barry was showing Lionel the birds.

Lionel enquired, "So, this was a deliberate attempt to hurt the girls, then?"

Barry nodded his head. "Yes, I'm afraid it was. And I don't know if Emily has kept you up to speed about why we needed to get in touch with her, but…" Barry went on to explain the story and the facts circulating about Jack Fleet House. By the time he'd finished, Lionel just sighed. "So, this effing Lord effing Mayor is the one behind this? What a bastard."

Barry was trying to be diplomatic. "Well, we don't have proof, and I don't expect we will get any. You saw SOCO examining the area. Let's hope they find something." The two of them started walking back to the house.

Lionel said, "By the way, that's a really impressive set up you have there. How much did you say? £500 each for chicks?"

Barry replied, "Yep, and it's ... well the demand is there too, but we don't want to be doing more than we are at the moment. It's hard work. Not physically; it's just time consuming. And yes, it is rewarding, but when the chicks are newborns, they need feeding every four hours. It's hard that way, ya know."

They walked into the snooker room. The girls were on the wine. Barry joked, "Oh yeah, starting early ain't ya, girls?" The girls both laughed. Who could blame them?

Lionel challenged Barry. "Do you want a frame or two then, Barry?"

Barry smiled, "It'd be rude not to. Do you want a beer, Lionel?"

"It'd be rude not to," he smiled.

Getting His Own Back

Davey McCallister was now a well-established superstar in the tiling field. It had been twenty years since he first came to Essex. He was now a pillar of the community, currently working on twenty-five underground stations. He had supermarket contracts coming out of his ears and was even working on Admiralty Arch at the end of The Mall in London. Oh yes, he was a Big Time Charlie now alright.

He made a real statement when he bought out Matchless Tiling Co, the company where he had his humble beginnings. By far his best acquisition, though, came about when he had offered to buy the company that was the sole distributor of a certain special tile. The England-based sole trader refused to sell to Davey, so instead he bought the Italian company that supplied that exclusive range of tiles. Oh yes, he'd made it.

He was now very much respected in the local community and, because of this, he was always in demand. The local council paraded him at every opportunity, as if he was one of them. Instead, he was the boy from the Falls Road in Northern Ireland who had made it, and made it good. He knew all the local councillors and they were in awe of him. Davey McCallister, in local business parlance, was a superstar. He had four children, all boys who, if Davey had his way, would carve their own futures. Of course, if they wanted, he'd bring them into the tiling game, but he really hoped they would go on to prove themselves in their own right.

He was a proud man, a loyal husband and a proper role model for his children. He admitted many times that he wasn't perfect; he had his shortcomings. Sometimes he would make the wrong decisions but, all in all, he was a sound, likeable businessman.

Recently, at the local business awards, where he again won the much coveted 'Businessman of the Year' honour, he was honest enough to play down his achievements in his acceptance speech. He noted that there were people in the community that deserved the award much more than he did. He was, business-wise, the local hero. The good thing for him also was that he had no skeletons in his cupboard. He had a distinct dislike for the local Mayor, who he found to be an irritation most of the time. When they were in the same company, Jock McBride was interested in only one thing, Davey thought to himself, and that was Jock McBride. He recalled an incident that occurred at the presentation night to a fellow award winner who had just won 'Businessman of the Year'. Jock McBride approached Davey about the contract for a new shopping mall in Grays Town Centre, making it clear to him that he was after a sweetener to ensure Davey's company won the contract.

Davey, without hesitation, put the Scotsman in his place, saying words to the effect that "I'm not for sale, Mr. McBride, at any price. So, you can put that in your pipe and smoke it."

Jock McBride's face apparently went as red as a beetroot and he very soon left the party. Davey was nobody's fool. Jock McBride was the only fool, expecting him to jump into bed with him. Jock, though, didn't take kindly to being snubbed when it came to local businesses and, on his way home, he promised himself he would get one over on the Irishman.

When Jock got home, Jimmy Miller was waiting for him.

"Hello, Jimmy. How are you?" Jock asked.

He was acting surely, Jimmy thought. "How am I? Are you kidding? You know that woman died in the accident, don't you? What you asked me to do has killed somebody, do you hear me? You've killed somebody. You did this!"

"Hold on just one minute, Jimmy boy. I haven't got the slightest clue of what you're on about. What woman? When? I don't know what you're saying." Jock seemed clueless.

Jimmy was fuming. "Jock, you asked me to cut the brake pipes on her car. You wanted to kill somebody, I guess. I know you've been there for me, but this is too much. I'm not going down for you or anyone. It's not my fault."

Jock just stared at Jimmy. When he seemed to have said everything he wanted to say, Jock just said quietly, "Check your bank account in the morning, alright my boy? Then you'll sleep, okay? Now fuck off."

Toast And Marmalade

Angie was the first to arrive in the kitchen after a crazy night. Barry and Lionel were playing snooker all night and drinking all night too. She put the kettle on and nearly jumped out of her skin. She shut the fridge door to see Emily standing there. "Morning, Emily. Did you manage to sleep okay?"

Emily answered, "Well, I did till Lionel woke me. It must have been about 3am. He was drunk and whinging that he'd lost to Barry at snooker. It took me ages to drop off again after that, especially since he was asleep in no time, snoring his head off."

Angie smiled. "Men make me laugh. They reckon they don't snore. I know for a fact that Baz's snoring has even woken him up, it's been that loud."

Emily was nodding her head in total agreement. "You're so right, Ange. Lionel's the same, exactly the same."

Angie made a pot of tea and asked Emily if she fancied breakfast.

"I'll just have some toast if there's any going," she replied.

"Of course, no problem. Brown or white?" Angie asked.

"Oh, white. Got to be white, please Angie."

Angie smiled and plugged the toaster in.

"I'm just going to see if Lionel's awake yet, Ange."

Angie said okay but wasn't sure if Emily heard her. She wondered how she was, you know, inside. It must have been a terrible ordeal, and to lose your best friend as well, that must be heartbreaking.

Emily came back into the kitchen. "He's sound asleep, Ange."

"Leave 'em to it, I say. They're not bothering us if they're asleep, are they?" Angie laughed. She felt so sorry for Emily. She'd come back to Essex to help everyone who wanted to keep the home open, and now she'd lost her best friend in tragic circumstances. If she was honest, she couldn't believe that Jock McBride was behind this. Surely it wasn't that big a deal, was it? No, it... There had to be another reason surely. She called to Emily, who was in the lounge. "Do you want butter or what?" Angie asked.

Emily came back into the kitchen. "I don't suppose you have any marmalade, do you?"

Angie smiled. "As a matter of fact, I do."

They sat at the breakfast bar. Angie wasn't confident that she could say anything to Emily that would make her feel any better, but she believed that, in times like these, you have to try to act as normal as possible. "Where did you meet Lionel, Emily?"

Emily was finishing her second round of toast. "Well," she smiled for the first time that day, "I went up to a favourite spot of mine in the north of Peru on the coast. I try to get there every year and stay in the same hotel. It's beautiful. Lionel was staying there, too. I suppose we just clicked. It's been difficult, though. He travels all the time, but we've just recently decided to make every effort to make what we have turn into something really special." Emily smiled again, stood up and took her plate to the sink.

"I think he got on okay with Baz last night, don't you?" Angie remarked.

"Oh, very much Angie. They got on like a house on fire. I didn't know he liked snooker, though. I'm not sure if he's any good or not, but they seemed to enjoy it, seeing what time they must have played till. I woke up at two-thirty and he still hadn't come to bed."

Angie smiled and said," That's probably Baz's fault. He doesn't get to play much lately and, like I say, he was the one pushing for one more frame, I reckon." Angie got up and loaded the dishwasher. "Would you like another tea, Emily?"

"I think I will. Could you let me do it? I'll make Lionel one. It's time he was up," Emily asked.

"No, you sit there. I'll make us all one. Baz should be up by this time anyway. He's late feeding the birds," Angie insisted.

Emily had forgotten the conversation last night about the parrots. "I remember now, you breed African Greys, don't you?"

Angie smiled, "Yes, it's a team effort. It has to be. They are very time consuming, especially when they are chicks; they need feeding every four hours. And believe you me, that is quite a commitment."

"I'm sure it is," Emily agreed.

Angie had gestured to Emily to enter the lounge, where she put the tray down and pointed to Lionel's cup. "Does he take sugar, Em?"

Emily laughed. "Oh, does he! He asks for three spoons in a mug. I never give it to him, though. Give him two; that'll do."

Angie did the needful. Then they both went to their respective bedrooms to wake the all-night playboys.

Investigation

The accident on the Fort Road had been a big talking point in the pubs and clubs locally. It even made a couple of national newspapers. The press didn't seem to have any information about the vehicle being tampered with though.

Ronnie Dexter brought in a freelance reporter he used when something like this happened. Although he was upset at the whole tragic event, he was looking forward to meeting his 'freelancer', as he used to call her.

Penny Lamb had worked for him on several occasions. She lived relatively local, but the only time Ronnie saw her was if he needed her services. He'd called her yesterday as soon as the story broke and was pleased she agreed to help. She said she would be in Grays around lunchtime.

Ronnie knew D I Carter and had called him first thing. "Well, Graham, what's the score then?" Ronnie asked, not expecting anything too useful.

He heard Graham sigh. "Ronnie, I'm not at liberty to say too much that is going to help you. I can confirm, off the record, that the vehicle had been tampered with, and it seems it was done the night before, outside the house, while the two ladies were out. Ronnie, I must insist you print none of what I say until I give you the nod, okay? I've had the nationals bending my ear and I gave them nothing, absolute zero. Please keep a lid on it. I'll get back to you and yes, you will know before the nationals, okay?" He was very stern with his words.

Ronnie knew not to let him down. "Of course, Graham, mum's the word." At that, he hung up.

Lucy entered the office. "Penny's here, Ronnie."

Show her in, Lucy love, show her in." Ronnie got up from behind his desk and was almost at the door when Penny walked in.

"Ronnie, how are you? You putting on weight, you old rascal?" she smirked.

Ronnie patted his stomach. "It's a wee beer belly, Pen, that's all. How are you doing? Still hitting the magazine trail?"

Penny had three or four magazines that seemed to like her work and, for the time being, that was the way she liked it. "Oh yes, Ron, still driving down that road. It pays the bills. I'm ready to spit feathers, Ron. Could we have a coffee, love?"

"Of course, Pen." He buzzed Lucy and ordered two coffees.

Ronnie spent the next couple of hours informing Penny of the whole shooting match. The crooked Mayor, the orphanage, everything, and then he played his ace card, the accident. He stressed that the facts regarding the accident were known only by a few. He wasn't sure yet if Emily had been informed but, anyway, she probably had a good idea, given all the forensic examination that had taken place. It was right up Penny's street, and she assured Ronnie that the investigations she was about to begin would remain between the two of them.

Ronnie totally trusted Penny, one hundred percent. "What do you say I take you out to lunch then, my treat?"

Penny loved coming to Grays. "As long as we go to the chippy, Ron... yeah?"

"But, of course, my sweetheart, of course," he replied.

As they walked through Lucy's office, Ronnie just smiled and said, "Lucy, I'll be a couple of hours. If you need me, we'll be round the corner in the chippy, okay?"

Lucy forced a smile. She didn't like Penny; she was full of herself. Lucy was sure this would be something to do with Jack Fleet. She would call Uncle Jock tonight, tell him what was happening.

Jock wouldn't admit to anyone that he had a little smile when he heard about the accident, but smile he did. It could have been Ms. Fleet, but he felt it would be enough to ensure that she just went and buggered off back to Peru or wherever it was she came from. He did, though, have another problem. Jimmy Miller.

Jock's secretary had lost count of the number of times this Mr. Miller had called. Jock wasn't too concerned; he could handle Jimmy Miller. He was a no mark, a nobody and nobody would give a stuff if he disappeared suddenly. "It won't come to that," Jock thought to himself. He'd sort it out. He always did get his own way, didn't he?

He opened the drawer, moved his handgun to one side and picked up his bottle of Famous Grouse. He reached over his shoulder for his favourite glass, which held the words 'Favourite Uncle Jock' etched into it. It was a present from Lucy. In the near future, he would be giving Lucy a very special present, one she could live in, rent free, for ever. He smiled and drank from the glass. "Not long now, Jocky boy, not long."

Goodbyes

Maureen's funeral was taking place tomorrow. Emily was pleased that Lionel was still with her. Barry and Angie had been brilliant with their support and letting them stay with them. Lionel, in a quiet moment, had thanked Barry and commented that it felt like they'd known them all their lives. Emily wondered if Maureen's brother, Laurence, would be there tomorrow. She hadn't been able to contact him. He was also a good friend of her brother, Peter. Maureen had a falling out with her mum a few years ago and never spoke of her. Maureen's father died when she was young.

It was the month of July and the weather was surprisingly hot. Barry suggested a barbeque to Angie, who said, "I don't mind. Do you think Emily would like it? I mean, we'll probably start drinking. I don't know if she's up for it. Better ask her, Baz."

Barry got up and replied, "Aye, Doll. I'll do that."

Lionel and Emily were in the garden. Barry walked through the open patio doors and said, "What a beautiful day. So you know what? I fancy a barbeque. What do you think, Lionel?"

Lionel smiled, looked at Emily and agreed with Barry. "Sounds like a plan, Barry. Okay with you, Em?"

Emily was deep in thought. Lionel said again, "Emily, do you fancy a barbie?"

Emily smiled and nodded her head. As he asked Emily, Lionel started laughing. Both Barry and Emily looked at him puzzled. "What's so funny, Lionel?" Emily said.

He finally stopped laughing, took a deep breath and said, "It just struck me, Em. Barry, if we weren't here, would you have said to Angie…" He laughed again and then stopped, "would you have said to Angie, do you fancy a barbie, Doll?" and burst into laughter again, only this time, Emily and Barry joined him.

Angie, on hearing the laughter stepped out onto the patio and said, "That's a sound I've not heard for a while. What you all laughing at?"

Barry said, "Oh Ange, it's nothing really. I'll tell you later. And yes, we're all okay for a barbie, Doll." They all started laughing again.

Angie looked at Barry, who chuckled, "Ange…. Barbie Doll."

Angie then saw the funny side too and joined in with the laughter.

Having a barbeque was a regular occurrence at the Wilson household. Soon the charcoal was turning from black to grey and, as if on cue, Barry arrived with his apron and his chef's hat on.

Emily was in stitches. "You look like the Swedish Chef from the Muppet show."

Barry obliged with a poor effort at impersonating the Swedish Chef in question.

The evening went well. Emily's spirits were lifted a little. Yes, tomorrow was going to be a sad day, but that was tomorrow. Tonight was for fun. Maureen would be smiling if she were watching.

There was talk of an early night but that's all it was, talk. The funeral wasn't mentioned and each of them relaxed, ate too much, drank too much and laughed a lot more than they had recently.

Lionel more or less carried Emily to their room. It was gone one o'clock in the morning. Lionel laid her on the bed and didn't bother covering her up as it was still a hot night. To his dismay, Emily was snoring before he even got into bed. Therefore, it took a little while before he was able to go to sleep himself.

Barry and Angie sat in the garden for another hour or so. They were chatting about the evening and they both said how Lionel and Emily were so well suited. Their thoughts turned to the funeral. "Emily wants us to go, Baz," Angie said.

"Yes, I know Doll. I think we should go… for her really."

Angie agreed.

They were to be at the crematorium for eleven fifteen. Barry was up before seven thirty, bright as a button. Lionel walked into the kitchen; Barry was cooking again. "Hello, mukka. Fancy a bacon sarnie?"

Lionel shook his head, smiling. "How do you do it, Barry? What time did you go to bed? Oh, and yes, I'd love a sarnie, thanks."

"One bacon sarnie coming up." Barry tried doing his Swedish impression again, which started Lionel laughing again. "How's Em this morning, then? She up yet?"

"She's just having a shower. She's a bit hungover, though," Lionel admitted.

"Angie is too, matey. The pair of them were proper on it, weren't they?" Barry said.

Angie walked in holding her head and, right on cue, Emily followed her in, also holding her head.

Sadly, there were not as many as expected at the crematorium but, nevertheless, it was a decent turn out. Emily held on to Lionel's arm virtually the whole time. Barry confessed to Angie that he felt a little out of place, but Emily had made a gesture to Barry and Angie with a whispered thank you in the chapel.

The service was pleasant and thoughtful. The local vicar who had taken the service asked if there was anyone who would like to say a few words. At first, nobody seemed to want to. But, at the last minute, a tall blonde-haired man, probably in his forties, stood up and walked to the lectern.

Emily looked and realised it was Maureen's brother, Laurence. He looked in good shape. The last time Emily saw him he was overweight, but here he seemed to look a lot healthier. His words were, unsurprisingly, poignant. He made a reference to Emily, stating that his sister was with her best friend when she passed over to the other side, so it was a blessing that she wasn't alone.

Outside the chapel, Emily was looking at the flowers and recognised a few names on them.

"Hello, Emily." Emily felt a hand on her shoulder. She held her arms open.

"Laurence, I'm so sorry," and the tears flowed.

They held a long embrace. Laurence, too, had tears and wiped his eyes as they let go of each other.

"How have you been, Em?" Laurence asked.

Emily was still linked arms to Lionel. "I've been good, Laurence."

Laurence smiled, "What's with the Laurence, Em? You always called me Lol," he laughed.

Emily chuckled too. "I know," she said, "We were kids then. Look at us now. Look at you, all slim. You look really well. Oh, I'm sorry. This is my man, Lionel. This is Laurence, or Lol," she laughed. "We met in Peru, where I live now."

Laurence smiled. "Peru, wow. What's it like there? I've never been."

Emily remembered home. "It's beautiful. You should come visit."

They reminisced until Emily mentioned that she needed to get in touch with her brother, Peter, but she'd lost contact with him.

Laurence solved her problem, "I've got his address if you want it."

Emily was in shock, "Wow, that would be great. How is he? When did you last see him? I can't believe you've got his address. Where is he living, still in Australia or what?"

Laurence held both his hands up "Whoa, hold on, Em. I didn't say I'd seen him, just that I know where he was living. Up to a couple of weeks ago, he was living and working in Melbourne. He works in a hospital there. I think he's nearly a fully qualified nurse. He's been studying for years."

Wow, Emily thought, he's making something of his life. "Lol, thank you so much. Have you got his address on you by any chance?"

Laurence shook his head. "No, but it's back at my hotel. I can call in there and get it for you on the way to Orsett. We are all going to Orsett, aren't we, The King's Arms? I'm sure that's the place."

Emily smiled and nodded her head. "Yes, that's right. We'll be there before you, so we'll save you a seat, Lol."

They all made their way to the cars and set off for Ronnie's pub. Barb had done Emily proud. The pool room had two pool tables, both with their covers on, with tablecloths on top of them. The shelves all around the room were full of sandwiches, sausage rolls and almost every kind of snack food you could imagine. Ronnie had thrown in a dozen or so bottles of red and white wine.

When Ronnie walked in, Barb was just topping the wine glasses up. "Fucking hell, Barb. There's enough food 'ere to feed a bloody army!"

Barb had never been any different. "Well, they deserve a nice spread, Ron. It's been a terrible thing to happen."

Ronnie smiled at her, "Aye, lass, it has that."

Near enough everyone came who was at the crematorium. Soon the pool room was bursting with people. Lionel and Barry went out to the bar and sat on a couple of stools. Angie and Emily sat on chairs in the pool room.

As Barb came in, Emily grabbed her arm. "Barbara, thank you so much for this. It's wonderful. I must owe you some more money. What I gave you would never cover this."

Barb smiled, "Don't mention it. Oh and, by the way, you and your two lover boys have got beer in the pump, okay!" Emily looked puzzled.

Angie explained, "She's not going to charge us for anything that we drink, Em."

"Really?" Emily said, "Not sure I can handle another drunken night, Ange."

Lionel and Barry were chatting away at the bar when they heard a bit of a commotion at the front door of the pub. By the time Barry got there, it was virtually over.

"What's up, Ron?" Barry asked.

Ronnie had a face like thunder. "Can you believe the nerve of that man? I don't believe it. I just told him to fuck off, how dare you turn up here, now fuck off."

Barry was trying to get Ronnie to say who. Eventually he shut the front door and was about to go into another rant when Barry got hold of both of Ronnie's shoulders. "Who did you tell to fuck off, Ron?"

Ronnie paused... "Jock fucking McBride! Baz, can you believe it?"

Barry was dumbstruck. "No, Ron, I can't believe that. What a total fucking bastard."

Emily and Angie had entered the bar and caught the tail end of the fracas. When Barry told them, they, too, could not believe their ears.

The bar was emptying out and the four of them found a table in the bar and sat down. The drinks were flowing. Emily was happy to talk about her best friend now. She'd paid her respects. She was in a better place was Maureen and, finally, Emily was too.

"What's everyone drinking, then?" said a voice at the bar.

Emily recognised it without turning around. "Mine's a JD and coke, Lol, please."

Laurence just smiled and said, "Good ole Em. You still like a short, then? Everyone else?"

Barry and Lionel asked for another couple of pints and Angie just had an orange juice. After a few minutes, the five of them chatted well into the early evening.

Barb and Ronnie had brought the rest of the food that was left over into the bar and Ronnie challenged Barry to a game of pool. Laurence and Lionel followed. Soon they were paired up, Ronnie and Barry against Lionel and Laurence. Oh, the banter. Lionel considered himself to be a well-travelled and educated man, but some of the banter flying around that room that night was legendary.

Angie and Emily were sitting at the bar now. Barbara was behind the bar, but only served customers that Carol couldn't manage. Their conversation concentrated on one thing, Jack Fleet House. Emily promised that she would write to Peter first thing in the morning. They were all hoping there would be good news arriving soon.

"Oh my, look at the time," Emily said, "It's quarter to twelve."

Barbara said, "That's okay, Emily. No rush." Within a minute or so, they heard the men folk returning from their pool room exploits.

Emily asked, "Well, who won then?"

Lionel was the first to comment on the events of the evening. "Well, it's going to sound like sour grapes but..."

Ronnie butted in, "Eight frames to two, Em. We proper stuffed 'em!" Ronnie and Barry were laughing.

Lionel tried again, "I've never seen such blatant cheating."

"Ah, leave it out, Line. You got your arse proper kicked by a couple of old'uns. Take it like a man," Barry teased. There it was, the laughter again. "You still serving, Barb?" Barry asked.

"Reckon there's nobody else behind here, Baz, so yeah, same again all round?" she said.

They were indeed all up for it. Laurence and Emily sat at a table and Laurence went to his suit jacket pocket and pulled out a diary. He flicked through the pages until he found Peter's address. "Here it is, Em. 391, Yale Drive, Epping, Melbourne."

Emily copied down the address in a note book. "Thank you," she said, as she placed the notebook back into her handbag.

"Emily," Laurence said. "Don't you want his phone number, too?"

"What! You never said you had his phone number. Of course, I want it." She was very happy, not just for herself, but for these lovely people who had been so kind to her during this tough time. They could have some positive news soon and, who knows, the news might just save the home that they were all so desperate to keep open.

Emily's mind was drifting. Peter, a nurse! Wow, he'd done well for himself if it was true. It must be true. Lol had said so, hadn't he? She couldn't wait for the morning to come. She remembered Australia was around ten hours ahead of the UK. So, she couldn't leave it too late to give him a call. She turned to look towards the bar. Oh dear, another round was arriving on the bar. Ah well, she thought, one for the road. "This one is for you, Maureen. Love you." Emily got up and went to get her drink from Barb.

Made It!

Davey was spending most of his time at home. He'd been able to keep hold of the reins by the odd visit to the office. He was in the middle of decorating. Well, not really decorating, more a case of refurbishing the downstairs bathroom. He had always been good with his hands, but he did struggle with some of the plumbing even though, compared to years ago, it was getting easier. His wife, Tricia, was out shopping but was due back soon, so he left her a note to say that he was going to Plumb Supply Co. and wouldn't be long.

He set off in his Jaguar XJR with a list of requirements. When he arrived at the shop in Tilbury, he noticed another XJR in the car park. He entered the trade counter and a tall, elderly man commented, "Nice motor fella. Had it long?" It was Barry.

"Yeah, about a year and a half now. Is that one yours outside, then?" Davey asked.

Barry smiled. "Yeah. I love my baby. I always said for years that when I had a nice Jag, I'd be content. I'd feel like I'd arrived, you know what I mean?"

Davey smiled. "Said the same thing myself. Always wanted one. A friend of mine has one that he only brings out in the summer. It's a red convertible, like the one that Morse had in the TV show. It's beautiful. I keep asking if he wants to sell it. It's only done twenty-three thousand miles. It's a sixty-five model, fucking beautiful."

Barry was equally impressed. "Sounds like it's worth a few bob."

Davey nodded his head. "You're not wrong there. He told me he was offered sixty for it and turned it down."

The two of them chatted some more, then Davey remembered why he was there. "I've got a list if you'd be so kind."

Barry looked at the list. "We've got most of it in stock. These two items should be in later today. Where do you live?"

Davey replied, "It's alright, I'll call in tomorrow."

Barry insisted. "Where do you live? My assistant goes one way from here, I go the other. There's a good chance one of us passes your area on our way home."

Davey smiled. "Okay, Orsett, I live in Orsett, near the hospital. I face the cricket ground."

Barry smiled back. "There you are, see. I live in Horndon. I virtually pass your house on the way home. That's sorted then. I'll drop these other bits off on me way home."

Davey said his thanks and settled the bill. After he'd gone, Barry said to Tom, "What a lovely fella, Tom, though I did struggle to understand everything he said with that strong Northern Irish accent."

Tom was stocktaking and laughed. "You don't understand me 'alf the time Baz, do ya!"

Barry's mind was elsewhere for most of the day, wondering if Emily had been in touch with her brother and if there was some good news to be had. The rest of the day was fairly busy, but summer wasn't the busiest time for the plumbing trade. Around four thirty, Barry said to Tom, "I'm gonna drop the rest of the stuff off at the Irish fella's drum, Tom, okay?"

Tom was used to locking up. He was generally the only one there most of the time, so it was nothing new. "Yeah fine, Baz. You in tomorrow, only I need to take my mutt to the vet's?"

Barry stepped back into the shop. "At the moment, I should be here most of the day, Tom. What time you gotta be at the vet's?"

"Eleven-thirty. Will that be okay?" Tom enquired.

"Yeah, I'll make sure I'm here before eleven. Okay, see you in the morning," Barry replied.

The house where the Irishman lived was one of less than a dozen beautiful places. Barry was envious as he pulled into the drive. It was huge, and you could drive in one side and out the other. He went to the boot of his car and sorted the remaining parts of Davey's order. He looked around. Lovely, he thought. He knocked on the door. It had one of those big brass knockers.

Davey answered the door. "Ah, thank you. Come in, come in." They walked straight through to a room adjoining the kitchen. Davey opened the door. "Anywhere here will do, thanks. Sorry, what's your name?"

Barry smiled. "It's Barry, or Baz, whatever. And yours?"

Davey shook his hand. "It's Davey, Davey McCallister."

They chatted, mostly about the improvements Davey had made to the house. Davey offered to show him around and Barry was only too pleased. If he was honest, it was a bit ostentatious for Barry's taste, but the one thing that really impressed him was the pool room. "Wow," Barry gasped when Davey opened the door to his sports room. "Now you're talking, Davey. I love a game of pool."

"Well, no time like the present. Fancy a frame?" Davey challenged.

Barry was definitely in the mood. Beer also came to the fore.

Barry and Davey played pool in Davey's lovely home, the two of them complimenting each other on their prowess on the pool table. "We should make a night of it," Davey commented. "How about a game at the King's Arms? It's a nice pub and their tables are in good nick. What do you say? If you've got someone to partner you, we could play doubles. What do you think?"

Barry didn't hesitate. "You're on, doubles it is. When do you fancy it, then?"

Davey smiled. "Any evening, or late afternoon may be better. Who's your partner, then?"

Barry looked at Davey with a grin. "Oh, it's Ronnie, the Guv'nor of the King's Arms. Is that okay with you?"

Davey was surprised. He'd seen Ronnie in action and was impressed with his talent around the table. "No problem. You haven't seen my partner yet, have you? We should be well matched. Can't wait."

They chatted some more and left it open until they could all make it. Barry, all in all though, was pleased with his new acquaintance. Davey McCallister was a good man and these days there were too few of them about. They'd played five frames. Davey won three but conceded that he'd had a little luck when Barry went in-off in the deciding black. As Barry was leaving, he said, "If you have any problems with the plumbing, give me a bell. I'll sort it, okay Davey?"

Davey waved and nodded his head. "You're a good man Barry, thank you. See you and let me know when we'll have that doubles match up, okay?"

"Okay," Barry agreed. On his way home, his thoughts turned back to Emily. Was there any news? He was home in less than five minutes. He parked the car and went in by the kitchen entrance. Angie was filling the dishwasher. "Sorry, Doll," Barry said. Angie never answered. "Doll, I said I'm sorry." He went on to explain where he had been and why he was late.

Angie wasn't amused. "It's been a month or so since you had the affair and then you go and do something like this. What do you expect me to think? It's such a thoughtless thing to do, especially when we have guests staying here. They felt uncomfortable, Barry, don't you see?"

"Doll, I said I'm sorry." He realised he was getting nowhere. He walked into the lounge. Emily, Lionel and Laurence were there. "Oh, I'm so sorry," Barry said, "I lost track of time. I didn't…"

Emily was abrupt. "Barry, it's not us you should be apologising to, is it?"

She was right. He went back into the kitchen. Angie was sitting on a stool. He walked over and hugged her from behind. "Ange, Ange babe. You should know, I'm never gonna fuck up again. It's you I love. It's you I've only ever loved. Please don't shut me out."

She spun around on the stool. "You ever do something like that again, Mr. Wilson, and we're finished. Do you get it? Finished!" She got up and went to her bedroom.

In the lounge they were sad. All they heard was the word 'finished'. When Barry walked in, they didn't know what to say. Barry sat down and put his head in his hands as Angie walked in. "I fancy the pub. What do you think, Bazza?"

He looked up at her. The guests looked at the pair of them and the hosts started laughing, joined very quickly by the guests.

"Ronnie's it is, then," Barry said.

"Oh no," Emily said," I'm going for my hat trick." Everybody laughed.

Next thing Angie was on the phone. "Yes, a mini bus please, straight away to the King's Arms. How long? Okay, that's great. Thank you. Ten minutes. He's dropping someone off in the village. Let's be having you then, guys and gals." They were all in a better place. The earlier atmosphere had gone, disappeared without a trace. Twenty minutes later, they were 'on it' again.

Barry finally got to ask Emily about contacting her brother. "I've left a message on his answer phone, Barry. I'm guessing he does shifts, so he could call me back literally anytime, so we'll just have to wait," she sighed

Barry nodded his head, "Yeah, hospital shifts. Logical, I suppose."

Carol was working again tonight. Barb was upstairs watching TV. Ronnie was out with the pool team on a cup match. Laurence was quiet, and Barry noticed something not quite right when Lionel tried to talk to Laurence. "Ah, maybe it's nothing," he thought. In reality, it wasn't nothing. Laurence had a crush on Emily when they were youngsters and it seemed like it hadn't gone away. Barry tried to form a bridge between them and, for a while, he seemed to be breaking down a few barriers. Lionel had noticed the way Laurence had been but, to his credit, it never phased him, and he continually made the effort to talk to Laurence.

Eventually Laurence started questioning Lionel, his work, where he was from. Lionel felt like he was being interviewed by Emily's father. He side-stepped most of the questions but found himself getting annoyed by his antics. "How about a game of pool, then?" Lionel suggested.

Laurence shook his head. "I'm no good at pool."

Lionel looked at the others. Barry looked at the girls. "How about mixed doubles then, girls?"

Emily laughed, "I've never even played pool. I'd be useless."

Laurence commented, "You've played snooker with your brother Pete before."

Emily remembered playing on a small table. "Ah yes, but I think I wasn't even ten years old then, Lol." They all laughed. Then Emily said, "Go on then. I'm game for it."

So, another evening of fun and laughter was kicking off. There were, however, no smiles and hardly any laughter from one of the crowd. Laurence looked, if he was honest, and felt out of place. He didn't fit in with these people. The only one of them he knew was well into a relationship with a Scotsman, who he didn't much like.

A part of him felt it was because he was with Emily, his Emily. All those years they'd spent together as kids counted for nothing now. She was gone. Oh yes, she was polite with him, more than polite some of the time. But, as soon as 'her man' was on the scene, Laurence felt invisible. He made a decision that night. He was out of there, away from this, this situation. He'd never felt so uncomfortable. He was a mixer, got on with anyone, so why now? Why was this situation so unbearable? He just wouldn't admit what the real problem was. He was totally smitten with Emily and therefore jealous as hell as she sat with a Scotsman of all people, a Scotsman. He resigned himself to leave Essex tomorrow for good. Good riddance.

Break In

It was four o'clock in the morning. Emily couldn't sleep. It was hot. Not as hot as she was used to, but hot just the same. She decided to get up after an hour or so of tossing and turning. She made herself a cup of tea and almost immediately it hit her. Sam! Sam's brother would have sent him the Gazette with the details of the accident. It was probably headline news and he would be worried about her. She had to call him, put his mind at rest. She would speak to Barry in the morning.

She quietly opened the patio doors and sat on one of the loungers. Her mind drifted from Lima to Australia. She had still not spoken to Peter. She was staring down the garden when she suddenly wondered why Barry had left the lights on in the aviary. "Ah well," she thought, "there must be a reason." She looked up at the stars; they had always fascinated Emily, especially on a totally clear night like this. She finished her tea and, as she got up, she noticed that the aviary light was now off. Her first thought was to go and check, but she changed her mind straight away. It wasn't a light, it was a torch.

She quickly ran inside, carefully closing the patio doors, and ran to Barry's room. "Barry, Barry, come quick." She was knocking on the door at the same time. Barry opened the door, still putting his dressing gown on. "What is it, Em?"

Emily was worried. "Barry, there's somebody in your aviary. I saw the light from a torch."

Barry went back into his bedroom. Angela was awake, wondering what was going on.

Barry whispered to her, "Ange, call the police. We've got an intruder. At that, Barry found a crowbar and set off to the aviary. By now, he was joined by Lionel. The two of them didn't speak as they approached the door, which had been forced open.

There was no light shining now but, as Lionel pulled the door open, Barry was knocked to the ground by the culprit, who ran towards the bottom of the garden or, at least, that's where he was trying to get to. Lionel ran after him and brought the intruder crashing to the ground and, not only that, he'd grabbed both his arms and pinned them to his back.

"Wow," Barry remarked. "That was impressive, Line. Now who are you?" he asked the intruder, who said nothing.

Angie and Emily reached the bottom of the garden. Angie was shaken. "The police are on their way, Baz."

"Okay, Doll. You two go back inside. We'll sit on this one till they get here."

Jimmy Miller just laid there. He was in trouble and there was no way out. This brute who had him pinned down was as strong as an ox. No, he was going nowhere. He had to think fast. He had to take the rap for this. Jock would deny any involvement, what with his position as Mayor. Nobody would believe he could have anything to do with this.

Jimmy had been in trouble before, mostly drug related, but had always managed to avoid doing time. A couple of suspended sentences hung over his head, but they had long passed the point where they would be acted upon now. He wished he'd stuck to his guns and refused to do anything for the Scotsman. When Jock offered him cash, though, he was never going to refuse. Even though he had told Jock, after the car business and knowing that he was responsible for the loss of somebody's life, that he was done, no more meant no more, here he was about to be arrested, all because of the Scotsman.

Lionel kept the pressure on. It had been about twenty-five minutes since they caught him. Barry looked up to the house to see two or three figures coming towards them. It was a woman PC and an officer shining a torch. "Well, Mr. Wilson, what have we here?" The first thing they did was handcuff the man and stand him up. "What you here for then?" the policewoman asked. Jimmy didn't speak. "Where was he when you found him, Mr. Wilson?"

Jimmy was looking at the ground. "He knocked me over as we opened the aviary door," Barry replied.

The female officer looked at Jimmy. "What were you doing in there, then?"

A thought struck Barry. What was he doing in there? He quickly opened the door of the aviary and walked in. When he turned the light on, he gasped, "Oh no!" There were at least a dozen of his African greys dead on the floor. He was in tears.

Angie heard his cries and came running in. "Oh my god, how could someone be so cruel?"

Barry rushed passed her and tried to get to this so-called gentleman. The officers stopped him as the woman PC was explaining what had happened inside the building. The officer, who Barry found out later was also a keen follower of birds, and had indeed many years ago bred his own African greys, looked at Jimmy and said, "Why would you do something as horrible as this? Do you have an axe to grind with Mr. Wilson? Either way, you are going down for this. Scum like you should be with your own kind, you horrible piece of shit!" They marched him away. He had still not said a word.

As Barry, Angie, Lionel and Emily walked back into the house, Angie broke down. She was in pieces. How could anybody be so cruel? Emily made some tea. Barry was numb. Lionel too was distraught. It had been a terrible ordeal.

Barry looked at Emily. "Thanks, Em."

Emily was confused. "Why thank me, Barry?"

Lionel cut in. "Em, if you hadn't raised the alarm, we would probably have lost all the birds."

Emily nodded her head. Yes, probably, but she'd done nothing that anyone else wouldn't have done, had she?

Barry piped up, "It's a bit early, but I'm gonna do something to eat. What do you lot think, bacon sarnies all round?" On the pretext that nobody said no, he set about cooking the bacon though, by the time he'd finished, it was a full English.

"A feast," Lionel commented as his plate was placed in front of him. Emily just said "Wow" as Angie put her plate on the table. It was unusually quiet at the dinner table. Deep down, they were all upset, yet it seemed the whole incident, for now, was best forgotten.

At Grays police station, Jimmy Miller was in a cell. The officer in charge, when booking him in, questioned him as to his name and address. He said nothing. Why had he done what he'd done? Again, he said nothing. Officer Barry Walker had been in the force for twenty-three years. Nothing surprised him anymore. His colleague, Vicky Price, was in her first year and was still trying to understand this latest incident. "What makes somebody do something like this?" she asked Barry after they booked him in.

Barry smiled and said, "If I knew the answer to that one, Vic, I'd probably be able to earn more money as a shrink. Honestly, it could be any one of a number of things. He might owe someone a favour and maybe Mr. Wilson had pissed somebody off and he's got this low life to cause some grief, but really, I just don't know."

By the time they'd finished breakfast, it was nearly seven. Angie had cleared away the breakfast dishes and was loading the dishwasher. Emily, who was by now really tired, asked Angie if she had a minute to chat.

Angie was more than happy to accommodate Emily. "What's up, Em?"

Emily explained that her old friend, Sam, back home in Lima would quite probably be concerned about her wellbeing. She explained that her friend's brother sent the local paper to Sam. When he saw the article about the accident that Emily was in, which was on the front page, it would give him cause for concern.

Angie was starting to get the picture and, before Emily could say any more, Angie said, "And you would like to call him to let him know you're okay, right?"

Emily nodded her head, "Yes, I'll pay for the call. You can do that thing that they call you back and..."

Angie butted in, "Emily, don't worry about the cost. It's just a few quid, so don't worry."

Emily thanked her, then added, "Well, I'm going to say this. You have been so kind to me and Lionel since the accident. You are going to have to let me treat you and Barry before we leave, okay? And I'm sorry, Angie. That's not negotiable!"

Angie laughed and nodded her head. "Okay, we've got a deal then, yes." They both laughed together.

It was another hot day. Emily was so tired. Angie suggested she lay out in the garden on one of the loungers and try to get some sleep. "Sounds like a plan, Ange," she added. She arose from her seat to enter the patio, and stretched out on the lounger. Lionel was in the aviary helping Barry. It wasn't an easy task. Barry was in tears virtually all the time, but he had to get the birds out of there.

There was a knock at the door. Angie answered the call and opened the door. It was the police. "Good morning." As the officer said it, he realised that 'Good morning' was hardly the right phrase, and his expression said as much. "Sorry. Not off to a good start am I? We are here to do forensics, if it's convenient."

Angie showed them in and escorted them to the aviary. Barry and Lionel had cleaned up. The officers seemed to be unhappy that things were not left as they were. Barry apologised, saying he could not leave his dead parrots on the floor. It was undignified. The officers understood and said it wasn't a problem.

SOCO, as they were called, were in the aviary for more than an hour. Barry was surprised, yet pleased. He hoped it meant that they were being thorough. Yes, they had their man bang to rights, but when it went to court, you didn't want the scenario where somebody got off on a technicality. No, this was the correct procedure.

The officers walked into the house via the patio and said that they had all they needed. Barry showed then to the door and waited till they got in their van to open the gates.

Barry walked into the lounge. "Well, that's it, then." Lionel mentioned the length of time they were there and that, surely, they had the man responsible, so what was the problem. "He was caught red-handed Barry. He can't wriggle his way out of this, surely."

Barry nodded in agreement. The culprit was bang to rights. What concerned Barry was why somebody would do what he did. Was there an ulterior motive? He even wondered whether Jock fucking McBride was the one behind it.

Angie seemed very quiet, which was hardly a surprise, given the last twenty-four hours. Barry noticed and was very aware that she needed an arm round her shoulder. "There, Doll. You're okay. We'll be okay. I've already been in touch with our supplier and he's looking for replacements as we speak."

Angie wasn't happy. "Barry, you don't understand. I... We were close to the birds that were killed. They were like family. You can't just bring other birds in and say that's it, everything's back to normal. Every one of those birds had their own personality. You can't just bring other birds in and say that's it, sorted." Angie was in tears.

Barry understood. Of course, she was right. There was a connection with all the birds. Barry was trying to get back to basics and Angie was struggling. It's just the way things were. They'd lost, in the final count, fourteen pairs of African greys. It was heartbreaking.

Lionel took Emily for a walk to the bottom of the garden. "Are you alright, Em?"

Emily tried to smile. "No, not really Lionel." He cuddled her, and she just squeezed him tightly.

Suspicion

Jock McBride was waiting for a call. It had been more than twenty-four hours since the job should have been done, yet he still hadn't called.

He was tempted to call him, though he was no fool. His number couldn't be associated with the goings on if things went 'tits up'. The likelihood was that the police would have Jimmy's phone, so it was prudent not to give them any ammunition. He thought about calling his contact at the police station but decided against it. Masons were masons and they kept their own counsel. If there was something he needed to worry about, he would be notified soon anyway.

His thoughts went back to the incident at the King's Arms. If he was honest, he wasn't unduly bothered. There was nothing to link him to the death of Emily Fleet's friend so, consequently, he was not bothered. After all, he was the local Mayor. His position in the community demanded respect.

His idea to get Jimmy Miller to 'nut' the plumber's parrots was probably ill conceived, but he had no time for Mr. Barry Wilson. He'd broken his niece's heart and thrown her away like a piece of toilet paper. For Jock, that had crossed the line. Nobody, but nobody, messed with his family. He was in his office when his secretary called and said that a police officer was on the phone and wanted to talk to him.

"Put him through, please," he requested.

It was Barry Walker. "Jock," he said.

"How are you, Barry? How's the family? All good?" Jock asked.

"Jock, your man..." He paused. "We've got him in custody, Jock."

Jock thought for a second. "And?"

"What do you mean 'And?' Didn't you hear what I said? We've got him bang to rights. There's nothing I can do for him, Jock. He's going down," Barry added.

Jock didn't share Officer Walker's concern. Jimmy Miller would never talk, not in a million years. "Barry," Jock was smiling. "Barry, take a breath. He is not going to say anything, okay? As far as it goes, he will say zip, nothing. Do you get it? He's mine, I tell you, mine."

Jock was ready to put the phone down when Officer Walker changed tack. "Jock, can you put my mind at rest?"

Jock was starting to lose his patience but said, "Go ahead."

"Jock, I'm going to ask a question, and I want the truth, okay?" declared the officer.

Jock replied, "Of course. What's the question?"

"Did you have anything to do with the accident at Gun Hill?" asked Barry Walker.

There was an eerie silence. Jock didn't like his tone. "What, are you crazy? Do you think I could be involved in a terrible tragedy like that? Quite frankly, Barry, I think you should take a long hard look at yourself before accusing me of such a terrible thing." Once again, Jock was smiling. He imagined Officer Walker's face not liking what he was hearing, but realising that the Lord Mayor of Thurrock would never stoop to this level, would he?

"Okay Jock, I'm sorry. It's just that, well, you know what I mean."

Jock replied, "I understand, Barry. I'm sure you're only doing and saying the things you have to. Now, you sort yourself out and get yourself home to your lovely wife as soon as you can, do you hear?"

Barry heard. He wasn't convinced but he was sure of one thing. There was no way any of this was going to come back on him. They said their goodbyes and agreed to let things settle down.

Jock was nonchalant. He was relaxed and couldn't see that anything was going to upset his plan. Indeed, it was time to move things along. He wrote a note to his secretary to forward the C.P.O to Jack Fleet House, making sure that the opportunity to lodge an appeal was not put in the letter. He did, though, expect there to be an appeal, but why should he make it easy for them? Phase two was under way. He'd meet Terry tomorrow to let him know the state of play.

Meanwhile, his niece, Lucy, was trying to make sense of everything that was happening. She'd had her suspicions but let them go, thinking there was no way her uncle would be involved in anything as serious as the death of a human being. The Gun Hill accident was simply that, a terrible tragedy. No, her uncle was not involved. She almost believed what she had just thought. There was doubt in her mind; she just wasn't sure. It was time to let it go, forget about it. She did consider leaving her post at the Gazette. She was still young. Love hadn't been kind to her. Maybe it was time she moved on. She'd saved well and could afford to travel for a year or so. She'd had enough of Grays. She'd had enough of Mr. Wilson. Basically, she'd had enough of everything.

The Writing On The Wall

The planned purchase of Jack Fleet House was entering, for all concerned, a critical stage. The Compulsory Purchase Order that the council was seeking to purchase the land that Jack Fleet House was on, and the surrounding area of around four acres, was under review by the Government. Jock McBride was so confident. In fact, you could say he was over-confident that his plans would come to fruition. At council meetings, there had been calls for a public meeting so that the public could have a say and ask questions like 'why' and 'does the council have a heart'.

Yes, Jock did control the council, but more than one or two had quietly asked him to give the locals a chance to ask the pertinent questions. They were given short shrift by their leader, as if to say, "How dare you question me! What the Mayor wants the Mayor gets. Don't you realise that I'm in control."

Due to the concern from his councillors, Jock was considering actually agreeing to a public meeting. His secretary entered his office. "There is a Penny Lamb to see you."

Jock looked up from his horse racing paper. "Who?"

"A Miss Penny Lamb. I think she's from the Gazette, but I've not heard of her before," his secretary added.

"Tell her to make an appointment for next week," Jock replied sharply.

"Okay," she said and left the office.

Penny stood her ground. "I'm here on behalf of the local paper and I'm not waiting a week. Christ, it'd be easier to see the Pope. Go and tell him I'm not moving and if he doesn't come out and tell me why he won't see me, it'll be front page news of the kind that he will not enjoy, considering he's public enemy number one out there at the moment!"

The secretary was about to go back and see her boss, when he came out of his office. "Hello, Ms. Lamb. Won't you come in? Would you like some coffee?"

Penny shook her head. She had met him before a few years ago for a similar reason and, straight away, had realised he was a smarmy piece of work.

"Take a seat. It's Penny, isn't it?" Jock smiled.

Penny sat near the window. "Yes, it's Penny."

"So, what can I do for you?" Jock asked.

Penny had worked for Ronnie Dexter on numerous occasions and one of the reasons Ronnie was happy to employ her services was simple. She didn't hold back. She explored every angle. She wasn't afraid to go for the jugular. Oh yes, Penny was a handful alright.

"Well, Mr. Mayor, I'll come straight to the point. Jack Fleet House. Why? Why, Mr. Mayor, when there are so many other areas ready for home building that would not require C.P.O.s, and certainly not mean the closing down of a very good and well supported children's home? The locals want an explanation, not sound bites, Mr. Mayor. They believe there is some skulduggery going on and that you, Mr. Mayor, are behind it. In fact, some would say, responsible, though I would rather say culpable, Mr. Mayor." She was measured, but her opening gambit was full of emotion. She was good.

Jock was like the proverbial swan. He didn't seem bothered, but inside he was fuming. He initially told himself to be tactful, but the underlying feelings surfaced. "You, you come in here. Who do you think you are? I'm the Mayor. Do you know what? Go and print what you like and then tell Dexter to get his solicitor ready to deal with the consequences. Now, if you don't mind. I've got more important things to do!" As soon as he'd finished speaking, he picked up the Racing Post and made sure Ms. Lamb saw the name of the paper he was choosing to read, rather than give her any more time.

"Thank you so much, Mr. Mayor. You've been a great help. Just don't be surprised if your plans fall at the last fence, like I hope your horse does!" She turned and left the Mayor with a huge grin. "Bye," she said sarcastically.

The Mayor put his paper down. He was angry. No, he was fuming. One thing the meeting had done was convince Jock that he was now ready to use one of the aces up his sleeve.

Yes, they can have their meeting and he would ensure that as many of the locals that wanted to attend would be able to. "Civic Hall," he mumbled to himself. "We'll have it at the Civic Hall."

Another thought crossed his mind. "Please, Mr. Parrot. Please be there."

****

Penny walked into the Gazette office. Lucy didn't look at her as she entered Ronnie's office.

"Well?" Ronnie asked, eager to know what had been said.

Penny sat down and gave a gasp. "I need a drink, Ron."

Ronnie got up. "I'll get Lucy to..."

"Ron, no. I need a drink!" she repeated.

Ronnie got her meaning and looked at his watch. "It's a bit early, but I suppose it won't hurt."

Twenty minutes later, they were in the King's Arms. Carol took their drinks to the table by the bay window.

Penny said, "Thank you. Have you got any sandwiches?"

Carol replied, "I'll see what we've got. I have to make them fresh." Penny thanked her and said that would be great.

Ronnie, still eager to find out what had happened, said, "Now Pen. What went on with our Mr. Mayor?"

Penny relayed the goings on and left Ronnie in no doubt that she had got under his skin.

She laughed. "His craggy face was as red as a beetroot. I don't usually do this Ronnie, but you know I've got a lot of time for you and your local rag. So, I'll let you into a little secret." She went into her handbag and pulled out the smallest tape recorder Ronnie had ever seen.

"You didn't!" he gasped.

Penny smiled. "I did!" Penny's sandwich arrived just after she had furnished Ronnie with a small pair of headphones. She watched the expressions on Ronnie's face as the tape played back the whole conversation.

"Wow," Ronnie said, "You really did get under his skin. That's my girl."

"I like to please my employer, Ronnie," she smiled.

Ronnie knew that he couldn't use anything from the tape due to Mr. Mayor not being informed of its use. Even so, it made the editor of a very popular local paper and his bulldog of a reporter more determined to prevent this horrible man from getting his own way and causing misery for a lot of people.

While they were sitting in the bay window, Ronnie noticed an XJR pull around the corner. He thought it looked like Barry's. Sure enough, Barry entered the bar from the carpark. He was joined by two other gents. Almost immediately, they were joined by Ronnie, the landlord. It transpired that a pool match was behind the meeting, some sort of challenge. Barry acknowledged Ronnie with a wave.

Ronnie had told Lucy where he would be until she finished work. Carol, who was behind the bar on her own, now beckoned Ronnie Dexter over to the bar. "It's Jock McBride," she said as she handed him the phone.

"Hello," Ronnie was curious.

"Oh, hello Ronnie. I thought you'd like to know that, after an impromptu meeting, my council have decided to hold a public meeting on the Jack Fleet House issue. We will confirm the date and time in a couple of days, okay?" Jock said.

Ronnie smiled but didn't let on to the Mayor how pleased he was. "Thank you for telling me. Okay, bye." He walked back to the table "Well, what do you know?"

Penny looked at him, expectantly. "What, Ron?"

"That was our Mr. Mayor. He's agreed to a public meeting." He smiled.

Penny punched the air. "Yes! That's great, Ron."

Ronnie was not punching the air. He was more reflective.

Penny wasn't sure why Ronnie seemed subdued "What's up, Ron?"

Ronnie sensed that the Mayor had something up his sleeve. He didn't have a clue what but, all the same, why would he agree to it suddenly?

While they were in this quiet moment, Barry came over after he'd ordered a round of drinks. "Hiya, Ron. How are you?"

Ronnie tried to be upbeat. "Well, our beloved Mayor has just phoned me to say that the council have agreed, no sorry, have decided, to hold a public meeting so the people of Thurrock can have their say on Jack Fleet!"

Barry was shocked. "Really? I can't believe it. He must have an ulterior motive, Ron. He's got something up his sleeve."

Ronnie was nodding in agreement. "That's just was I was thinking, Barry."

Penny didn't understand why these two were so down. "Hey guys, surely you've enough about you to tie him up in knots. I mean it didn't take much from me to get to him this afternoon."

Ronnie explained to Barry that Penny had a bit of a showdown with the Mayor a couple of hours before.

"Okay Ron. Gotta get back to the pool room. Big challenge match on. Keep me posted, mate," Barry said.

"I will Barry. See you later."

Penny asked to be notified when the meeting was and then she was on her way. "See you soon, Ron. Don't forget to let me know."

"No, I won't forget. Thanks, Pen. Bye love," he replied.

The Pool Match

Barry said, "Okay then, Davey. Yeah, I'll pick you up around 4:30ish. Will your mate be at yours, then?"

Davey told him that yes, he would be at his place in time and thanked Barry. Barry hung up the phone. It was 3:15. He just about had time to nip home, have a quick shower, then on to Davey's to pick them up. Then on to the King's Arms for the 'game of the century'. He laughed quietly to himself.

Tommy laughed at him. "You're a nutter, Barry." He was being a mate and Barry laughed with him.

Barry asked him, "How did you get on at the vet's the other day, Tom? Not seen you since."

Tommy stopped smiling. "I should have been a vet, Baz. Robbing bastards! Do you know it doesn't matter what it is they do for your pet and, dare I say it, it doesn't matter what pet you've got. They charge you £149 for nearly every treatment. God help you if your pet has to stay with them. I could stay at the Hilton for less money."

Barry nodded in agreement. He knew only too well the sense of extortion when paying for vet fees. "Anyway, Tom, I'm off. Got a pool match tonight. Why don't you come over and watch?"

Tom looked at Barry, smiled and said, "Baz, I'm sorry. Not a pool fan. I'm old school. Snooker, yes. Pool, no. No comparison. Sorry."

Barry had to agree. "Completely agree, Tom. Do you know, I reckon if you or me played the world champion pool player, say ten frames yeah, I reckon we'd win at least one or two of them, maybe more. How many frames would you win if you played the best snooker player in the world, eh? Absolutely zip, zero. You probably wouldn't win a frame if you had a fifty start. They both concurred. Barry said his goodbye and set off home for a quick shower.

Angie was expecting him.

"Looking forward to this, Doll. A good session with nice people and we're sure to have a laugh, too. Are you coming over later or not?"

Angie smiled and nodded. "Actually, we're all coming over around six, Baz. Lionel has promised us a meal in the restaurant. I'm really looking forward to it."

"Well, that's alright then. I'll probably grab a burger or something, Doll. I'm sure we won't be playing all night," he said.

Angie raised her eyebrows. "Really, Baz, I don't mind how long you play, but don't tell me you will only play for a couple of hours, please!" She laughed.

It was the fastest shower he'd ever had and, in no time, he was kissing Angie. "See you in a bit then, Doll," he said as he walked out the front door.

Angie laughed to herself "Bless him. He loves a challenge and, to be fair, he's not a bad loser, but it's still a matter of life or death."

He was pulling into Davey's drive as a taxi was pulling out. Davey and Scouse Andy were at the front door, ready and waiting. As they got into the car, Barry said, "What you got there, then? You got your own cues?" He laughed. "You must be pro's then, I reckon."

Davey introduced his partner for the contest. "This is my right-hand man, Barry, Scouse Andy, but you don't have to use the 'Scouse' every time, okay?" he laughed.

Barry turned and shook Andy's hand, and said, "So, what colour are you then, Andy?"

Andy gave a little grin. "The only colour you should be when you're a Scouser, Barry. I'm red through and through."

Barry wanted to test him out, so he said "Well, that's probably a good thing, Andy, because you're going to have a red face tonight, red with embarrassment." He laughed, and Davey saw the funny side too.

It was a five-minute drive to the King's Arms. They parked in the carpark at the rear of the pub and entered the bar. It was quiet. Thankfully the pool room was empty. Ronnie had told his regulars that only one table would be available from around five in the afternoon. He'd done them proud too. The table looked immaculate. It had been brushed and ironed and even marked as well.

There was a couple sitting at the bay window table who Barry waved to. They ordered their drinks as Ronnie turned up. He'd been having a nap upstairs, he said. Barry introduced Davey and Andy and the four of them set off for the pool room.

"So, we get a free table then do we, as the landlord is playing? Is that right?" Barry laughed.

Ronnie was quick with his reply. "You spend some dosh over the bar tonight, you can have a free table. No problem."

They hadn't started yet and Barry was off to the bar for another round.

Ronnie said, "So, you've played together a while then?"

Andy said, "Yeah, we've been working together for most of our working lives and yes, socialising too. So, the answer to your question is yes."

Davey wouldn't have been so open about their experience on the pool table, but there we go. It was done.

Ronnie said, "What's keeping Barry? He's been ages." He walked out to the bar. While he was gone, Davey said, "Listen, these two are probably going to be the hardest we will have ever faced, so don't go for silly shots, okay? If you can't pot, tuck 'em up, okay?"

Scouse Andy nodded. "We'll take 'em, Davey boy. Don't worry. Have they said anything about cash, you know, per frame or what?"

Davey smiled and shook his head. "I don't think there's going to be any cash changing hands, Scouse."

Ronnie didn't make it to the bar, as Barry was already on his way back with a tray of drinks. When they entered the pool room, Ronnie said, "Okay then, let's get this road on the show!"

Davey and Scouse looked confused.

Barry commented, "We were thinking a fiver a frame or play till we drop. And the losers pay for the food as well as the sherbet. What do you think?"

"Whatever," Davey replied, "let's get it on."

At that, Barry held a coin and asked the two young pretenders, "Heads or tails?"

Davey quickly said, "Tails". The coin dropped; it was tails.

Barry said, "Up to you. Who's gonna break?"

Davey thought for a second and said, "Okay, your break."

Ronnie didn't give Barry a chance to say anything and hit the most powerful break shot that Davey and Scouse had ever seen. When the balls stopped rolling, two reds had gone. Inside three minutes, Ronnie was on the black. He looked at Barry, who just nodded. Ronnie lined up the shot and doubled the black.

"Yes," Barry shouted, as Ronnie offered his hand for a high five.

Davey and Scouse looked at each other and realised they were in a proper match.

Angie, Emily and Lionel got into the taxi. Lionel was okay, though he was restless. Emily sensed that all was not quite the way he wanted it to be. She promised herself to broach the subject at the first opportunity. When they arrived at the pub, the bar was relatively quiet. Barb was serving, and Angie asked how the match was going. Barb started laughing, "It's like the World Pool Championships out there. Some of the pub's pool team are here and they are out there watching the game."

Angie asked, "Who's winning, Barb?"

Barb's smile said it all, "Who do you think, Ange?" Angie knew by the expression on Barb's face that Barry and Ronnie were winning.

They ordered their drinks and decided to go and watch the game. When they walked in, you could have heard a pin drop! Barry was at the table. He had three yellow balls left. Davey and Scouse had the black adjacent to the middle pocket. The first shot left, two yellows, the next, one! Barry walked away from the table and took a drink. Ronnie sat on his stool as smug as you like. Barry returned to the table. The next and last yellow wasn't difficult, but to get a decent position on the black would be more of a problem. He and Ronnie whispered, well, who knows. Suffice it to say that Barry just rolled behind the yellow, leaving Scouse and Davey snookered. The watching crowd applauded. This really was being played at a very high level.

Scouse and Davey looked at the table and whispered their options. It was clear that they had to go for it, no question. Davey was next to play. The crowd murmured as he seemed to be looking at going off three cushions to hit and more than likely pot the black. Scouse leant over and said something to Davey, who stood up, walked around the table and then got into position. You could cut the atmosphere with the proverbial knife. Davey settled on the shot, drew back the cue, one cushion, two cushions, finally three cushions and stopped, half an inch short of the black. The crowd sighed.

"I believe that's two shots, Ron, don't you?" Barry was smiling. The next shot was Ronnie's. While they were now favourites, he still had to pot the last yellow and land on the black, though. Having two shots meant, really, that the pressure was off. Barry lined up over Ronnie's shoulder and they chatted quietly and agreed on the next shot.

There was quite a crowd now, and you sensed that the pressure was mounting. Ronnie walked around the table, making remarks that were his trademark. He never took pool seriously, but this was as good as it gets. He'd been deliberating for nearly five minutes by the time he addressed the cue ball. Three or four forward and backward motions with the cue, then smack! The yellow rattled in the pocket and came to rest against the cushion behind the black spot.

The locals sighed together. Still one shot. Davey and Scouse looked happier and sensed a victory in this long drawn out frame. Ronnie stepped back from the table, never said a word, looked along the cushion and promptly hit cushion and ball perfectly. The yellow rolled along, hugging the cushion until virtually stopping right over the corner pocket. The crowd sighed, then cheered as it fell into the hole. By then the cue ball was mid table three or four inches from the black and, as the black disappeared, Ronnie took a bow.

"I need a drink," was all that Ronnie said. He put his cue on the table and walked to the bar.

Scouse and Davey were gutted. They were now down three frames to none.

Barry went over to Angie with a big smile on his face. "Hello babe, you okay?"

Angie smiled, "I guess that you're winning, then?"

Barry was beaming, "Yes, I believe we are three up so far. Early days though, Doll." Angie wasn't surprised. The two old codgers had a habit of winning. She didn't really understand the game, but she was used to seeing her man on the winning side.

Ronnie returned with a round of drinks. Lionel was enjoying watching this duel between the young and old and it seemed clear to him that 'old' would win the day.

They decided to have a break for some food. Once they returned to the bar, the pool table drifted in their memory and three nil was to be the final score.

"We must do this again," Barry said.

Davey disagreed. "No, we mustn't. We must beat you next time. That's right, isn't it Scouse?" Andy nodded. "First blood to you guys, but we'll be back."

Consequences

Jimmy Miller was a mess. He was certain to go down for the offence of aggravated burglary, but his day was just about to get worse.

D I Carter visited him on remand at HMP Feltham. D I Carter looked at him as he walked in and sat on a stool opposite. Now D I Carter was holding all the cards and sat with a superior, almost smug, expression on his face. "Well, Jimmy, how are you? I do hope you are getting used to life behind bars, you know, as that's where you are going to be for the foreseeable."

Jimmy looked down at the floor. He was in the brown stuff alright.

"I've got some news for you, Jimmy; would you like to hear it?" the D I asked.

Jimmy never acknowledged the question.

D I Carter went ahead anyway. "Did you hear about the tragic accident near Gun Hill, Jimmy?"

Jimmy almost choked, but he managed to remain aloof.

"Well? Well, I'll tell you what I know and please tell me if I'm wrong won't you, Jimmy, please?" The D I went on to explain that somebody had tampered with the car that ended up in the ditch at the bottom of Gun Hill. "Now I wonder," he said, "where were you the night before the accident, Jimmy?"

Jimmy never spoke. In fact, he'd hardly said two words since being arrested over a week ago.

"Okay then, let me give you a, well, let me rephrase it. I think you did the damage to the vehicle that ended up killing the owner and injuring her passenger in that tragic accident." D I Carter's voice changed when he said the word 'accident'.

Jimmy was worried. It seemed that he'd been rumbled. He wondered how. He was careful. No, he was bluffing.

"Well?" D I Carter asked.

Jimmy, again, didn't speak.

"Jimmy, I'm going to let you in on a little secret. Do you know what DNA is?"

Jimmy sat not saying anything or letting on that he was listening to what was being said to him.

"Well, I'll tell you Jimmy. It's a foolproof system that is going to nail you good and proper. And do you know what? Your silence is going to guarantee a maximum sentence when you go to court tomorrow. You are done for, fella, done for. Do you hear?"

D I Carter moved his stool nearer to Jimmy. "Do you realise what I am saying, Jimmy? Now I know that basically you were a decent man. Sadly you moved in the wrong circles. But do you know what, Jimmy? I don't believe that these incidents are of your own volition. What I mean is, I'm of the opinion that you were asked to do these things by somebody. Who, I'm not sure. But you must ask yourself, why should I go down on my own for doing somebody else's dirty work."

Jimmy never flinched. He wouldn't, couldn't grass on anyone, but he couldn't argue with the words that would keep recurring in his head, "Why should I be the only one to go down?" He did, however, manage to remain expressionless.

D I Carter said one more thing as he left. "Jimmy, think on this. When we nail you for the accident, well, I guess it'll be a case of throwing the key away. You need to ask yourself, why me alone. See you in court, Jimmy." He got up and left.

The warden opened the door back to the cell. Jimmy was really troubled, but he still said to himself, "I'm no grass."

D I Carter was convinced that somebody was pulling the strings where Jimmy Miller was concerned. He'd listened to a few people who all had the same opinion. They were convinced that, as hard as it was to believe, the local Mayor was behind these recent incidents. He had promised to investigate their suggestions, but he felt it would be fruitless.

Jimmy was back in his cell. He had never been this low. Why, oh why did he not just say no when Jock asked the question. Yes, Jock had rewarded him, but now he was destined for prison, probably for most of his life. He considered the consequences of being a grass. It didn't sit well with him. It wasn't really about 'honour amongst thieves' but he just couldn't bring himself to do it. He looked at his watch. His children would be round the dinner table. He missed them. He thought he had never been in such a difficult position.

He lay back on his bunk and tried to sleep. As he lay there, he considered calling Jock, but he wasn't sure he would answer. Jock was as shrewd as they came, and he wasn't about to let his guard down. Jimmy had a choice to make. Really, it was as simple as that. He might do a few years less if he grassed.

Here it was again, that feeling, that feeling of being in a hopeless place. At that moment, he decided what he was going to do.

D I Carter was back at his office, working late as usual, when his colleague, David Buxton, entered his office. "Well, what's the score on Miller, then?" Buxton asked.

D I Carter looked up from his desk. "I'm not really sure, Dave. Part of me wants to believe the locals but, in truth, we are not going to get anything from Miller, so the link from the Mayor point of view is going to be a non-starter. I know we should probably bring the Mayor in but, for the time being, I think we should leave well alone. We might lose ground with him if he is involved. Really, we need Miller to come clean. It's as simple as that."

The two of them discussed the case for another half hour or so, then decided to call it a day.

The hearing at Basildon Magistrates Court was due to take place at around eleven o'clock. From the police's point of view, it was a formality. Jimmy Miller was going to the Crown Court at Chelmsford after today's proceedings.

D I Carter was in court two at Basildon when, a few minutes before the case was to be heard, Dave Buxton waved and motioned for Carter to leave the court room.

"What's up?" D I Carter asked.

"It's Jimmy Miller, Graham. He's topped himself," said Buxton.

D I Carter just sighed. "Do you know, Dave. I did give it a thought, you know, that maybe he needed watching. He was in a hopeless position and, because of this, we are no nearer to solving this case. One thing, though..." He stopped his walk back to the court room. "One thing, Dave. For me, this makes me think even more that there was somebody behind these crimes. So, let's look at the case from a different angle. Let's presume that there is a third party involved. Yeah, that's what we'll do."

They made their way to the carpark and headed off back to Grays nick. Carter was quiet on the drive back. Buxton had rarely seen him so thoughtful.

"I'll tell you what, Dave," Carter commented, "Let's have a look at Mr. Mayor. Discreetly, though. You know he's a mason, don't you?"

Buxton nodded. "Yes, I had heard as much. Is there a mason's lodge in Grays, then?"

Carter continued to look at the road ahead and said, "Oh yes, you'd better believe it."

Up North

Emily was restless. Lionel couldn't wait to get her out of this situation. He wanted to ask her to leave and go to Glasgow with him, but he was considerate of her predicament. She had lost her best friend at the end of the day. Part of him wanted to not ask, but tell, Emily that he was taking her to Glasgow, end of subject. The problem was that, to do that was out of character for Lionel. He loved Emily and felt he couldn't be as pushy as that.

Angie entered the lounge where Emily was relaxing on the sofa. "You know what you need Emily, don't you?" Angie didn't wait for a response. "You need to get away from here, love. You've had a terrible ordeal. It's time that you gave yourself a lift. Why don't you nip up to Scotland with Lionel before you go back to Peru?" Angie had tried to make her suggestion sound like it was her idea, but she wasn't sure she was that convincing.

Emily looked up from her magazine. For a moment she didn't speak. Then, just as Lionel entered the room, she said, "Well, I'm waiting to be asked, Angie!"

Lionel interrupted. "Waiting to be asked what, Em?" Lionel stood looking at Emily, anxious for her reply.

"Angie was just saying we should go to your beloved homeland for a few days. What do you think?" Emily asked.

Lionel tried to hide his true feelings. "If that's what you want, Em. It goes without saying that I'm looking forward to taking you back home, but it's your decision, love."

Emily didn't delay her response. "Okay then, let's go. Can you sort it, Lionel?"

He smiled. "What do you think? Just one thing. Do you want to fly or drive?"

Emily felt drawn to the idea of driving up. She'd see some of the old country. Yeah, that would be good. "Drive," she replied.

"Okay," Lionel said. "leave it with me. Do you want to leave as soon as possible or what?"

Emily was looking forward to this mini adventure. "Yes, why not? We can book or just turn up at a B and B on the way. Yes, that's what we'll do, Line."

They were both happy. Lionel went to the front lounge to book the car hire. Angie was pleased because she sensed that Emily needed a break, and Lionel had confided in her that he wanted to take her away for a few days.

Lionel had been given the number of a national car hire company that would come to your address, rather than vice versa. Sure enough, within the hour, there was a buzz from the gate intercom.

Barry opened the gate. He'd just returned from tending to the birds. "Okay then," he said as Emily and Lionel took their cases out to the car. "You've had enough of Essex, then. Well, if I wasn't so busy, I reckon we'd have come up with ya!"

Lionel smiled. "And you'd be more than welcome, Barry. You've been a wonderful host. You and Angie are the best."

The hosts walked back inside. Angie asked, "How long will that take, Baz? It's gotta be a long drive."

Barry nodded his head. "Probably looking at a good eight hours, Doll. Though they are going to stop on the way rather than drive all night."

They were on the A1 in no time. It was early evening. Lionel had looked at his map and worked out an approximate halfway point. Emily was comfortable. Her seat was reclined, not all the way back, but she was more than ready to sleep.

The weather was fine. Lionel liked the car. It was not by any means a small car. It was a smooth ride. Emily drifted off to sleep. Lionel saw a sign, Blyth Services. He was now looking for the slip road. He'd booked a room in a town called Bawtry. Blyth Services was the junction he needed to get to the B and B.

A few minutes later, they were in the carpark of the B and B. It was a little after nine-thirty. They'd made good time. When they checked in, Lionel asked if they could get a meal, maybe here or nearby. The receptionist gave them directions to a restaurant that stayed open late. They literally dropped their bags in the room and headed off to the restaurant.

It was a quaint little place with a rustic décor. The lights were low and the menu was quite varied. Lionel, when asked if they were ready to order by a young blonde-haired lady, said, "Have we got time for a couple of drinks or…"

The waitress replied, "You have indeed got time, sir. What do you fancy?" Her accent was very strong Yorkshire.

Lionel smiled. "Emily, what would you like?"

Emily thought for a moment. She couldn't even remember a time when she had drunk as much as she had in the last few days. It was session after session. Nevertheless, she said, "JD and coke, please; a double."

Lionel laughed. "Do you know what, Em? I'll have one of those too!"

It turned out the restaurant didn't close until one in the morning, so the two of them took full advantage and had a few drinks before their meal and a bottle of vino with their meal. The walk back to their B and B was quite long as Lionel couldn't remember where it was and unfortunately, at this late hour, there wasn't a soul around. They eventually arrived and tried unsuccessfully to go up to their room quietly. Emily's giggles would have woken the dead, as would the 'shhh' sound that Lionel was making to stop Emily giggling. There were no bedroom Olympics tonight. They were both sound asleep within minutes.

Emily woke with a start and looked at her watch. It was four-thirty. She couldn't get Maureen out of her mind. She cuddled up to Lionel, who initially didn't move. Emily was hungry, but not for food, and her hand was exploring Lionel's body. It had the desired effect and they had, what Lionel called in the morning, 'a quickie'.

Emily fell asleep again. This time she slept uninterrupted. After breakfast, they set off on the road to Glasgow. The journey was largely without incident. When they pulled up in a housing estate in the suburbs of Glasgow, Emily said. "What are we doing here, Lionel? We're in the middle of nowhere."

"Hardly," Lionel replied, "This is my Aunt Jenny's place." Emily was a few paces behind Lionel as he rang the doorbell. There was no answer.

"Well?" Emily asked.

Lionel smiled. "Don't worry, Em," and walked around to the kitchen door. He lifted a pot to retrieve the back-door key. "You're not down south now, Em," he said as he opened the door.

On first view from the outside, Emily was unimpressed about the standard of accommodation. She was no snob, but the building wasn't what you'd call salubrious. Once inside, however, she was pleasantly surprised. The kitchen was stunning, as was the rest of the house. Beautiful. Lionel took the lead and beckoned Emily to follow him upstairs. After entering the wrong bedroom, he eventually led Emily into their room, which was, as was no surprise now, given the quality of the rest of the house, a beautiful room.

They heard someone talking downstairs. Lionel announced. "She's home, Em."

As they returned to the downstairs living room, Emily was laughing at the accent of Lionel's Aunt Jenny. "Hello darling. You must be Emily. How are yah, girl? Is 'e lookin' after ya?" Jenny had no airs and graces. She was from the southeast but nearer to the east end of London. Emily took to her straight away. "Jenny, it's lovely to meet you. Lionel hasn't said a word about you!" She winked at Jenny.

"Bertie," Jenny called out so loud everybody jumped. "Sorry, Emily. Bertie, you get that kettle on, and don't forget the cakes and biscuits." She leant over and whispered to Emily, "I have to shout love, 'e's deaf as a post." Emily smiled, then laughed as Jenny marched into the kitchen, dishing out her orders.

By the time the tea arrived, there was enough food at the table to feed the whole street.

"Wow," was all Emily could say.

Jenny commented. "I know, pet. You don't get this down south, do yah? Lucky to get a fucking cup of tea in it, Bert?"

Bert looked up and said, "What Jen?" They all laughed.

Jenny said, "I said, ain't the weather been crap, Bert? Yeah, raining every day for the last week, 'cept today 'cos you're 'ere Lino, ain't ya?"

Emily looked at Lionel with a huge smile. Lionel shrugged his shoulders. Jenny went upstairs and Lionel asked Emily what her first impression was of Jenny. Emily said, "I think she's a proper lady, Line, a real down to earth proper lady."

They sat chatting for ages. It must have been a couple of hours or more. Jenny showed the compassionate side of her nature while they reflected on the accident, saying yes, it's a tragic thing to happen, but it'd be wrong to dwell too long on it. The best cure for it is to move on, put it behind her. She'll never forget what happened, but her friend wouldn't want her to be sad all the time, so we all have to move on with our lives.

"So, what we gonna do for the rest of the day then, Lino?"

Lionel looked at Emily and thought that a quiet evening might be the order of the day, though how quiet it would be in the company of Aunt Jenny was anybody's guess.

Honesty

Angie was changing the sheets on the spare bed where Lionel and Emily slept. She really didn't mind them staying. Having said that, she was glad they had the place to themselves again. It had been hectic to say the least, and alcohol had been too much in evidence. Even when they had stayed in, the evenings were all too often built around another drinking session. Still, now they were back to some kind of normality.

They'd be okay. To be honest, Angie found some company a good thing, mainly because she didn't have much time to reflect on Barry's affair. As she was thinking these thoughts, she still couldn't believe that he'd actually been unfaithful. Sure, she had been culpable, inasmuch as she had closed the door, so to speak, on the sex side of things. It wasn't done intentionally. It was just one of those things. Since the affair, she hadn't apologised and a part of her asked why should she? But there was a feeling that was growing inside that his behaviour, in a way, was understandable.

She had known that Barry loved the company of women, always had done. Yet, this had never happened before. Or had it? She was sure that this was the only time her man had strayed. She remembered a time when Lucy first came to learn about the task of looking after the birds. She said to herself then, "Wow, she's a stunner; Barry will be loving this." But never did it enter her head that he would stray with anyone, least of all Lucy! Oh well, crack on Angie, you silly cow! A few minutes passed, then it hit her. Surely not Lucy. No, she wouldn't. No.

The mind is an unbelievable thing. You can literally concentrate on one thing, but you are not really in control. And here she was, determined that it couldn't be Lucy, no way. Yet her mind wouldn't play the game she wanted. She started to doubt herself. Why does Lucy not want to come here anymore to help with the birds? Coincidence? Or had she got something to hide? Angie was still of the opinion that Lucy wasn't involved in any way, but there and then she decided to meet up with this young beautiful girl.... No, she was a woman. Any man would fancy her. She was sure that she wouldn't just ask her straight up. No, she would just assess her reactions as they spoke about everyday things, including Barry. She would be able to tell. Yes, that was the right thing to do.

She carried on tidying the spare room and finished up by getting the hoover out and, before she knew it, she was virtually spring cleaning the whole house. She sat down with a coffee and looked at the grandfather clock. It was nearly half past four. She didn't have a phone number for Lucy, but she would still be at work.

A couple of minutes later, Lucy's phone rang. "Hello, Thurrock Gazette, Lucy speaking. How can I help?"

"Good," Angie thought. "Hello, Lucy. It's Angie. How are you?"

Lucy was not prepared for this and, try as she may, she was unable to answer her caller's question comfortably. "Oh... An, oh hello, Mrs. Wilson, I'm good... How are... Is everything okay?"

Angie was looking in the mirror in the hallway at herself and couldn't hide how she was feeling. "I was wondering if we could meet up for a coffee sometime. No rush. Just have a chat, you know."

Lucy needed to avoid a confrontation. She wasn't confident she could hide her feelings if cornered by the wife of the man she fell for. "Well, Mrs. Wilson..."

Angie butted in, "Lucy, it's Angie. Call me Angie."

Lucy thought that Angie wasn't making this easy. "Okay. Sorry, Angie. I'm really very busy. I don't know when I'll be free, but I'll try. Give me a few days. Would that be okay, Angie?"

Angie said that would be fine and the call ended. She walked back into the lounge and picked up her cup of coffee. Was she sure? Not really. She did seem to be flustered at first, but it could have been anything that caused that. She was at work and she was always very busy. To call her out of the blue like that, well, maybe it was a natural reaction.

Angie walked into the kitchen, rinsed her cup and picked a wine glass from the rack. She went to the fridge and opened a bottle of Chardonnay. Her mind was in control now and she just couldn't get Lucy out of her thoughts. By the time Barry got home just after six, she was about to burst. Barry's day had been busy. After pecking Angie on the cheek, he grabbed a beer from the fridge.

Angie was on her third glass of wine. The red mist was rising in her. There was nothing she could do to quell the rising tide of emotion. She just had to say what was on her mind.

As yet, she hadn't spoken to her man since he'd come home, but what she was about to say would shake the foundations of their marriage. "Did you sleep with Lucy?" There, she'd said it.

She was expecting a firm denial and Barry didn't disappoint. "What!" he said. "Did I sleep… Ange, what on earth gave you that idea?"

Angie didn't respond. She wanted to hear what he had to say, and listen and look at his body language.

"I really don't know why you would say something so crazy… Lucy? Really, Ange, I promise you, I.." He stopped talking as if he was in shock.

Angie then spoke. "I spoke to Lucy earlier and…"

Barry butted in. "And she said I slept with her?"

It was Angie's turn to butt in. "No, she didn't, but she, to me, seems to be hiding something. Anyway, we are meeting up for a coffee. I'll sort it out then."

Barry went quiet. He wished now he'd come clean right from the start. There was only one way this was going to end. Now, though, it was too late to confess. Or was it? He had wondered whether Lucy had told her uncle about their affair. Surely, if she had, he would have used it by now. He loved to be in control. Maybe, though, he did know and was waiting for a better time to drop the bombshell.

Angie opened another bottle of wine and sat in the lounge. Barry finished his beer, poured a drop of whiskey in his favourite glass and added a couple of ice cubes. He sat opposite his wife, the love of his life, and was about to confess, when Angie said, "Baz, I don't know if you slept with Lucy, but I'm going to say this. If it was Lucy or not, I just want things to get back to normal. I want you to know that I will defy anyone who tries to throw a bomb under our relationship. They will get a short shrift from me. I will not now speak to Lucy. As far as I'm concerned, the matter is closed."

Barry didn't know how to respond but, once he started crying, Angie knew her hunch was correct. It was Lucy. She had forgiven him. She would not let on to anyone. Why should she? It was nobody else's business. She felt responsible on an equal level. Sure, he shouldn't have done what he'd done, but, if she had been her normal self, he wouldn't have felt the urge to be unfaithful. Tomorrow was a new day. Yesterday had gone.

Evidence Possibly?

D I Carter was informed of the death of Jimmy Miller a day or so ago. At the time, it seemed a clear case of suicide. However, SOCO investigated the incident over a longer than usual period of time, some twenty-six hours. The findings were passed to the Crown Prosecution Service forthwith and D I Carter addressed his team.

"It now seems that Jimmy Miller was murdered. I want each of you digging deep into all facets of this case. Leave no stone unturned. There are, sorry I should say there is, an open book on the hours you can spend on this case. What I want to see is one or two of you who are hungry enough to delve into the relevant issues surrounding this and other incidents which are most definitely linked. I want answers people. Now go to it!"

There was a buzz, which was music to the ears of the D I. He'd had the bulk of his team together for a number of years now and, though not always successful, they were diligent and methodical in their approach to whatever case was ahead of them. He retired to his office.

The biggest concern for him, though, was not related to his staff. He'd encountered problems before when dealing with secret societies. He'd heard mumblings that a senior officer was casting aspersions on the validity of his claims that one of the suspects, namely the Lord Mayor, could well be involved.

The Mayor was a member of the 'Free Masons', as was the senior officer. D I Carter quite frankly didn't give a shit if you'd committed a crime. He didn't care if you were the Pope or the Queen, he would take you down.

Inspector Buxton knocked on his door and entered when beckoned. "Sorry I missed the meeting Guv. I just got back from Feltham. It's a turn up for the books, isn't it!"

D I Carter was nodding in agreement. "What did they say was the cause of death, then?"

Inspector Buxton handed his D I the sheet of paper from the Forensic Investigation team. They had itemised their report. D I Carter read it out loud.

"On first impression, it appeared that Mr. Miller had hung himself. However, he had severe bruising to his upper arms and thighs which all pointed to foul play as it was physically impossible for Mr. Miller to inflict the injuries on himself. Added to this are statements from the prison officers who were on duty at the time, a P O Bloss and P O Wilson, who stated that a fracas took place at the recreation room around the pool table on or about the time that Mr. Miller was found to be deceased. It is the decision of the below Forensic Officers that the death of Mr. Miller was not of his own doing and also not accidental."

He entered the form into the case file and looked up at Inspector Buxton. "Well Dave, what do you think?"

Inspector Buxton paused for a second, "I'm with you. We need to dig the dirt on the Mayor, track back into his past. I believe he's originally from Glasgow. I'll get on the phone to CID up there and bang some heads together."

D I Carter was happy, happy that his lad, who he'd brought through the ranks, was thinking straight. It was looking bad for Mr. Mayor but, as yet, they had nothing concrete on him. He was, as everybody knew locally, a slippery customer. You could almost say 'smarmy', like a smiling assassin.

Inspector Buxton spoke to a couple of colleagues and got the ball rolling as to pulling out all the stops in the Glasgow history of Jock McBride.

****

Lionel and Emily had been in Glasgow just over twenty-four hours. Lionel had been on the phone for most of them, at least that's the way it seemed to Emily. Jenny, to her credit, had taken Emily by the hand and took her into town to get her away from Lionel's constant domination of the phone. They ate lunch and shopped to their hearts' content. Lionel, meanwhile, was convinced he'd met Mr. Mayor on the day of the funeral. He just couldn't remember who he was with that seemed to know him. Ah well, it would come back to him.

Emily arrived back after five hours of shopping, laden with carrier bags and designer boxes of shoes and clothing. Jenny said to Lionel, "Bloody hell, Lino. She can shop for England."

Lionel laughed and said, "That's my girl."

Jenny helped Emily upstairs with the fruits of her day's shopping. When she came down, she said to Lionel, "Hey Line, bumped into an old friend of yours in town."

Lionel asked, "Who's that then?"

"Oh, that Jimmy Mahoney. You know, you were at school together, weren't you?"

Lionel smiled. "Jimmy Mahoney! That's who it was. That's who was sitting with Jock, Jock McBride, the day of the funeral." He quickly found his diary, located Jimmy's number and gave him a call. There was no answer. He tried a few more times over the next hour or so, but to no avail.

Meanwhile the officers entrusted to get information on the Mayor from the CID in Glasgow were also not having any luck.

There were a few people with the surname McBride on their books, but all were accounted for in various ways. One had passed away three years ago. One had emigrated to Australia many years ago. Of the other three, there was nothing tangible to get hold of. It seemed they had hit a brick wall.

Lionel called Jimmy around seven in the morning. Just when he was about to hang up, a voice answered, "Who the fuck is this? Do you know what fucking time it is? Who the fuck are you?" He hadn't changed.

"Jimmy, it's me, Lionel," Lionel laughed.

It took a moment to sink in. "Lionel. Fuck me. Where are you? Don't you know there is a time difference? Where you calling from?"

Lionel laughed again. "Glasgow, Jimmy. I'm in Glasgow."

Jimmy muttered something about, so why call me so early or something like that. Then he said, "Ah well, I suppose we'd better meet up for a few bevvies then, Lino."

Lionel didn't argue. They arranged to meet at the venue where the funeral wake was held.

Lionel asked Emily, "You'll come, won't you, Em?"

Emily was already shaking her head. Her alcohol consumption in the past few weeks was out of control. "No Lionel, you go. I'll stay here with Jenny. She turned to look at Lionel's Aunt, who was nodding her head. "That's fine, Em. Fine by me."

Lionel went upstairs to have a shower. Around half an hour later, he was ready.

Emily was in the kitchen with Jenny. "I'm off then, Em, okay?" Lionel said.

Emily smiled. Jenny commented, "Don't be late, Lionel. You've got to show the city to your lady. Glasgow at night. What a sight." As she looked at Emily, she said, "So, what we going to do then, Em? I know…" A few minutes later the photo albums were out. Lionel as a kid. Hilarious.

Jimmy Mahoney was sitting at the bar on a stool when Lionel arrived. "Well, look at you, Lionel bloody Mason." He got off the stool and nearly fell over. He was only five feet tall.

"Jimmy, how are you?" Lionel asked.

"Well, I guess. Things are about the same as the last time I saw you, lad, at your uncle's funeral, except I'm six months or so older, ha ha, fucking six months older!"

Lionel beckoned Jimmy to sit at a table in the corner.

"Oh Lionel, are we talking about someone doing a dirty deed? Why are we in the corner?" Jimmy asked.

Lionel went back to the bar for a shot of whisky for Jimmy and a pint of Guinness for himself. After a couple of minutes of catching up on gossip, Lionel said, "Now, Jimmy, do you remember at the funeral you introduced me to Jock somebody. What was his name?"

Jimmy thought for a moment. "Can't remember, Line. Didn't you go into the other bar and sit on your own? Do you know what, I can't fucking remember. Fucking getting too old, that's what it is."

Lionel was getting frustrated, but he hoped Jimmy's recollection of that day would come back to him soon.

They had a couple more drinks then, when Lionel was about to leave, the barmaid who he had chatted to previously arrived for her shift.

He wondered if she remembered and decided to have another drink and have a chat with her.

Jimmy was slowly getting drunk, so Lionel left him at the table and sat on a stool at the bar. "It's Lisa, isn't it?"

The barmaid was filling the dishwasher. Lionel, unlike his old mate, could remember names. "I'm sorry, I'm not sure I know you. Have we met before?" she asked.

Lionel smiled and said, "Aye, lass. I came around to this bar when I should have been in the other one at a wake, about six months ago. Don't you remember? I said something like, "It's a big world out there Lisa, go and grab it girl' or words to that effect."

"Aye, got you now. The jet setter. Well well. Never thought I'd see you again. What you come back to this shithole for then?" She smiled.

Lionel laughed and said, "I love your accent. Really miss the home lingo. No Lisa, I'm visiting my Aunt. Do you remember when I sat in this bar? I was talking to a couple of locals. One was Jimmy Mahoney and the other was Jock."

Lisa cut in. "McGregor, Jock McGregor it was. I remember because he's not been around for years, since it happened."

Lionel's head turned. "Sorry, since what happened, Lisa?"

Lisa was reluctant to explain, but she asked Lionel to wait till it quietened down as it was fast approaching five and the bar was filling up. Lionel was okay with that and said he was going to nip out for an hour or so, but he would one hundred percent be back.

He exited the pub through the other bar. He noticed that Jimmy had paired up with some guys playing pool. He slipped out the door and set off to Jenny's.

It was only a ten-minute walk and, when he got there, he explained to Emily what had happened at the pub. Emily seemed keen and wanted to go back with him to find out more.

Jenny piped up, "Aye, lass, that den of iniquity ain't no place for a lady, especially not in the evening, let me tell ya!" Lionel agreed with Jenny. Reluctantly, Emily admitted defeat.

"I'll knock you some grub up Lino, okay?" Jenny asked.

"Okay then. I said I'd only be an hour, but she isn't going anywhere is she?" Lionel added.

Emily looked at Lionel with a sideways glance. She couldn't believe how lucky she was.

Twenty minutes later, Lionel thanked Jenny for his 'marvellous meal'.

Jenny joked, "You taking the fucking piss. I'll brain ya, Mason!"

Lionel was taking the piss. She'd done him beans on toast. Anything to fill a hole. He kissed Emily on the cheek and whispered he wouldn't be long and left, whistling as he shut the front door.

The pub was still fairly busy, but the landlord had arrived back from his golf society day earlier than expected due to somebody having a heart attack.

Lionel ordered a pint from Lisa. When she'd served him, she crossed over into the other bar and said something to her boss. When she returned, she said to Lionel, "Right, Mr. Jetsetter, I've got half an hour. Let's get a table."

"Do you want a drink, Lisa?" Lionel asked.

"No, I'm fine, though, I can't remember your name. What is it now?" she asked.

Lionel smiled, "It's Lionel."

"Ah, Lionel. Okay, it will have to do," she giggled. "Now, I'm not one hundred percent on all the facts, but I'll do my best for you."

Before she started, she changed her mind and asked Lionel for that drink. Lionel duly obliged. A few minutes later, Lionel sat next to her and asked the question, "You were going to tell me something about Jock... are you sure his name is McGregor?"

Lisa was sipping her glass of Chardonnay. "Yes, oh definitely yes. He was as slippery as anything. I always felt like he was undressing me, you know what I mean? Anyway, there's a name for people like him. Quite simply, he's a confidence trickster, a real nasty person. He didn't care who he conned but took great pleasure in stealing thousands off the old people. He used to tell them that investing money into stocks and shares was foolproof. He'd show them all the fancy brochures on new companies that would be 'floated' on the stock exchange in six months' time, and that the shares were estimated to start at £11 to £14 each. 'The opportunity' he said was to get shares now at a maximum £3.50. This meant that there was a fantastic opportunity to buy now and make three to four hundred percent profit, and the more you invest now, the more you make in six months' time."

Lionel sat open mouthed. Then he had to know. "What happened then, did he get caught?"

Lisa smiled, then frowned. "It seems that our mutual friend had been, at some time, a member of the Masons. Now I'm sure even you know that the Masons have police officers, judges and the like in their midst. The only good thing that came out of it, I mean some of the pensioners lost thousands, many thousands of pounds. As I said, the only good thing was he was told by his fellow Masons that yes, they'd manage to keep him out of prison, but he had to leave Scotland. He wasn't given a choice and that's it, Lionel. Good riddance, I say."

Lionel looked up at the ceiling. As helpful as this was, he needed concrete proof and getting that was a different problem. He thanked Lisa, who returned to the bar. He went to the bar to say thank you again, and gave her a ten-pound note. "Buy yourself a drink, Lisa, and don't forget that world is still waiting for you."

She smiled, "Thanks Lionel. Take care."

When he returned to Jenny's, he quickly told Emily and Jenny what had happened. Bertie was there, too, but he'd been at the whisky while Lionel had been out. The two of them sat listening to Lionel's news. Jenny couldn't believe she hadn't heard anything about it.

Emily eventually wondered out loud whether this could help the Jack Fleet problem. "Sadly," Lionel said, "We don't have proof. It was all swept under the carpet." They continued talking about the conman and suddenly, at the mention of Jock McGregor's name, Bertie shouted out, "Jock McGregor, cheating bastard, conned my dad out of ten grand, fucking pig of a man."

Jenny said, "Bertie, what you on about? Did he con your dad, then?"

Bertie was half asleep, but he seemed sure about what he said.

"Do you know what, Lionel?" Jenny added, "Now you come to mention it, I vaguely remember something about the father-in-law getting done by somebody. The trouble was he was a proud man and he kept quiet about it. Pride, eh!"

Lionel and Emily looked at each other, then Emily said, "Is your father-in-law still alive, Jen?"

Jenny replied, "I'm afraid not. His wife is though, and she still lives in Glasgow."

Lionel was racking his brains for an answer that would sort out Mr. McBride or McGregor, whatever his name was. Bertie was on his way up to bed, followed by Jenny, who was questioning him all the way up the stairs, trying to get something out of him that would help.

Lionel was thinking of any angle. Then he said to Emily, "What I don't understand, Em, is... If you'd done something in your home town, something as horrible as this, no normal person would have the front to return, would they? No way. So why would he come back? There's got to be a reason. I think we need to do two things tomorrow, Em. I'll try to get more out of Bertie, and two, have another chat with Lisa from the pub."

Emily agreed and commented, "I want to call Barry, and tell him what we've discovered but..."

Lionel cut in, "But we don't have proof. We need proof. No, don't call him just yet Emily. Let's have an early night, love. I've got a feeling it's going to be a busy day tomorrow."

Conned

Barry and Angela were having a lie in. It was a Sunday morning; the sky was blue. Another warm day lay ahead. For a couple of minutes, they both tried to get their other half to make the first move towards the kitchen for a cup of tea.

"You make the tea, Ange, and I'll do breakfast. Alright Doll?"

Angie was reluctant but, in the end, she agreed. The kettle was boiling as the phone rang.

"Hello." Angie was wondering who it could be as it was not yet eight o'clock.

"Hi, could I speak to Emily, please. I'm her brother, Peter."

Angie replied, "Well, I'm afraid she isn't here at the moment. She's in Glasgow with her friend." Angie wasn't sure why she didn't say boyfriend but anyhow Peter replied.

"Oh, okay. Do you know when she's due to return or is she going home from Scotland?" he asked.

Angie was apologetic in her reply. "I'm sure she will be coming back here, Peter, but I'm not sure exactly when." There was a slight pause. Then Angie continued, "I do have a number for her in Glasgow, if you'd like it?"

Peter said he would and Angie reached for her diary and gave Peter the number. They had a brief conversation, but Angie didn't say too much as to the events of the last couple of weeks. Minutes later, Peter was calling the number he'd been given.

A very broad Scottish accent answered. "And who the fuck is ringing this time of the morning? Hello!" Bertie could hear an echo on the line.

"Hello, my name is Peter. Can I speak to Emily, please?"

Bertie was hungover and not really awake. "Emily who? There's nobody of that name that is living here."

Jenny took the phone off Bertie saying, "Give it here, Bert. Hello, hello." Jenny, too, could hear an echo.

"Hi, my name is Peter. I'm Emily's brother. I'm calling from Australia. Could you…"

"Hold on love, I'll get her." Jenny looked at Bertie. "Don't touch that phone, right!" She ran upstairs and knocked on the spare room door. "Emily, quick, your brother's on the phone."

Emily slipped one of Jenny's dressing gowns on and ran down the stairs. "Hello Peter!" For the next couple of minutes, Emily said the occasional "yes". Eventually she was able to ask the questions relating to their old home. She listened intently and, again, she was listening more than she was speaking. "I did wonder. It's been a couple of weeks since Laurence gave me your number. Yes, I guessed that you must have been on holiday or something, yes… Okay …. Right. So, you might have them, then? Okay. Well, I think by then we will be back in Essex… Okay… What?… His name is Lionel. We met in Peru, and no, we are not or have not got any plans to get hitched…. No, Pete. Okay, I'll speak to you soon, okay?… Yeah, good to hear your voice, too. Okay. Bye. Love you."

By this time, Lionel had made it downstairs. "Anything useful, then?"

Emily said she wasn't sure because Peter himself wasn't convinced that the property still belonged to the Fleet family. But he did say that he'd taken a small leather wallet with him when he emigrated, and there were some old documents in it. He couldn't honestly say what they were. So, he was going to check and get back to her.

"So, we haven't any good news then?" Lionel sighed.

Emily quickly said, "Not yet, Lionel.

Lionel wanted to show Emily the city centre. Jenny said, "Don't go down there at night, Em, not unless you've got a gun in your bag." She had a little chuckle after she said it.

Lionel took offence. "Just a wee bit over the top there, Jen. Emily, it's nothing like that. Sure, there are places you should avoid, like any city, but I'm not about to take you to them places now, am I?" Emily was laughing, not at Lionel, though. Jenny was behind Lionel, circling her hands in a wind-up motion. She was still doing it when Lionel turned around. "I knew exactly what you were doing, you cow!" Lionel then joined in the laughter.

They sat and had breakfast. Bertie, who had been cat-napping since the phone call, woke and said, "Who was that on the phone, then?"

Jenny remarked, "It was the Queen, Bertie. She wants you to go down to Windsor Castle to clean the windows."

Bertie opened his eyes. "Aye, tell me when her private jet turns up and I'll grab me bucket!"

Emily loved Bertie's banter. He was a real character and she could imagine the two of them having some real laughs over the years. She'd said as much to Jenny, who agreed, though she did say she worried about Bertie's drinking. He seemed to be getting worse.

Around lunchtime, there was a knock at the door. Lionel opened it to see Lisa, the barmaid, standing there. "Hello, Lisa. Come in."

Lisa followed Lionel momentarily. Then he beckoned her into the kitchen, where Emily was making a drink.

Lionel introduced them. "Emily, this is Lisa from the pub. Lisa, this is Emily." Emily smiled and shook her hand.

"To what do we owe the pleasure, Lisa?" Lionel said and pulled a kitchen stool away from the front of the fridge and offered Lisa a drink.

"Well, you know the conversation we had about your friend, Jock?" Lisa started, but Lionel stopped her. "Yes, but he is no friend. Anyway, carry on."

Lisa took a deep breath. "Right. I didn't want to say anything yesterday because I wasn't sure that… Oh, sod it. My father was conned by our mutual 'enemy' and my father is very much alive. And before you ask, yes, he will do whatever is required.

Lionel and Emily hugged each other. Then they hugged Lisa, who was overwhelmed by the response that her short statement had created. They chatted for about an hour and arranged to meet Lisa's father, Rory, the next afternoon.

Emily was bursting with anticipation. The news that they were going to take down to Essex was going to make so many people extremely happy. Lisa said her goodbyes after Lionel said he'd be at her house around 2:30pm the next day.

Lisa said, "Okay," walked a few steps and then stopped, "Lionel, you'd better have my address, yes?"

Lionel laughed and stepped back into the hall, picked up a pen and paper and took the details down. "Okay, then," he said, "See you tomorrow, love."

Lisa smiled and replied, "See you!"

When he re-entered the house, Emily was ecstatic. "Lionel, do you feel as happy as I do. I'm so pleased. This will do it, won't it?"

Lionel, probably due to his career, wasn't about to go overboard with excitement, but he told Emily that it was, to him, highly likely that the Mayor's position would be untenable. "However," he said, "I'm not pouring water on the news we've discovered, but I've learnt that when you don't expect too much, you are more likely to be pleased with the outcome."

Emily understood the logic and agreed. They also agreed they would return to Essex the day after tomorrow.

"Emily, that's just a day before the public meeting, isn't it?" Lionel asked.

Emily was nodding her head, "Yes Lionel. Maybe we can travel down on tomorrow night's sleeper train. What do you think?"

Lionel agreed, "It'll give us a bit more time, I suppose."

The trip to Glasgow city centre was put on hold. Jenny, sensing that this was Lionel's last night, suggested a night in and invited a few close friends. It wouldn't be a party as such, just a family get-together. All agreed it was a great idea, even Bertie, who was between hangovers and obviously up for a few bevvies! Three hours later, he was his old self, drunk and asleep in the corner.

The morning arrived. There were a few hangovers and a couple of lodgers, also with hangovers, in the lounge. It had been a good night, Emily thought as she tidied up the kitchen. She'd held back and didn't drink too much so she could be up early. She had the kitchen all cleaned by the time

Jenny surfaced. "Christ, girl, what time did you get up? You shouldn't have done this, but thank you. Honestly, I dread the morning after, so I owe ya!"

They both laughed and chatted about life in general. Emily was missing Lima, but Lionel more than compensated for it.

Jenny probed with the question, "Well then, Em, is Lionel the one for you? Sorry for asking but he's never really settled. I think you're a perfect match, if you want my opinion."

Emily didn't mind the question, but wasn't sure what to say, so she just said, "We both decided to just get on board and see where the ride takes us, Jen. He is very special to me but, as I say, we have to be patient."

Jemmy admired Emily. "I think you're perfect for him, and I do understand. I think you're right to adopt the attitude that you have, and I wish you all the best." At that, she held her arms out and gave Emily a tight squeeze and patted her on the back and said, "Bless ya."

Emily thought the world of Jenny. Yes, she was loud, but she had a heart as big as the sky. No wonder Lionel wanted her to meet his Aunt. They had only been in Glasgow a few days, but she felt at home straight away. When the dust had settled, she thought, she'd love to come back, but she, too, worried about Bertie's drinking. Whenever he was questioned about it, his response was always the same. "I've fucking worked all me life, and now it's time to enjoy the early retirement. I've earned it."

They had told Lisa they would be there mid-afternoon, but now that Lionel and Emily were leaving this evening, they rang Lisa and arranged an earlier time. They were anxious about the conversation they were going to have while still trying to be positive.

"Lionel," Emily said. "do you think her dad will be willing to come back with us. I mean, it's the meeting tomorrow and we really need him there, don't we?"

Lionel understood Emily and tried to reassure her. "Worst case scenario, love, he's unable to come and we still make the accusations. I believe the Mayor will be so cock-sure of himself, he won't be ready for what we have on him. Yes, he might swerve out of it, of course, but we will cause enough doubts in people's minds to stop any further action until the true facts come to light. And let's remember that, Em. The truth is on our side love. He can try to waffle his way out of it, but I think even he will find it a tall order to convince everybody that what we are telling the local people, most of whom disagree with the CPO, is actually true."

Emily listened and smiled. Lionel was still that smoothie she first saw in Peru. He could charm the uncharmable, no doubt about that.

It was only a short drive to Lisa's dad's and, sadly, it wasn't the nicest area of Glasgow. As they walked up the path, some kids started to gather around Lionel's hire car.

Lisa opened the door. "Hi. Come in," she told them. Then she stood outside to let Emily and Lionel in. While doing that she shouted out to one of the kids, "Josh Campbell, look after that car for me. If there's no damage when my guests come out, I'll give you a fiver."

Josh shouted, "I'll do it for a tenner, Lisa!"

Lisa walked down the path and whispered in Josh's ear. She then patted him on the back and said, "Okay then, Josh." Josh was already moving the rest of the kids away from the car when he turned and said, "Okay Lisa, nae problem."

When Lisa entered the living room, her father was already getting red faced mentioning the name of the swindler, Jock McGregor. He went on and on. Luckily, Lisa managed to calm him down by telling him that the slower he recalled the events that led to being conned, the more likely it was that he would remember everything and that could only be a good thing.

As he told the story, Lionel's hatred of this vile man was growing noticeably. Emily sensed it and had a quiet word with Lisa when her dad had to visit the bathroom. Lionel had gone to the window to check on the car.

Emily asked Lisa, "Lisa, I know it's a lot to ask, but do you think your dad would come with us to Essex? You can come, too. It'll be on us. You won't spend a penny, I promise."

Lisa smiled, then gave a slight frown. "I'm okay with it, Emily, though I'm not sure dad will be. But if he is, then okay. When are you going then?"

Emily whispered as Lisa's dad was coming down the stairs, "Tonight, on the sleeper train." Lisa nodded.

When, maybe half an hour later, Lisa's dad had finished the task of telling these people what a mug he'd been, Lisa said to him, "Dad, Jock McGregor is now Lord Mayor of a place in Essex. What's more, he's blackmailed half or more than half of the councillors on the board of the council and now wants to knock down an orphanage that Emily's family started thirty-five years ago. My friend Lionel would like you and me to travel to Essex, so you can face this horrible man and expose him for what he really is."

Lisa's dad thought for a few moments. Then he stood up tall and proud and looked at Emily. "My dear, I'd be delighted. Shall I go pack?"

They all clapped. Emily stood up and gave this wonderful man a big hug.

Lisa was already darting about. "How long have we got, then?" she asked Lionel.

"No panic, Lisa. Train leaves at 10:30 tonight. We have plenty of time. Right now, we'll leave you to get sorted and we will ring you when we're on our way round. Oh and, by the way, thank you and thank your lovely dad again." Lionel gave her a cuddle.

The clock was showing eight-thirty. Emily was packed, Lionel, not quite. Jenny had just given Bertie his dinner, which he wanted as soon as he woke up, drunk again. A few minutes later, Lionel was ready. "It's a bit early, but I've got to get the car back to the hire company, so we'd best be off."

Jenny was a little down, but cheered up when Emily invited her to come to Peru. They all said their goodbyes and a couple of hours later, they were all on the train to London.

The train journey was as comfortable as it could be. Lisa's dad declined the use of a bed, deciding to have a nap with his feet up on the bench seat. Lisa, once she felt that her dad was asleep, made her way to the buffet car, where Emily and Lionel were waiting for her.

"Oh, I'm sorry I've been so long. I just wanted to be sure he was asleep. He sleep-walks you know, not particularly a good thing on a train is it?" Lisa laughed.

Emily grabbed Lisa's hand and squeezed it. "I'm sure he'll be fine, Lisa."

Lionel had told Emily that he wanted to ask Lisa why she never mentioned that her own father had been conned by McGregor, so she prompted Lionel. "You wanted to ask Lisa a question?" Lionel took a sip of his drink and slid over a white wine spritzer to Lisa. "There you go love, you've earned it."

Lisa smiled. "Oh, just what I need, thanks Lionel."

That done, he went on to ask the question. Lisa replied that, when Lionel first mentioned Jock's name, her initial response was to jump in with both feet, as her dad had really suffered. But she refrained and decided to ask her dad first and really just sound him out. After all, he'd kept it quiet by choice when it happened. Lisa's dad's reply to the questions that Lisa asked was that he would think about it. And so it was two or three hours later when he told his daughter that he wanted to meet these people who were being conned or crossed by this same man.

Lionel and Emily completely understood why Lisa did what she thought was right. Emily would have certainly done the same in her shoes. They had one more drink each, then they retired for the evening.

The journey from London to Essex took around an hour and a half. Lionel was cursing not finding a car hire company that actually had something to hire. Emily phoned Barry from Fenchurch Street and, before she could say anything, he said he'd pick them up at Grays train station.

In less than an hour and a bit, they were pulling into Barry's drive. Lisa was full of admiration, firstly at the electric gates, then the house itself. But when, after they'd had a coffee, Angie showed her the birds, she was loving it.

Once Angie and Lisa returned to the house, Barry, after being teased by Lionel that he had some good news, no, great news, asked, "Well, what's the good news then?"

Barry and Angie listened to Lisa's dad's story and were pinching themselves every couple of minutes. They could see that this little, frail old man in front of them was going to dethrone the Mayor and most likely save Jack Fleet House. The pair of them were so emotional. Angie managed to control her feelings, but Barry couldn't. He got up from the lounge and walked into the snooker room, with tears flowing down his face.

Angie followed him. "Baz, you silly sod, don't Baz." They were crying and laughing at the same time.

"Got the bastard, Ange. We've only gone and got him!" Barry cried.

Emily said when they had all sat back down again, "What time is the meeting, Ange?"

Angie replied, "Seven o'clock tomorrow."

Emily gave Angie a quizzical look. "I thought it was tonight?"

Barry still had his hankie in his hand. "No love, it's tomorrow, so you know what that means don't you?"

Lionel smiled. Emily smiled. Lisa wondered why they were all smiling.

Barry said the usual words, "So, do you fancy a Barbie, Doll?" And they all started laughing, except Lisa's dad who really didn't get it.

Barry popped into his bedroom and sat on the bed. He couldn't believe it. They were, it seemed, going to save Jack Fleet. He was shaking his head. He and Angie decided not to reveal it to anyone, even supporters of the battle to keep Jack Fleet open. Instead the cards would be dealt tomorrow evening.

He did remember that Angie gave him a message from Davey McCallister, who needed to speak with him as soon as possible. So he called him from the bedroom. The conversation lasted a few minutes and, when he said goodbye to Davey, he was even happier. Some more good news.

It was going to be a momentous day tomorrow, a momentous day indeed. He joined the others, putting on his apron. He did his Swedish chef impersonation. Everybody laughed.

The Public Meeting

Barry wasn't confident that everything would go the way they wanted. They had evidence, true; witnesses, also true. It was just hard to believe that the Mayor wouldn't wriggle his way out of it. He was also surprised that he even called a public meeting, and further surprised that he'd arranged the largest venue possible, the town's Civic Hall.

Emily sat having her lunch on the patio and was soon joined by Lionel, Lisa and her dad Rory. It soon became clear that Rory was a bit of a comedian. Soon they were in a jovial mood.

Barry decided to do some gardening. Angie had been vocal about the weeds taking over the front garden, so off he went with his yellow gardening gloves and his tools. Angie watched him through the snooker room window. She jumped when Emily put her hand on her shoulder. "Sorry, Ange," Emily said. "That's okay, Em. I'm just making sure he's not loafing," Angie replied, laughing as she said it.

"You've a good man there, Angie, a real good one." Angie started to nod her head and turned to look at Emily. "You've not done so bad either, Em, have you?" The pair of them laughed together. "Would you like a drink, Em?" Angie asked. "I know we've got the meeting tonight, but I thought a couple of drinks and a little siesta would fit the bill. What do you think?"

Emily had promised herself she would reduce her alcohol intake, as she seemed to be "on it" far too much. She didn't answer straight away, but then decided to join Angie in her plan for the afternoon.

Angie did the honours and they moved into the kitchen. By the sound of it, Rory was on top form judging by the laughter coming from the patio.

Barry was almost finished with his weeding duties, when he heard the "toot" of a car horn. He looked up and saw Davey getting out of his car. Barry walked over to the fence. "How's it going, Davey?" Barry asked, as they shook hands. "Grand, Barry, just grand. Really looking forward to finishing the Mayor off tonight, that's for sure." Barry was nodding in agreement. "If I'm honest Davey, I'm a little bit anxious. I'm confident that we have enough ...but it's just that he always seems to wriggle his way out of things and comes up smelling of roses." Davey didn't hesitate with his reply. "Baz, there's no reason to be anxious, I tell you. He is going down tonight, 100%, I'm sure of that!" They chatted for a few more minutes more, then Davey was off. He never stood still very long for anyone.

Barry was about to come back into the house, when D I Carter pulled up. Angie had come back to see how Barry was getting on. She saw them exchange a few words before the officer left. She asked him what he wanted, but it seemed he was just passing and stopped to say hello.

Barry and Angie popped their heads out of the patio doors to apologise to the others, as they were going to have a "siesta". Rory chuckled. "Is that what they call it now? Okay, we believe ya! "

Emily, too, decided to get a couple of hours. After all, it could be a late night.

Lisa, Rory and Lionel were still chatting. Actually, Rory was doing all the talking, relating back to his younger years. One of his stories was about when he was an apprentice in the shipyard. He stood up to explain his point at one stage, bent over and then just froze. Lisa jumped up. "What's up, dad. Is it your back?" Rory was screaming with pain. Lisa was crying. Lionel was encouraging him to try to stand up, but he was in too much pain. They managed to get him into the lounge and laid him down on the floor. He was, though, bent in two. Lisa had to leave the room; she was getting hysterical and not really helping.

Angie, on hearing the commotion, came out from the bedroom. "What's happened, Rory, are you...?" She stopped herself from saying the obvious. "Where's Lisa?" she asked. Lionel pointed to the snooker room. Angie entered the snooker room to find Lisa in pieces. "Come on, sweetheart, he'll be okay." Lisa was sobbing. She tried to talk but couldn't get the words out. Angie told her to wait there and went back into the lounge.

Rory was in a bad way. He was struggling to breathe. By this time, Barry was on the scene and straight away was on his mobile. "Yeh ..right ..he can't move, Andy ... okay..not really ..sorry ..it's a long story... he just has to be ....okay...you sure? ..Thanks, you're a diamond. You know where I am. Okay, see you in a bit." Barry looked at Rory with a troubled expression. "That was Andy Warren. He's a physio, a good one, too. He's on his way round." They all knew the implications of what was happening here. If Rory couldn't get to the meeting, well, it didn't look good .The mood had changed. Half an hour ago, they were all in a different place, laughing and joking, looking forward to the possible end of a long journey that had seemed hopeless but only recently had turned in their favour.

They awaited the arrival of a man that most of them didn't know and prayed for a miracle.

Angie went into the kitchen and put the kettle on. Emily followed. The pair of them were quiet. Lisa joined them. The last time this happened," she said, "he was literally on his back for ten days or so!"

That did little to change the mood.

It was now approaching five thirty. They were indeed getting into the "miracle" time. It was starting to look like the dream could be over.

Angie was in the front garden. She'd been there since Barry phoned Andy. Finally he arrived; it was ten minutes to six. They all left the lounge at the request of the man who was their last chance to win the day.

They waited. And waited. A good half an hour passed before the lounge door finally opened. Andy motioned for Barry to come back into the room. The others naturally tried to follow. Andy just held his hand up to stop them.

When they re-entered the room, Rory was laying on his stomach. He was still mumbling about the pain, but not as much. "Barry, I need you to help. He won't like what we are going to do. I've explained it to him, so he is sort of ready, okay?"

"Okay, Rory, are you ready?" Andy asked. "Fuck off," he replied. "I'll take that as a yes. Okay, Barry, grab him under the shoulder. When I say pull, you pull, okay? Don't listen to him." "Fuck off," Rory repeatedly said as the two of them lifted his shoulders far beyond where they should be, until finally Rory let out a huge fart!

The smell was something neither of them had ever smelt before. As disgusting as it was, he farted again, and then it happened. He followed through! The smell was revolting. Rory was still swearing and cursing, but he wasn't complaining about the pain anymore. In fact, he rolled over onto his back and sat up. "How's the pain, Rory?" Andy asked. "What pain? I've got no pain, but what's that smell. It's disgusting!"

The pair of them left Rory sitting on the floor and found Lisa and explained what had happened. "Oh my god, I'm so sorry. He does this sometimes. I'll sort him out. His back is okay, though, yes?" Andy nodded. "As long as he takes it easy, he should be fine."

They were all extremely relieved. He would be able to do what he had wanted to do for years; bring the man down who had conned him all those years ago.

****

Jock was in a confident mood. He was sitting on the edge of the stage at the Civic Hall. He was confident to the extreme. Otherwise, why would he have booked the largest venue around?

As seven o'clock was approaching, he felt for the first time that he may have got it wrong. There were still twenty odd minutes to go and already the hall was over half full.

Barry, Angela, Davey, Ada. In fact, everyone who supported Jack Fleet was there. Lisa and her dad were on the end of a line of seats.

Davey had his move planned but, when he spoke to Barry, he felt as though Barry would rather he didn't try to bring Jock down himself.

The meeting was chaired by an outsider, a councillor from Suffolk. Edward Simmonds had been on the Ipswich Council for seventeen years and he seemed to have an open mind. Barry had his doubts, but he, too, was confident the support from his team would be enough to win the day.

The Chairman called the meeting to order. The hall was bursting at the seams. Jock was looking increasingly nervous.

Mr. Simmonds briefly ran over the point of the meeting and then invited the Mayor to open the debate.

The Mayor stood up, only to be met by a chorus of boos.

The Chairman quickly interrupted. "Ladies and Gentlemen, if this is the way it's going to be, we may as well stop now." Barry stood and gestured to everyone to be quiet.

The Mayor talked briefly, saying how important it was that new homes were built. There were more than a few hecklers, but he did manage to get through his speech.

The Chairman listened to a few remarks from the floor, but it seemed to the supporters that he was just paying lip service.

Davey was really getting annoyed, so much so that he jumped up and made his way to the stage and climbed the four or five steps. He started talking and somebody shouted, "Can't hear you, Davey. Someone give him a mike!" Sure enough, a mike was put in Davey's hand.

He told of the conversation he had with the Mayor. He was told in no uncertain terms that, providing he greased the palm of the Mayor, he would benefit from future building projects, especially the new shopping centre at Stanford-Le-Hope. Jock just sat, shaking his head.

While this was going on, Lisa and her dad got up out of their seats and started towards the stage, mostly unnoticed.

Davey was losing his temper, and the argument, till he uttered some rather hash words aimed at the Mayor. The Chairman was trying to be diplomatic, but felt he had to ask Davey to sit down.

By the time Davey left the stage, Lisa and her dad were at the foot of the steps. Rory could see the man who conned him all those years ago, and his anger was replaced by the desire to bring him down.

The Chairman finally noticed them and gave Lisa a microphone. Jock was talking to somebody stage-left and hadn't noticed the arrival of Lisa and her dad, Rory.

"Ladies and Gentlemen," Rory said. The Mayor turned to look at the new possessor of the microphone and squinted his eyes, but was unable to identify the speaker.

"I've known your Mayor for thirty-five years. Jock McGregor, how are you? It's been too long." Jock was still baffled.

"Ladies and Gentlemen, this man is a con-man. He swindled me and nine other people from Glasgow out of thousands. He had ten thousand from me alone and do you know what? Because he was a freemason, all that happened was that he had to leave, not just Glasgow but Scotland.

"He didn't go to prison, but he was found guilty in a court, and you can check the records. How you feeling Jock? Remember me? Rory, your old pal, you lying bastard. I hope you rot in hell."

Jock rested his head on the table and held his hands over his ears, so he couldn't hear the abuse from the majority of the crowd.

Barry was ecstatic. Everyone was hugging each other.

"Well, well," Barry said as the noise quietened down. "I've got a feeling the beer may well flow. What do you think, Doll?"

Angie smiled and hugged him. "Most definitely, Baz."

Lionel shouted, "Is somebody gonna phone Ronnie at the King's Arms and let him know we're on our way?"

"I've already done it. Let's go!" cried Ada.

The Joy And The Pain

Ada woke early. It wasn't even six, but she was wide awake. Yesterday was immense. The miracle had happened. She was still pinching herself. Percy was sound asleep and no surprise there, she thought. The get together at the King's Arms after the meeting went well into the early hours. She had left Percy at the pub around one o'clock and the place was jumping. Ronnie and Barb somehow managed to get a buffet out in no time. It was as if they knew the course the evening would take.

Ada walked around the ground floor of Jack Fleet. Yes, it needed some work done, but it was still home for the kids and it was going to remain a home for the kids. She was so happy, not just for herself and Percy, but for the kids too. The numbers had dwindled recently because of the expected closure, but now things were back to normal and she was sure that they would, once again, have the ominous task of caring for a home full of deprived children. Sad as it was, it meant that she and her lifelong partner would be the rocks and cuddles for these unfortunate souls that landed at Jack Fleet. She decided to make another cuppa and to take one up for Percy.

When she walked into their room, he was still asleep. She placed the cup on the bedside table. On the floor was a crumpled piece of paper. She unfolded it and read the words and started crying.

The words were written by Davey McCallister, who had decided that he was going to modernise Jack Fleet House. His words seemed to indicate no expense spared. She was choked. Why didn't Percy say anything? Then she remembered that he had made an attempt to say something when he came home, but, as she was woken by his entrance, she told him to wait till the morning. So, it was looking even better. She wondered if Barry and Ange knew. They'd be so happy to hear this. In fact, she thought to herself, everybody she knew would be so happy, because everyone wanted the same thing and now they had got it.

She shook Percy's arm. "Perce," she said, "Perce, wake up." Percy mumbled. He wasn't ready to face the world, she thought. So she whispered, "There's a cuppa for you, Percy," and left him to waken in his own time.

Barry and Ange were the last ones to leave the King's Arms, along with Emily and Lionel. By the time they 'hit the sack', so to speak, it was nearly four o'clock.

The sheer joy of getting the result they all wanted meant the rest of the evening was buzzing. Everyone was ecstatic. Emily and Lionel announced their engagement, though Barry wasn't surprised. He was expecting it, to be truthful. Sure they were a lovely, well matched couple. Lionel himself had really settled in with the local crowd, with his sense of humour and wit. Emily was slightly less 'out there', so to speak, due understandably to the loss of her best friend, Maureen.

Ronnie and Barb had been brilliant, getting a buffet from nowhere. 'Keeping everyone happy' should be their motto.

In a quiet moment during the evening, Ronnie, who was sitting with Lionel, Barry, Percy, Ada, Emily and Angie, said, "I'd like to make a toast." He paused. "Shut up, Baz. I'd like to make a toast. I hope the Scottish wanker's cell shrinks by an inch every day he spends in it." They all shouted their approval. "Here, here," was heard, as well as "Love it".

Almost straight after Ronnie's toast, Lionel stood up and said, "Ladies and Gentlefolk." The 'gentlefolk' brought some "ooh's and aah's" from the group. He continued, "Listen. I've been, I mean, I'm new here but I'm fast getting used to the lot of you. So I'm not going to beat around the bush." At that, he turned to Emily and dropped to his knee, put his hand into his jacket pocket and pulled out a small velvet box. "Emily, my love, would you do me the honour of becoming my wife?"

Barry piped up, "If she don't want ya, I'll say yes, Line." They all laughed. Angie put her hand over Barry's mouth.

"Well?" Lionel said.

Emily was not expecting it, but she answered the question from the heart. "Yes, Lionel. Yes." Everybody cheered and, before you could say Jack Fleet House, a bottle of champagne appeared on their table.

Davey McCallister was bringing it over to celebrate the result at the meeting, but he was more than happy to donate it to the happy couple. "All the very best to you both," he said and joined in with the cheering.

Lionel popped the cork and, once the cheering was over, proceeded to pour everyone a drop. He was so happy. She'd actually agreed to marry him. He was over the moon. Emily was surprised at the proposal, but she knew in her heart that he was the one.

Shortly after, Percy left the table. He walked around the bar and into the empty restaurant, found a seat and sat down. He'd been there a few minutes when Davey said, "Percy, can I join you?" Percy nodded. "Percy, I've been thinking and I'm confident that I can do you a favour." Percy looked at him curiously. Davey continued, "I can see you're wondering what's next, Perce. Right, I've been living in this area for a long time now and, to be fair, we are very happy, me and my family. So I was thinking, well, right, let me tell you. My accountant says I'm making too much money and so I've got to spend more on my business. So, what I was wondering... Well look, Percy, I want to do a refurb on Jack Fleet House. I'm not saying a total refurb but just to modernise it, you know. Improve the décor and facilities, kitchen, etc. What do you think?

Percy was in shock. He couldn't speak.

"Percy?" Davey said.

Percy's head was down. When he looked up, his eyes were full of tears. "I... I... Davey, thank you."

Davey gave him a piece of paper. "Here's my plan, just a rough draft. We'll talk some more in a couple of days."

****

Jock McBride went straight home after the meeting. He walked into his four-bed detached house. He didn't turn a light on. He just walked into the lounge, got a glass and a bottle from the cocktail cabinet and poured. He was finished, done for. Not only that. There were sure to be repercussions due to his fake name and the threats to his fellow councillors, let alone the scam in Glasgow, which, until an hour ago, was a distant memory.

He had never been so low. The phone rang and rang and rang. Eventually it stopped, only to start again straight away. He answered it. "Hello," he said in a stern voice.

"It's me, Terry," the caller said.

His face was distorted. "What the fuck do you want?"

Terry Watson had heard about the meeting. "I just want to know that you are going to keep quiet about our arrangement. I know the deal is off, but that's life. We won't worry too much, will we?"

Jock was fuming. "Why the fuck should I keep quiet? This is all your doing, your fault, you fucking hypocrite. If I'm going down, you're fucking going with me, do you hear?" And he slammed the phone down. Jock was shaking. He reached into his drawer and took out a bottle of pills. He didn't ever dream in his life he would ever contemplate such a thing. The next thing he heard was a loud bang from the front of his house.

Before he could react, he was surrounded by police officers.

One of them said, "Mr. McBride, I'm afraid you'll have to come with us to the station to answer some significant questions."

Jock looked at him and laughed, "Look at you. What's your name? How old are you?"

The officer replied, "My name is Detective Inspector Graham Carter. My age is of no consequence. Now would you kindly come this way?"

Jock took the rest of his drink in one gulp. "Aye, I'm coming," then muttered under his breath "Bastards". He sang like a canary over the next twenty-four hours.

Terry Watson was questioned and released some eight hours later.

****

Printed in Poland
by Amazon Fulfillment
Poland Sp. z o.o., Wrocław